Moreno Valley
Public Library
25480 Alessandro Blvd
Moreno Valley, CA 92553

September 26, 2012

D0457775

MVFOL

SHUNNING SARAH

ALSO BY JULIE KRAMER

Killing Kate
Silencing Sam
Missing Mark
Stalking Susan

SHUNNING SARAH

A NOVEL

JULIE KRAMER

EMILY BESTLER BOOKS

—

ATRIA

New York   London   Toronto   Sydney   New Delhi

Moreno Valley Public Library

ATRIA BOOKS
A Division of Simon & Schuster, Inc.
1230 Avenue of the Americas
New York, NY 10020

This book is a work of fiction. Names, characters, places, and incidents either are products of the author's imagination or are used fictitiously. Any resemblance to actual events or locales or persons, living or dead, is entirely coincidental.

Copyright © 2012 by Julie Kramer

All rights reserved, including the right to reproduce this book or portions thereof in any form whatsoever. For information address Atria Books Subsidiary Rights Department, 1230 Avenue of the Americas, New York, NY 10020.

First Emily Bestler Books/Atria Books hardcover edition August 2012

EMILY BESTLER BOOKS / ATRIA BOOKS and colophon are trademarks of Simon & Schuster, Inc.

For information about special discounts for bulk purchases, please contact Simon & Schuster Special Sales at 1-866-506-1949 or business@simonandschuster.com.

The Simon & Schuster Speakers Bureau can bring authors to your live event. For more information or to book an event, contact the Simon & Schuster Speakers Bureau at 1-866-248-3049 or visit our website at www.simonspeakers.com.

Manufactured in the United States of America

10 9 8 7 6 5 4 3 2 1

Library of Congress Cataloging-in-Publication Data

Kramer, Julie.
  Shunning Sarah : a novel / by Julie Kramer.—1st Emily Bestler Books/Atria Books hardcover ed.
      p.   cm.
  1. Spartz, Riley (Fictitious character)—Fiction.   2. Women television journalists—Fiction.   3. Murder—Investigation—Fiction.   4. Amish—Fiction.
I. Title.
  PS3611.R355S5 2012
  813'.6—dc23   2012011246

ISBN 978-1-4516-6463-8
ISBN 978-1-4516-6465-2 (ebook)

Moreno Valley Public Library

For my mom—Ruth (Spartz) Kramer—a fan of the Amish

SHUNNING SARAH

PROLOGUE

The missing face unnerved me. No eyes, nose, or mouth lent personality to the cloth doll clutched by the little Amish girl. My own Raggedy Ann exuded charm while this toy sported a plain dress and an empty facade. It was spooky, even.

I felt sorry for my playmate, but could express no true condolences because we didn't share the same language. Instead, I set four cups and saucers on a tree stump for a makeshift tea party.

Our fathers were inside the barn arguing about the price of an old crosscut saw. Mine didn't want to sell the saw because my great-grandparents had used it to build the house where we now lived. While the dusty tool hadn't been used in two generations, the saw told a cherished story from our family history.

The other man had immediate, practical plans for the device. The visit ended badly when it became apparent that no deal was forthcoming and the saw would remain behind. Though his beard and wide-brimmed hat masked his expression, he walked like an angry man. Untying the horse, he commanded his daughter to join him. She hurried over, absently leaving her plaything behind.

As I stood to return the doll, my eyes fell to a basket of crayons on the ground. A good deed came to mind. Round black eyes. A red triangle nose. Smiley mouth with center lip. Had there been more time, I would have added red striped leggings.

I rushed the doll over to the other girl and handed it up to her in the black buggy. The fresh face greeted her like a new friend, but instead of a smile of gratitude, her eyes grew wide with dismay.

I watched the pair ride out of our farm yard, never to return.

The next day, when I walked to the gravel road to check the mailbox, something caught my eye. The head of the doll rested among the weeds, the cloth body nowhere near.

I didn't tell anyone what I saw, not even my parents.

That night, as I tried to sleep, the image haunted me. But somehow, by morning, I had pushed the incident from my mind and didn't think about it for twenty-five years.

CHAPTER 1

What do you smell, Bowser?"

Josh Kueppers, wearing a neon orange stocking hat and carrying a shotgun, chased after his dog.

"Maybe bear?"

His voice sounded hopeful as he dreamed of returning home with such a trophy. He'd watched the news the night before and seen reports of a black bear sighting in southeastern Minnesota. So while unusual, his goal wasn't impossible. At least, that's what he told himself during the pursuit.

The school bus had dropped the ten-year-old off outside his family's farmhouse. As he dumped the mail on the kitchen table, he found a note from his mother that said she'd been called to work an evening nursing shift.

She instructed him to bike over to an older friend's place down the road, spend the night, and go to school with him the next morning. Josh smiled at the prospect of fun.

But his mother's absence also presented another opportunity. For a hunt. So he threw on his camouflage jacket and was out the door.

Josh and Bowser, a tan mixed breed, ran through a lightly snow-covered farm field. The corn had been harvested, but not yet plowed under. An early cold spell had hit just as the calendar touched October. He stumbled a couple of times before reaching a line of trees growing in a depression in the ground.

His dog bayed, just like a real hunting hound.

Josh's eyes grew wide.

He held the gun steady, finger on trigger, as he glanced around to see what had attracted the animal's attention. He didn't want to be ambushed, although theirs did seem to be the only tracks, so he figured they were safe. He looked upward hoping to face off with a raccoon in the branches . . . but they were empty. No masked opponents.

He didn't have enough experience to realize that broad daylight was less conducive to hunting wildlife than dawn or dusk. Bowser barked some more and Josh noticed a hole in the earth that looked curious. He hoped for a bear den. He moved closer, his eyes cautiously scanning back and forth for trouble, when the ground beneath him collapsed.

Josh tumbled downward amid a cascade of dirt and snow. Gradually, through a reassuring gap of sunshine, he became aware of his dog still above, sounding an agitated alarm that he feared would go unheard by anyone else.

Something smelled awful, and as his eyes adjusted to the blackness he realized he was not alone in the bottom of the pit. Fumbling for his gun, he aimed the weapon toward the sky and pulled the trigger in a calculated call for help.

Nothing happened.

Then he realized the safety was on, and tried again.

Almost immediately, he wished he hadn't.

Instead of alerting someone of his whereabouts, the shot caused an avalanche of dirt that buried both Josh and the grisly secret beside him.

CHAPTER 2

Two nurses had called in sick with the flu, so the emergency room was already understaffed when a semitruck smashed a minivan on the highway outside Rochester. Even though Michelle Kueppers was scheduled to be off for the rest of the week, and even though she normally worked days, she answered the hospital's call for extra hands like a good trouper.

She tried phoning her son, Josh, at home during her break, but heard ring after ring. He was probably on his way to the neighbor's. She'd catch him there during supper.

But her shift turned into one during which she saved a life instead of eating or calling her son. The whole floor cheered her like in one of those breathless medical dramas where attractive people in scrubs muscle a cart and IV down the hall in a race with death.

Popular television plotlines aside, directly saving a life was not an everyday occurrence on the job for Michelle. Mostly, she prided herself on her skill for assessing patients to avoid such crises. Staying ahead of trouble was considered smart nursing.

But every once in a while a patient codes, signaling cardiac arrest. That night, lights flashed. Alarms sounded. And suddenly Michelle was kneeling on a hospital bed for better leverage while pounding the victim's chest and cracking some of his ribs to restart his broken-down heart.

She was sore and sweaty, but looked forward to celebrating a job well done with Josh the next day.

CHAPTER 3

The woman's cloudy eyes freaked Josh out. Her head was crooked, and parts of her face had black splotches. She reminded him of a zombie from a movie he'd seen once at a friend's house. But the creatures in the film were billed as living dead or walking dead. He had no doubt this woman was dead dead. And would never walk again.

Because she could not shut her eyes, he shut his. Every time he opened them a crack, she was still there—staring back. The rest of her body remained wrapped in a colorful blanket. Terrified, he stayed on his side of the pit, breathing fast and cringing.

"Bowser!" He cried for his dog, but no answer.

Josh hoped his pet had gone for help. He pulled his stocking cap over his tear-streaked face. That improved the view, but did nothing for the smell. Hours passed and he began to wonder how much time would slip by before he resembled the lifeless woman trapped beside him.

His fingernails hurt from clawing his way free of the dirt. He wished the landslide had buried his companion. Though some of her body had been covered, her head had been spared. Josh thought about kicking soil over her face so he wouldn't have to look at her. But that seemed wrong.

He pushed his cap back so he could see better to dig, and minutes later he found the shotgun. He was afraid to pull the trigger again, but just clutching the weapon was like holding a security blanket.

Josh sensed the sun going down. By nightfall, he wouldn't be able to see the dead woman. But maybe knowing she was in her corner was better than imagining her coming at him in the dark.

By now, his body was shivering and his teeth chattering. Rubbing his hands over his arms didn't help. He decided the corpse didn't need her blanket anymore, and creepy as the idea was, huddling under it might bring him warmth. He was sure he'd feel safer. He stood, grabbed one end of the bedding, and with a few jerks, tore the cover, dirt and all, from her body.

The back of her head hit the ground, then her body rolled onto its side, and landed facing Josh. And even though the light in the pit was dim, he could tell the woman was naked, and still staring at him. Horrified, Josh crawled under the blanket and pulled it over his head to escape the mortifying view.

CHAPTER 4

Josh's mother got home just after midnight. She smiled, pleased to see the mail on the table—even though it was mostly junk and bills. Her son was becoming responsible in his father's absence.

Brian Kueppers was overseas, on active duty with his national guard troop, and wouldn't be home for about six months. He'd been gone about a week. Eight days to be exact. Every morning she said the new number out loud as she brushed her teeth. Sometimes, if the mirror was steamed up, she traced it with her finger.

Brian's absence was hitting his young son hard. At ten years old, this was the first season Josh could legally hunt. He'd even received a special slug shotgun on his birthday. Now there was no dad to take him scouting for deer or pheasants.

Even before the actual deployment, Brian was off training with his military unit, so they had little family time. Once, Michelle caught him lecturing their son on acting like a man while he was away. She stayed out of the conversation to avoid a fight. She'd prefer Josh remain a little boy.

Later that night, when she'd brought up not putting so much pressure on Josh, Brian scowled. She'd backed down quickly, not wanting to provoke him. He left the house for a few hours that night, as was their protocol when he became angry. But when he returned, he was calm and gentle. And when they said their goodbyes Michelle felt that she would miss him and that when he came back they would have a fresh beginning. All three of them.

Brian had developed a temper over the last couple of years. Sometimes he blamed Michelle. Sometimes Josh. She had struggled with doubt concerning their future, but their last months together had been much better. Yet she realized this separation was a crucial test for their marriage. She wanted them both to pass.

Michelle had a hard time falling asleep after her shift because the dog kept barking outside. Once she even got up to check for signs of trouble, but the yard was empty except for Bowser.

The telephone woke her the next morning. On the other end of the line was the school attendance office.

"Hello, Mrs. Kueppers. Just calling to confirm your son's absence. Is Josh sick today?"

"What do you mean? Josh isn't home, he's in class."

But the professional voice on the other end insisted Josh was not present. "If he's playing hooky, he will be disciplined."

That put his mom in a panic. "I need to call you back."

She scrambled out of bed and rushed down the hall. Josh's bed hadn't been slept in, but his backpack lay on top of the covers. Downstairs, his coat hung in the closet. She dashed out the front door, calling his name wildly. The dog was barking and chasing after her. She looked in the shed. Josh's bike was parked inside. She ran to the barn, the garage, and two other outbuildings. By this time she was screaming for her son.

She knew that kids in the country were vulnerable to perils ranging from rusty nails and grain bins to strange cars along open roads. Not a mother in Minnesota didn't know that Jacob Wetterling was still missing more than two decades after being kidnapped while biking home from a convenience store with friends.

She rushed back in the house and grabbed the phone. First

she misdialed and got a wrong number. Finally, she reached the grocery store where the neighbor who had agreed to watch Josh worked.

"Did Josh go to school?"

The other mother seemed puzzled. "We didn't see Josh last night. He never showed up. We thought your shift must be tonight."

Michelle slumped against the wall as the strength left her legs. She slid to the floor in a crouch.

"Are you there? Michelle, are you there?"

"Josh is missing."

She said the last word softly. Because "missing" is such an urgent word. And saying it with a lack of urgency makes it less likely to be true.

Her friend couldn't understand her. "What did you just say?"

Michelle breathed deep and spoke fast. "Josh is gone. I need to call the police." Then she hung up, dialed 911, and forced herself to pretend she was on duty at the hospital, calmly discussing a patient's prognosis and not the fate of her only child.

"Fillmore County Sheriff's Office," the voice said. "What is your emergency?"

"My son is missing. He didn't go to school and appears to have been gone all night."

"How old is the child?"

"Ten."

"Do you think he might have run away?"

"No." Her attempt to stay professional failed. "I know something bad has happened to him. Please find him. Now."

She told them when she had seen him last, what he was wearing, and answered all their other questions.

"No, he doesn't have a cell phone. He's only ten."

"No, he hasn't been upset about anything."

The dispatcher on the other end persisted. "Have there been any recent changes in his life? A divorce, perhaps?"

"No, nothing like that." Michelle paused for a few seconds.

"His father left for Afghanistan a week ago. But Josh understands that he's coming back."

Then she remembered one other thing worth checking and opened the door to a back hallway closet. Josh's coat, bike, and backpack were all in their usual places. But his gun was gone.

She almost dropped the phone as heartbreaking theories flooded her mind, but she briefed the dispatcher about the missing weapon and was assured that someone from law enforcement was on their way.

"Please locate a recent picture of your son."

Michelle glanced at the kitchen clock. She hadn't seen Josh in more than twenty-four hours.

CHAPTER 5

The house was full of photographs of Josh. School. Sports. Holidays. Some clipped under refrigerator magnets. Others mounted in frames hanging on the entry wall. Several buttons pinned to a kitchen bulletin board featured Josh wearing basketball, baseball, and soccer uniforms, holding each matching ball. Michelle also had a stack of scrapbooks starring the blond, freckled boy. She grabbed a current school picture and stuck it in the front door in case the cops got there before she got back.

The dog kept barking and getting in her way while she tried to concentrate on where best to search for her missing son. And suddenly Michelle realized she'd been stupid all morning.

"Come on, Bowser. Where is he? Where's Josh?"

The dog let out a howl and started running toward the farm fields, eager for her to follow.

"Good boy. Take me to him."

She vowed that if Josh had run off, she would hug and not yell. "Just let him be safe," she prayed. She said "safe" louder than the other words. Because "safe" is such a comforting word. And saying it with a ring of confidence made it more likely to be true.

Soon, she noticed a trail of footsteps on the ground—mostly beast, but definitely some boy feet had passed this way, too. She was relieved the dog stuck to the path of tracks in the snow.

The last signs of her son.

CHAPTER 6

Josh woke cold, scared, and hungry. He had been dreaming of breakfast when he realized he was still trapped in the pit. The thought of another day underground with a dead body was unbearable.

Michelle heard a gunshot.

The noise seemed to come from the direction the dog was headed. Her heart pounded as she moved faster, uncertain what she would find.

A few minutes later, she grabbed Bowser's collar and pulled him back before either of them slid down the hole where the tracks ended.

So while the dog woofed their arrival, she dropped to her knees hysterically screaming "Josh!" "Hello!" and "Are you down there?"

It wasn't until her throat grew sore and she grew quiet that she could hear his small voice.

CHAPTER 7

My name is Riley Spartz and I'm a television reporter in Minneapolis—one of the most competitive news markets in the country.

The tip about the trapped boy came from my mother.

She was always calling with local gossip she hoped might qualify as news in a bid to get me on the phone for a long chat. I almost ignored her call because most of the time her ideas were more of a nuisance than they were news.

But not this time. This time she had something good. "A kid the next county over fell in a sinkhole."

A phone call to the Fillmore County Sheriff's Office confirmed they were trying to rescue a young boy, but provided few other details.

I was supposed to be reporting about why so many Minnesotans—Walter Mondale, Hubert Humphrey, Eugene McCarthy, Harold Stassen, Tim Pawlenty, and Michele Bachmann—have run for the White House. That idea came from my new boss during the morning news huddle. Even though I thought the assignment lacked originality (every four years the station seems to broadcast a version of it) I had volunteered for the story to try to get off to a good start with him on his second day as news director.

There was still a risk, though, that I could work my butt off and he might still think my story sucked. A career in news had taught me that bosses never think their ideas suck, just the execution of them. But I had enough confidence in my reporting skills to take the chance. I was supposed to be picking the brains of political analysts from various universities when my mother called about the trapped child.

News value has to be high these days to merit Channel 3 sending a crew more than a hundred miles. Media is in a recession meltdown and cost of coverage is a real factor on what events make the news. I had to sell my boss on a game change. That happens all day long in the news world; better stories come along and push others out of the lineup. But he balked over me hitting the road.

"I'm not convinced yours is the better story." Bryce Griffin was overseeing the redesign of his news director's office—making it his own turf. "By the time we get there, the news could be over."

That was a risk for any story. Talk like his made me miss my first news director. He ran the station under the Child Struck Directive—meaning anytime anyone hears a report of a "child struck," they run. "I don't care if you're interviewing the governor," he used to say. "Drop the mic and race to the kid."

"We have a child in jeopardy, Bryce, and if we wait, he'll be someone else's lead story. Don't you remember that little girl who got trapped in that well in Texas?"

Bryce didn't react. And I realized he was probably no older than "Baby Jessica" herself when the live video coverage of the well that almost became her tomb mesmerized a nation for fifty-eight hours and made CNN a household name.

I tried a more recent example. "Don't you remember the Chilean miners?"

That example got his attention. Every news manager in the business knew that covering that particular life-and-death story was sixty-nine days of ratings gold.

"Do we have this alone?" he asked.

At least he appreciated the value of an exclusive. "A local

source tipped me. And the sheriff gave no indication that any other media had been in touch."

Bryce chewed on his lower lip before nodding affirmatively. "Bring me back some news."

He held his hand up for a high five and even though the gesture seemed cheesy, I obliged. Mostly because no one else could see us and roll their eyes.

Previous news director Noreen Banks had insisted on keeping a close eye on all that happened in the newsroom, so she had her office walls replaced with glass. With such a transparent policy, we could observe her as well, but that often proved demoralizing as we watched her intimidate our colleagues over perceived news-judgment lapses.

Bryce's first act as boss was to order the office walls boarded up. Clearly he preferred to keep those kind of conversations private. And having been verbally beaten down numerous times in Noreen's fishbowl, I saw some benefit to this change.

While her departure was most cruel and unfair, Bryce had nothing to do with her being gunned down on the job. So I was willing to give him a chance to repair our battered morale following the recent shooting spree by a wacko pissed over our news coverage.

Bryce was much younger than me. He'd come with a hotshot, whiz-kid reputation for turning around a foundering TV station out west. The network had snatched him up to perform the same magic with us.

I suspected more changes were coming to Channel 3, but I figured he couldn't be any worse a boss than Noreen. Of course, I'd only worked for him a couple of days. I hoped Bryce would take things slow and get to know the market—and us—before unveiling grand ideas while we were still emotionally walking wounded. But I also knew—and so did he—that the average tenure of a television news director was about eighteen months.

So he was up against a deadline of his own.

CHAPTER 8

My photographer, Malik Rahman, slept most of the drive south. I could have woken him to chat, but I had plenty to think about these days and didn't mind pretending I was alone for a couple hours.

My mind kept flashing back to the newsroom horror. As journalists, we'd all covered breaking news of rampage killers opening fire in schools, post offices, and shopping malls. We just never thought it would happen at Channel 3, but the target of a story made us targets of his rage during a surprise shooting spree. He'd made news after leaving his dog locked in a car on a hot day. It wasn't my story that made him come after us, but our anchor's live interview about his dead pet.

I'd urged Noreen not to let the man in the building. Not because I suspected him capable of murder, but because I thought meeting with him would be a waste of time. "Let him sue," I'd said. "Tell him we'll see him in court." Because of my negative attitude, I'd been banned from the meeting. And that decision probably saved my life.

The police labeled the killings as one of those cases in which the perpetrator apparently "snapped." But I disagreed. Our assailant didn't surrender to impulse, but came armed and ready for revenge in the guise of threatening legal action over a story gone wrong. Minutes later, bodies on the floor gave fresh meaning to the TV term "dead air."

If I hadn't been on a highway going nearly eighty past farm fields just then, I would have closed my eyes to shut out the memory of him shrieking outside my locked office door, while I cowered behind a desk, trying not to confirm my presence by breathing too loud.

I didn't pull the triggers that killed anybody that day, but I felt plenty of survivor's guilt. As did all my colleagues who lived through that fatal afternoon. The dead were dead physically; but the rest of us were dead emotionally. Especially the guy who stepped in and executed our attacker. Once upon a time, he and I were in love. But that seemed so long ago.

The first week after the station rampage, Channel 3 had broadcast the news from its State Fair building using a remote truck to transmit the signal. The Minnesota State Fair functions like an entire city for twelve days a year. Each of the local media outlets—newspapers, TV, radio—has its own building on the fairgrounds. The station retreated there, broadcasting newscasts on schedule, until the network managers could determine how best to react to the shoot-out.

Police had cleared the murder scene almost overnight. There was no "whodunit" drama surrounding this triple homicide. Crime scene decontaminators were brought in to remove all forensic traces of my coworkers and their attacker.

But still, business couldn't possibly run as usual. As long as any of the staff working that dark day continued to be employed at Channel 3, hints of the ambush would linger. I still remembered the shots and screams vividly. And nobody wants to stand over the spot where a colleague bled to death, even if the carpet has been replaced.

Physically altering the newsroom might be the only way to begin to help us repair emotionally. So the floor plan was remodeled, and the anchor desk where Sophie Paulson lay, a bullet in her brain, was thrown out. A new one was designed and moved to the opposite end of the space. Noreen's news director's office was also torn down and her formerly prime office space became a copy center/storage closet that no one liked to enter.

If we needed copies made, we asked an intern to perform the task.

Some of the newsroom remained unchanged. The assignment desk, where Ozzie had crouched on the floor with a telephone and a 911 operator tight to his ear, looked just the same.

Maybe because my office is down the hall from the murders, there are moments when I forget the violent assault. But each day, when walking into the newsroom for the morning huddle, it still feels like a chamber of death.

CHAPTER 9

By the time Malik and I arrived on the scene with a camera, the little boy was safe.

My first reaction was that in missing the rescue shot, Channel 3 had made a long drive for nothing: my new boss would be pissed, and I would be toast.

Then I was ashamed of myself. It wasn't that I wasn't rooting for a happy ending. But a happy ending this early in the news cycle decreased suspense, and hence viewership.

Audiences love stories of lives in peril, but they need to get to know the victims before they begin to care about their fate. Right then, neither they—nor I—knew anything about Josh Kueppers.

It had taken a while to find the location. Unlike in cities, where addresses are precisely marked with street signs and house numbers, out in the country, drivers must rely on landmarks like a red barn or a broken windmill.

A large brown sign in the small town of Fountain caught my eye. It read: Sinkhole Capital of the USA. I pulled over on the side of the road and shook Malik awake, then pointed the unusual slogan out to him.

"Weird," he said. "Are they bragging or warning?"

We used the opportunity to grab thirty seconds of video for the story and switch places in the van. I knew we were getting close to the action and wanted to be free to take notes. For the next several miles we veered from one country road to another, slowing once to pass an idyllic scene of a horse-drawn Amish buggy, driven by a bearded man with a boy wearing a matching straw hat beside him.

The area has one of the fastest-growing Old Order Amish communities in the country—a population of more than a thousand plain folk. The public was very curious about their conservative faith and quaint customs; thus a successful tourism industry was helping the region economically.

A farm girl myself, I was familiar with the simple ways of the Amish, and had long envied them their peaceful lives . . . especially now that my own life was beyond complicated. If not for the edict that women part their hair in the middle, going Amish was tempting.

Malik was Muslim and had never encountered Amish before. He wanted to stop for video. I nixed that idea, explaining that Amish do not like being photographed and further had nothing to do with our story at hand.

"Someday we'll come back and do a timeless feature on the Amish," I promised. "But right now, we need to concentrate on this trapped kid."

Just then we spotted several emergency vehicles with flashing lights and determined we were in the right place. And that we were the first media on the scene.

A yellow backhoe loader—a piece of excavating equipment— was parked near some trees, away from the road, its bucket extended as far as the arm would reach. I noticed it because my parents kept one on their homestead. Backhoes came in handy for carrying, digging, or reaching.

While Malik sprayed the scene for video, I chatted up Sheriff Ed Eide, who delivered the news that we were too late. I immediately concluded the worst. "I'm so sorry."

But he quickly corrected me. "Not that. Got the kid out more

than an hour ago. Story's over. You might as well move along
and head on back to the Cities."

I pried Josh's name out of him, but was surprised the law
wasn't more enthused to see us. Sheriffs, as elected officials, are
generally congenial to the media. They appreciate their voters
watching them on TV doing their job. Especially when they've
apparently done it well. Sheriff Eide seemed almost reluctant to
gloat about his successful rescue.

And that seemed odd.

Malik started moving toward the clump of trees—and backhoe—but was ordered to keep away from the action.

"How about telling us what happened here, Sheriff?"

I purposely referred to him as "Sheriff" because professional
and personal experience has taught me law enforcement types
appreciated being called by their title—our way of acknowledg-
ing that they outrank us. Even if he had asked me to call him Ed,
I never would. And he didn't.

"Soon as we get the story, Sheriff Eide, we can be on our way."

Another problem with rural news events is that fewer witnesses are generally available to interview out in the sticks than
in the city. And the sheriff made it clear no one on site except
him was authorized to talk to the media. And he wasn't in a very
talky mood.

"We can wait while you finish up." Malik set up a tripod and
smiled like we had all the time in the world. Only he and I knew
we didn't. I purposely kept from checking my watch to avoid ap-
pearing impatient.

The sheriff looked peeved that we weren't packing up. "All
right, media miss, let's get this over with."

I clipped a wireless microphone to his uniform, not bothering to ask him to run the cord up under his shirt. I just draped it
over his shoulder and down his back, figuring, good enough.

Being so near his holster made me nervous. I didn't like being
around guns anymore after the newsroom massacre. Even

though I knew the sheriff's weapon was part of his uniform, the steel on his hip made me tense.

Meanwhile, Malik continued fussing, framing the shot, and holding a reflector to improve the light. I was anxious to get the interview under way, but he wanted perfect visuals.

We'd argued about this numerous times. I'd say, "In color and in focus. Let's go, Malik." And he'd say, "Patience, Riley."

Finally he signaled ready.

"So Sheriff Eide, what happened here today?"

The sheriff swallowed before speaking, almost as if he was uncomfortable being on camera. "A local woman called to report that her son was trapped in a sinkhole. By the time we arrived, she had moved that piece of equipment to the scene." He pointed to the backhoe and Malik followed his gesture by panning with the camera.

"Did she dig him out?" I asked.

The sheriff shook his head like I was crazy for even asking. "The ground is too unstable. It had started to collapse around the boy. We tied one end of a rope to the scoop and made a loop on the other. She lowered it into the ground. The child grabbed onto the line, she pulled him up, and we untangled him."

Fast thinking and smart. I looked forward to interviewing the mother. Our female demographics would be torn between cheers and tears. "Sounds like a team of heroes."

The sheriff nodded, but gave me nothing verbal.

"Not too many people can be that sharp in a crisis," I said. "You must see a lot of cases that end badly. How does this one compare?" I was trying to get him to elaborate on the mom hero angle.

He shrugged and said, "Sometimes we get lucky on the job."

And some people just aren't very good interviews. I wondered how Sheriff Eide had ever gotten elected. So I stopped going for color and went for nuts-and-bolts questions that would help flesh out the tale.

"How deep was the pit?"

"At least fourteen feet. Maybe more. Some of the walls caved in."

"Tell me a little about the sinkhole, Sheriff. Was it already there and did Josh slip in? Or did it open up suddenly and trap him?"

"It appears to have been there for some time, but was overgrown. Locals apparently once used it to dump trash. The boy fell in while chasing his dog."

Viewers love dogs. I made a mental note to get a shot of them together. "How did Josh seem when he got out?"

"Scared. Real scared." That was the most emotional I'd seen the sheriff. He almost seemed scared himself. The camera does that to some people. "And cold. He spent the entire night in the hole."

He filled in some details about why Josh wasn't reported missing until morning.

"Which hospital was he transported to?"

I wasn't sure if Winona or Rochester was closer. I hoped Rochester, because that particular highway was on our way back to Channel 3 and would save us time.

"No hospital." Apparently the mom was a nurse and the family had waived all medical attention. "The kid just wanted to go home."

That wasn't a half bad sound bite, I thought to myself. We all want to go home. Viewers would relate. "Where's home for Josh?"

The sheriff glanced at a farm in the distance before quickly shutting down the interview. "That's enough here. We need to get back to work. We have to secure the scene." He started to walk away, but Malik stopped him to unclip the mic first.

"We just need one more thing, Sheriff." I eyeballed the direction where he had been heading. "A shot of the hole."

"Nope." Sheriff Eide held his hand in front of the camera lens. "Can't let you out there. Too dangerous."

"We'll take our chances," I said. Out of the corner of my eye I saw Malik mouth "We?" with a disapproving look. If anyone's going to get hurt covering the news, it's usually the photographer.

But returning to the station without a picture of the hole would doom the story. After all, this was TV. And that shot was basic journalism.

"How about if we climb one of those trees and get a shot from above," I offered.

Malik gave another disapproving look while the sheriff continued to shake his head.

"We have a telephoto lens," I continued. "We don't have to get real close."

"Good," he said. "Because this is as close as you're going to get."

Figuring he might ease up later, I handed him my business card and asked him to call if he learned anything useful. I told him I'd let him know what time the piece would air.

"Are you going to fill in the hole?" I asked. "So no one else gets trapped? We might want video of that."

The sheriff said no decision had been made, then turned and walked toward the rest of his team. He glanced back once to make sure we weren't following. Subconsciously perhaps, he slapped his gun as if checking to make sure he was armed and ready.

I had to settle for taping a standup of me with the sinkhole far in the distance, for insurance, since we didn't know what direction our story might take. Quickly, I scripted a standup.

((RILEY STANDUP))
SOUTHEASTERN MINNESOTA IS
KNOWN FOR SINKHOLES, BUT
NOT KNOWN FOR TROUBLE LIKE
THIS. WHERE THAT GROVE OF

TREES DIPS IS THE SCENE OF
TODAY'S DRAMATIC RESCUE.

As far as standups go, the content and visuals were fairly lame. Especially for a story of salvation. "Dramatic" might end up being an exaggeration. I was banking on the interview with Josh making this tale memorable and viewers weepy.

But I knew that goal might be a journalistic long shot. Some kids are good talkers, but most aren't, uttering one-word answers and looking down during the interview. We set out to meet Josh and hear his tale of spending the night in a dark and dirty pit.

CHAPTER 10

The good thing about chasing news out in the country is that the only posted signs banning trespassers apply to hunters. And they don't generally count those of us hunting facts.

So Malik and I headed toward the homestead a mile from the sinkhole. The one the sheriff seemed to eye without thinking. The mailbox indeed read Kueppers. A tan dog announced our arrival and stuck to our heels as we approached the front door. We knocked confidently; me armed with a smile, Malik with a camera.

A woman answered, then cut us off when she realized we were media. "He's fine," she blurted, closing the door in our faces.

"Maybe he'd like to thank his rescuers?" I suggested in a loud voice I hoped could be heard beyond the porch. "Maybe you would? Mrs. Kueppers?"

I was a little surprised at another negative reception. Happy-ending stories usually result in happy interviews for all parties. Victim expressing gratitude, hero murmuring how it was nothing, really. Hugs for all.

Since we missed the riveting rescue shot, video of the boy was crucial to the story. And heading back to Channel 3 with a big fat nothing was not going to sit well with the new boss.

"Technically," Malik said, "we haven't been ordered to leave the premises."

"That's exactly what I was thinking."

Years working a job together can keep you on the same page whether you're caught in a moment of drama or comedy. And lately, in the news business, it's becoming harder to tell the difference.

Each year Malik and I covered thousands of miles of news together. We'd seen each other at our worst, but liked each other anyway. The trendy thing was to call us "work spouses," and that was definitely an accurate title for us.

So I slipped my Channel 3 business card under the door and we perched on the edge of the white covered porch waiting for Josh's mother to change her mind and welcome us or direct us off her property pronto.

Apparently used to us by now and unaware we had been spurned, the dog stopped barking and started sniffing us. The animal's wet nose reminded me that I am also a new dog owner, and Husky was probably out being walked by the neighbor boy.

I was still hoping to get video of Josh and his pet together, but Malik shot some solo dog footage for backup.

The early coating of snow clashed with the brilliant autumn colors still in wide view. A combination of sunny days and unseasonably cool evenings had made this season's hues the best in years. We appreciated the vivid contrast with a fir tree grove that functioned as a farm windbreak.

Because Malik fancied himself an artist and not merely a photojournalist, I was guiding his gaze to an unusual quilt hanging on a clothesline by the barn when a small piece of paper blew across the porch.

I bent over and picked up a photo of a freckled face with a gap-toothed grin. Josh, perhaps? He was adorable. Viewers would love him. Just then I heard the front door opening again, so I quickly stuck the picture in the pocket of my jacket.

The woman exited cautiously, making it clear that we were not being invited inside. She was unhappy to see we had lingered. She looked right at me, and read my business card out loud.

"'Riley Spartz. Reporter. Channel 3. Minneapolis.' Do you have any children, Ms. Spartz?"

That was a sensitive question, and certainly unexpected. Part of me was tempted to point out that my motherhood status had nothing to do with her son's sinkhole accident, but another part of me sensed that my answer mattered to her and to my chances of landing the interview.

Twice, I'd thought kids were part of my future. Once, with my now-dead husband, Hugh Boyer. He had been anxious to be a dad and even had a baby-name book he kept in his squad car for amusement during speed traps. Later, with my ex-fiancé, Nick Garnett. He had already raised two boys, but would have embraced fatherhood one more time for me. We'd had the talk.

Now, out in the news field, was a bad time to be reminded that I lived alone and would probably die alone, too.

Malik realized I was stumbling for an answer and jumped into the conversation. "I've got a little boy and girl and they're sure a handful." He pulled out his wallet and was in the process of flashing a proud parent picture from some holiday gathering when she interrupted. "Not you, her."

My moment to lie had passed. Moms didn't need a minute to remember if they had children.

"No. I don't have any children," I replied.

She nodded like that was what she expected. "Then you're not going to understand what's at stake. My priority has to be protecting my son, not going on TV."

I was more confused than ever. People who have survived a crisis sometimes have reasons to avoid the media. Guilt. Holding out for a book deal. None seemed to apply here.

"But your son is safe."

Now she was the quiet one, staring into my eyes with a daunting intensity.

"Josh's accident is now part of your family history," I continued. "He will always remember what happened underground. Why don't the two of you sit on the couch together and tell us the story? You can save the video to remember this day years from now."

"Remember?" she said. "Remember this day? I need Josh to forget what he saw down that hole."

By the time I'd processed her answer, the door had slammed in our faces again. Her next words came muffled, from inside. "And I need you both to go away."

And because we'd been ordered to leave, we did. Without interviews of victim or family. Without pictures of the hole. Yet even empty-handed, I was now convinced we had stumbled upon a potentially more interesting story than a trapped boy.

Malik and I headed back to the scene, determined to find out what Josh saw down in that hole.

CHAPTER 11

Back at the site, one of the state's crime labs on wheels was parked near the backhoe. High tech and low tech side by side. Several technicians stared down at the ground. The presence of the van told me complicated evidence collection and analysis was taking place while we watched.

Deputies had strung yellow-and-black Police Line Do Not Cross plastic tape to keep people back in case any showed up. The hole was no longer the backdrop of an unfortunate accident, but the scene of a possible crime.

The county's top cop stepped into view from behind the cluster of trees, but ignored my wave. "Sheriff Eide," I called out. "What's going on?"

Malik nudged me and pointed toward the lens of his camera. I put my eye to the viewfinder and noticed a taut rope hanging from the backhoe scoop down into the hole.

While we watched, a white horizontal object was hoisted up and swung over to the side where two people teetered while reaching for a grip. As they loaded it on a gurney, a corner of fabric fluttered in the wind like a sheet covering . . .

"A body?" I asked.

"That's just what I was thinking," Malik answered.

"Now we know what Josh needs to forget."

• • •

Eventually, Sheriff Eide confirmed that authorities had recovered the body of an unidentified woman from the bottom of the sinkhole.

"Do you believe she also fell in?" I asked. "Or do you suspect foul play?"

"We have reason to believe the woman's death is suspicious and we are investigating it as a homicide."

"Cause of death?" I asked.

"We'll leave that for the medical examiner."

That didn't surprise me. Unless a cop actually sees a perpetrator pull out a gun and shoot a victim, or finds a knife sticking out of the chest of a body, they don't like speculating on cause of death. "What's the closest town?"

"Harmony."

A small town with a mellow name. "Have you had any reports of missing women in the area recently?"

He shook his head, unwilling to disclose other details. But that moment gave me the opportunity to show him the photograph we found outside Josh's house. I didn't ask him if the boy was Josh. I pretended I knew it was.

"I bet he looks better here than when you pulled him out of that hole." That's a little reporter trick to confirm things we suspect without sources realizing their information is crucial.

Beside verifying Josh's identity, Sheriff Eide assumed because we had the photo, we had the cooperation of Josh's mother.

"She thought it best he not go on camera just now," I said.

The sheriff agreed, explaining they needed to interview him again, once he calmed down. "What a mess for the kid. Spending the night with a corpse."

That was a keeper of a sound bite. "How was Josh found?"

"His dog got him in trouble and his dog got him out. The animal led his mother to the sinkhole. She went straight home to get the backhoe."

Then the sheriff started warming up to me and digressed from the case at hand to tell me about a backhoe theft he investigated a few years earlier. He solved the crime in a matter of days when the culprit parked the stolen vehicle in his front yard with a For Sale sign.

"Wish they could all go that easy," he concluded.

Haunted by some cold cases myself, I knew just what he meant. But I also knew that violent crime—particularly homicide—seldom happened in places like Fillmore County. Residents might be uneasy once word spread and that was probably why the sheriff was nervous when I first arrived. I assured him media coverage often brought tips from the public.

"When was the last time a murder happened in your county?" I asked.

"Not in my lifetime." He had to be nearly fifty. A long time for an area to be homicide free.

I knew that first cops on the scene to rural murders seldom had homicide training. They spend much of their shift writing speeding tickets, giving drunks Breathalyzer tests, and investigating drug sales. I hoped they hadn't done anything to mess up the evidence before the forensics team arrived.

"So Sheriff, how long have you been in office?"

"First term."

I tried to be positive. "Maybe you'll get lucky and solve this killing fast. Then you can count on smooth reelection for the rest of your law-enforcement career."

"Somehow I don't think so." He glanced back to the commotion going on at the crime scene van. "We're missing an important clue."

"What's that?"

"Her face."

CHAPTER 12

Down in the pit and down on his prospects, Josh Kueppers had blasted the dead woman's face away with his shotgun. The sheriff hadn't gotten a conclusive answer whether the boy's finger slipped on the trigger or whether Josh simply wanted to end his stare down with death.

It really didn't matter. Either way, the investigation was stalled because the victim is the starting point for most homicide cases. The face, the chief means of identification in most murders. So who was she?

All this rich debate over identity would enhance my story. Might even make it a two-day story.

So I was surprised when the news desk ordered us to drive back and package the piece for ten. I'd expected them to send the satellite truck and have me broadcast live from the scene for that feeling of immediacy that producers relish in newscasts.

That would also have allowed me more time to try to land an interview with Josh. Instead, I'd have to settle for neighbors with no real firsthand information.

I tried arguing, but Ozzie, the assignment editor, told me not to bother. Then he confided in me the real reason for pulling back on my story. "The new boss is mad at you."

"But I haven't done anything wrong yet," I insisted. "I've actually done something right. Landed an exclusive."

"It's not what you've done or not done, Riley, it's where you've done it."

"You lost me."

Ozzie explained that Bryce had seen a state map showing Harmony, Minnesota, built by the graphics department for my story, and concluded the murder was outside Channel 3's primary viewing area. "He seemed upset that you had not been clearer about the location when you pitched the idea, and that you might have been taking advantage of him being new to the area."

"But we're a major-market station," I said. "We report news around the state, not just in our viewing area. Otherwise we'd never cover medical breakthroughs at the Mayo Clinic, or the record forest fire up in the Boundary Waters Canoe Area."

"I'll let you explain that to him when you return," Ozzie said.

I told him we'd head back, and hung up just as my parents arrived with beef sandwiches and snickerdoodle cookies, hoping to turn the crime scene into a picnic zone. They were disappointed when they heard we were leaving and their plan for an impromptu reunion was a bust.

"We don't get to see you often enough," my mother said.

She had a point, and I could tell she put some effort into this impulsive get-together, even packing a plastic checkered tablecloth to drape over the tailgate of their pickup.

My mother complimented me on my hair. "I like that you're letting it grow out."

My locks hung just past my shoulders. "I just haven't had time to have it cut."

All day my parents had been phoning with rumors. Luckily the sporadic cell service kept them from being in constant touch with me. Their neighbors had already locked into a theory that the killer must be an outsider because no one in these pleasant parts would ever commit such a horrific crime.

"Probably one of those truckers," my mother said. She disliked their large rigs passing her on the road because they made the car shake. She also blamed them for potholes. And now apparently homicide.

"That makes the most sense," my father said, agreeing because that was easier than disagreeing.

I didn't question her theory, but I was betting that the murderer would turn out to be local.

While the sinkhole was actually not that far from the road, I couldn't see a stranger stumbling on the pit just when he needed a place to stash a body. And my guess was, the criminal investigation would take that direction and the killer would turn out to be a registered voter in Fillmore County.

In the meantime, Malik and I took our sandwiches to the van and headed back to Channel 3 with video of a body being recovered, a picture of a boy, his dog, and a look down the hole.

In a relief reversal, Sheriff Eide had let Malik come close enough to get a decent shot of the hollow. So Channel 3 had distinctive elements for the story.

Later, I would realize that the sinkhole was like Alice's venture down her rabbit hole into a world of symbolism and danger.

CHAPTER 13

Malik climbed behind the wheel so I could concentrate on writing my story. The downside was that driving always put him in a grumpy mood. But brilliant writing might help Bryce see the merit in covering this particular story even if the crime fell outside the Channel 3 viewing area.

"Do you have a pen?" I usually kept a couple in my purse, but couldn't find any just then.

"You're asking me for a pen?" Malik said. "A pen? Out in the field, I'm responsible for camera, tripod, microphone, lights, and video discs. All you have to remember to bring is a pen and notebook. You have it so easy. Do your job and don't ever ask me for a pen again."

So much for our contemporary working-spouse relationship. Now we were bickering like an old married couple. I tuned him out and dug around in the glove compartment until I found a chewed-up pencil.

TV news is always scripted in a narrow column for easy reading. The lines time out to a second apiece. The format allows anchor eyes to stare straight ahead with authority rather than dart back and forth like a felon.

((ANCHOR MAP BOX))
THINGS ARE NOT HARMONIOUS

IN THE SMALL MINNESOTA TOWN
OF HARMONY TONIGHT. WHAT
STARTED AS A YOUNG BOY'S
ACCIDENT IS NOW A HOMICIDE
INVESTIGATION. RILEY SPARTZ
HAS MORE IN THIS EXCLUSIVE.

As we drove through town, Malik recognized a now-familiar name on a blue campaign sign that read Reelect Sheriff Ed Eide.

"Isn't that our guy?" he asked.

"You're right," I said. "He didn't mention being up for reelection. I wonder if he has an opponent."

Our question was answered a couple of blocks later where we saw an orange lawn sign reading Laura Schaefer for Sheriff. A woman challenging the incumbent? I was curious what the backstory was on the election, but went back to my sinkhole murder script.

((RILEY TRACK))
THIS HOLE WAS THE SCENE
OF A FREAK ACCIDENT AND A
GRUESOME CRIME IN WHICH
THIS BOY SPENT THE NIGHT
TRAPPED WITH A CORPSE.

"Slow down, Malik," I warned from the passenger seat.

Rounding a curve, we closed in on the rear of an Amish buggy—harder to spot this time because the sun was setting. Some Amish mount orange reflective triangles to the back of their rigs to warn of slow-moving traffic. But others resist, claiming the flashy color violates their religious beliefs. This one was solid black. We waved at the man and woman in the front of the buggy, but both adults gazed straight ahead. I did see a young girl in the rear seat turn to watch us as we passed. I wondered where they were headed and where they had been.

Malik noticed both females wore bonnets. The child's was white, the woman's black. "Their caps are similar to Muslim women and *hijab*," he said.

I hadn't thought about that before, but he was right. I figured the head coverings in both cultures had roots in modesty.

"Beards, too," he continued, noting that the man we saw earlier in the buggy also had a long beard, same as this one. Like Jesus. Or Muhammad.

"That may be true, Malik, but despite such similarities, they would not consider your religion any more Amish than mine. The Amish call all outsiders 'English.'"

I wasn't sure how that word came to be used, but knew it to be long-standing and quite rigid. When I was growing up, Amish sometimes stopped at my parents' farm to water their horses. I'd watch and listen, and heard the word "English" bandied about, and not in a complimentary fashion.

"Viewers would find your comparison of the two faiths interesting," I told my cameraman. "We should make a story out of these similarities someday."

I wondered if Islam and Amish shared much else, but couldn't dwell on other possibilities then, because my murder deadline beckoned.

Since the tale had several complicated points and I'd only get two minutes to tell it, my writing needed to be tight.

((RILEY TRACK))
THE MURDER IS BIG NEWS
IN THIS SMALL TOWN.

Every once in a while I'd read a line out loud to Malik, who'd nod his approval. Technically, I was in charge of words and he was in charge of pictures. But sometimes I'd tell him what to

shoot and he'd tell me what to write. That sort of teamwork oc-
casionally made our stories into hypnotic television.

Back at the station, I voiced my track and then learned my story
was slated for section two in the newscast lineup. Section two
was like the cheap seats. I stormed over to the newscast producer's desk. "Why are you burying the lead? This is fresh news we
have exclusive about a boy who spent the night in a pit with a
murdered woman. All three network morning shows will be trying to book him once they hear about this."

The producer looked uncomfortable, especially when I noted
that the top story—whether the Minnesota Vikings should get a
new football stadium when they had such a lousy record—was
nothing special and had been reported by every other news organization and sports blogger in the state for weeks.

"Sorry, Riley, this is one of those nights when I'm following
orders, not instincts. Take it up with the new boss."

Just then, Bryce stuck his head out of his office and motioned
me over. A large laminated map of Minnesota with a big circle
around the Twin Cities hung on his previously empty wall.

He didn't ask me how my story went; he delivered a lecture.
"This is our DMA—designated market area." His finger traced a
round line that extended about seventy miles north and south of
Minneapolis, just missing Rochester and clipping western Wisconsin.

"Here's where your story is located." He drew a red star near
the Minnesota–Iowa state line, far outside the magic circle. "Our
news coverage resources need to be concentrated in this area."
He pointed inside the circle at the Twin Cities. "That's where the
majority of our viewers live."

His other hand swept across much of southern and northern Minnesota. "This territory gets no over-the-air signal. Only
cable."

I nodded to show I was paying attention to his lesson, even though I was already familiar with the information. But the DMA had never had any impact on Channel 3's news coverage. If a good story broke in Minnesota, we chased. DMA had always been more of an advertising sales tool. That's why even though most Channel 3 viewers were urban, we also ran commercials for seed corn and fertilizer.

I'd often thought of Minneapolis as a big town full of small-town people. I was one of them. And that made me unusual in the competitive world of television. Most journalists don't get to work in their home market. News is an industry of transplants.

"Bryce, I don't think Twin Cities residents are so self-centered as to not care about happenings outside the viewing area. I've lived here my whole life and our audience is hungry for the latest news across the state."

"That's your opinion," he said. "But as news director, I make the calls on what gets covered. And if I had known the trapped-boy story you pitched was so far out of the DMA, I would never have approved it."

Bryce moved away from the map and sat down on the edge of his desk, motioning for me to take a chair. I settled uncomfortably across from him. No personal photos graced his desk. Like most newsies, including me, he probably didn't have much of a personal life. If he did, he might not want his underlings to know about it. Or maybe he simply hadn't had time to unpack items that defined him.

I'd already noted he wasn't wearing a ring on his left hand. That meant he probably didn't have anyone to rush home to and would routinely scrutinize the newsroom to see who else stayed late, working extra hours. And he'd see me.

"I just want to be clear about something," he said. "I may be unfamiliar with this market, but when it comes to running a newsroom, I'm the man to save this sinking station."

"We're lucky to have you." I had no idea if that was true or not, but I had to say something. If our current dialogue was a job review, I'd probably only score "meets expectations." But that's not enough to fire someone.

"I'll try to do better down the road," I assured him.

"That's the kind of attitude I like to see on my team."

He raised his hand for another high five. I followed his lead, but instead of simply slapping our palms together, he grasped my hand and caressed my fingertips.

My impulse was to pull away and I did. A flash of displeasure crossed his face. Quickly, I pretended to be looking at my watch, checking the time.

"I really should check the story edit," I said. "And now that I understand your priorities concerning coverage, I'll be very clear about story geography."

He smiled at my surrender to his terms. "Because I sense we can work well together, I'll make your homicide the lead story tonight after all."

I thanked him for his confidence in me and returned to my office, trying to figure out what had just happened between us.

CHAPTER 14

When the shotgun slug tore into the sinkhole lady's face, it destroyed her nose and blew her brains out the back of her head. Because she was dead, the wound didn't actually bleed. But chunks of flesh, hair, blood clots, and bone pieces spattered behind her on the wall of the pit.

Josh didn't get covered with much gunk, but he abandoned gun for blanket, convinced if he wasn't already in hell he was headed there fast.

While his mother hoped he would forget the ordeal, a woman with a sketch pad was making him remember the most vivid details.

"You got the best look at her of anyone, Josh," Sue Senden said. "While it's still fresh in your mind, I'd like you to describe her face."

Sue was a forensic artist who worked with the police to draw composites of suspects or victims. Her favorite role was helping give the unnamed dead their identities back.

"Let's start with the mouth. What can you tell me about her mouth?"

Josh closed his eyes and the frightening face floated before him. He opened his eyes quickly to make the image go away. He wished his mother didn't have to wait so far down the hall.

"It's okay, Josh. We just need your help. We have to find out who this woman is. What can you tell me about her lips?"

He shut his eyes again. "They sort of look sucked in."

"Excellent." She held her sketch pad so he couldn't see her drawing.

Sue actually had more to work with in this Jane Doe case than usual. Many of her clients were skulls, recovered years after their deaths. She often used clay to reconstruct their faces.

Before driving down to southern Minnesota to meet Josh, she'd stopped at the Hennepin County morgue to stand over the body in question. Medical examiner Della Sax pulled the corpse from the cooler, leaving the two of them alone. While authorities were able to pull fingerprints from the corpse, so far they'd not had any cold hits from their crime computers. They'd also taken dental X-rays, but that wouldn't help unless they had a name to match.

That's why Sue's job was so important. Even though her final creation only dealt from the neck on up, and even though many forensic artists settled for photos of the deceased from the crime scene, Sue always insisted, whenever possible, on viewing the entire body.

Subtle hints gave her perspective about the victim's habits. In this case, the absence of tattoos, manicure, or pierced ears struck her as unusual for a young woman in this society. A chart on the shelf by the body read that her skin did not appear to have had any makeup—neither foundation, blush, nor mascara.

"How about her eyes, Josh? Do you see anything special?"

Josh didn't like this question. The eyes were the scariest part of this face. He didn't want to see her eyes ever again. Yet whenever he closed his, hers were watching him.

"Take your time," she cautioned.

Sue had already sketched the outline of the woman's face from her visit to the morgue. The center of the face was damaged by gunfire and had undergone some decomposition in places, but Sue had the bone structure down. Even chin. And long dark hair. She needed the witness to fill in the missing pieces.

Josh closed his eyes again. He was back in the pit, face to face with death. He cringed at the memory.

"You're not alone, Josh. I'm right here. Without you, she would still be in that dark hole. You helped rescue her. Set her free. But she needs more help. Don't think about what color her eyes are." She knew eye color changed after death. "Try to recall how far set back they were, and how they were shaped."

"I can't remember." She didn't believe him. Experience told her trauma victims never forget the eyes. But she didn't push him.

"How about her nose, Josh? What can you tell me about the shape of her nose?" This was the most critical element of his description because the nose was gone.

He'd barely shut his eyes when he answered. "Skinny. Her nose was skinny."

Sue showed him a book with pages of noses.

"This one," he pointed.

Sue sketched some more, adding shadow and contrast before asking Josh if he'd like to see the drawing. He thought for a while before nodding. She handed the picture to him. He glanced at the illustration for just a few seconds before giving it back.

"It's okay, Josh. What I'm drawing is what I think she looked like when she was alive. Hopefully, the police can show this sketch to people and see if anyone knows her name."

Josh reached for the picture again and pointed at her eyes. "Bigger. They were bigger than this."

Sue put her pencil to work. Josh paged through the book and looked at different pieces of faces before giving his approval to the final version.

"You have a good knack for detail," she said. She shook his hand, thanked him for his assistance, and turned him back over to his mother.

"Josh was a huge help." Sue showed Michelle the woman's face. "Police will likely put this on television and in newspapers in the hopes someone recognizes her."

No women even remotely resembling the sinkhole corpse—Caucasian, age fifteen to twenty-three, five feet four inches tall, about 115 pounds—had been reported missing in Minnesota recently.

So the victim was either from out of state, or no one realized or cared that she was gone. Already, detectives were swamped with queries from families of missing women across the country.

The picture would help narrow the field.

Josh definitely seemed calmer on the drive home. Neither mother nor son mentioned the sketch session, but Michelle Kueppers had a nagging feeling that the dead woman's face looked familiar.

CHAPTER 15

Covering a case in Minnesota's Amish country prompted me to buy a paperback bestseller with a demure blonde wearing a bonnet on the cover. I figured I'd learn more about their culture, and maybe it would be a fun read. That night, one chapter in, I realized I was reading a romance about forbidden love.

An innocent young woman was torn between a world promising tranquillity and one offering titillation. Two appealing men symbolized her contrasting futures. The following pages assured me that the narrative was no bodice ripper—any sex that happened, happened offscreen. So far, the most explicit dialogue was debate over open-mouth kissing before marriage.

By the time I went to bed, I'd gained some practical insights that I could share with Malik, such as the fact that only married Amish men grew beards.

As I drifted to sleep, I made a mental note: bearded = married; clean shaven = single. I preferred a smooth chin myself, not that I was looking for a date in a wide-brimmed hat and a buggy. But I had admired how the author had hinted that physical labor led to physical perfection in Amish men.

The next morning, an email was awaiting me at the station with a forensic sketch of the sinkhole victim attached. No scoop. The drawing was being sent to all media with a standard request to ask viewers/readers to contact law enforcement if they recognized the victim.

I printed the picture for the morning news huddle.

Thoughts of what the woman's face might have looked like before death, and her final moments of life, distracted me from the day's headlines for a few minutes. Details of her facial damage had not been disclosed, only that her face was missing.

I found myself mulling a centuries-old St. Jerome quote: *The face is the mirror of the mind, and the eyes without speaking confess the secrets of the heart.*

What secrets might this murder victim confess? And were any of them enough to cost her her life?

The medical examiner's official cause of death listed "blunt force trauma to the head with fracture of the cranium, cerebral contusions, with subdural and intracranial bleeding."

For viewers, I'd simply rewrite the science to say the woman had died from a blow to the head. There was no sign of any murder weapon. And if evidence existed as to what type of material caused the fatal injury, the cops were keeping quiet. That was routine. They liked to withhold those specifics to weed out false confessions.

Despite Bryce's insistence that stories outside our viewing area added no value to a newscast, I'd noticed—as I was sure he must have—that the overnight ratings showed that Channel 3's homicide lead held the audience of a popular crime drama with no drop-off.

But when I laid the depiction of the dead woman's face on the table, he picked up the drawing and stared into her eyes as if suddenly fascinated to meet her. "So this is our victim?"

"As described to a forensic artist by Josh, yes," I explained. "The cops need leads for the investigation, and right now the media is their best hope in identifying the victim. No doubt, the newspapers and other stations will air the picture."

That was a no-brainer. Free news content. Then I stopped talking. I left the advocating of specific coverage for someone else at the table to suggest. But no one was brave enough to speak about what had proven to be a risky story to embrace. Everyone waited for Bryce.

To my surprise, he proposed running the picture on all newscasts and displaying it prominently on our website. "Then if someone recognizes this woman we can take credit. Each version should remind viewers that we want to follow up on our exclusive last night."

Everyone else at the morning meeting nodded in agreement. I was beginning to think my new boss was sounding a lot like Noreen and that news directors must share some chromosome glitch that makes them immediately weigh audience payoff when making even relatively simple decisions.

Then Bryce commanded, "Make it so." Thus ruining *Star Trek* for me forever.

The station had yet to designate a main anchor to replace Sophie after she was gunned down. Each week, someone on staff would rotate in the anchor chair for a live on-air audition. Sort of like a reality show. But that was no guarantee Channel 3 wouldn't ultimately hire from outside.

These days, I just typed "anchor" on top of my scripts since I never knew who was going to be reading the news. The medical reporter had her turn this week.

((ANCHOR BOX))
POLICE HAVE RELEASED A
FORENSIC SKETCH OF A MURDER
VICTIM WHOSE BODY WAS
DISCOVERED IN A SINKHOLE IN
SOUTHEASTERN MINNESOTA.

((TWOSHOT ANCHOR))
RILEY SPARTZ NOW JOINS US WITH
A FOLLOW TO HER EXCLUSIVE LAST
NIGHT ABOUT THIS MOST UNUSUAL
HOMICIDE.

((RILEY CU))
DO YOU KNOW THIS WOMAN?
IF SO, THE POLICE WANT
TO HEAR FROM YOU.

I tagged off the story with the law enforcement phone number. Then, all we and the cops could do was wait. Someone, besides the killer, had to know the victim. Some murders—like those involving robbery or rape—hold little mystery concerning motive. In this case, someone took time to stash her body, rather than simply leaving her where she died or dumping her by the side of the road. Sure, some killers hide the evidence. Others don't want to risk being caught transporting it. This felt like one of those cases where understanding the victim's life might help make better sense of her death.

Later, I checked in with the sheriff. Still no answers. While my parents were confident the killer was an outsider, he told me citizens of Harmony were dismissing the victim as an outsider, too. I'd seen that type of denial in other slayings because people in small towns feel safer if the prey was not one of them.

That night, I dreamed I wasn't alone. The eyes of the woman in the drawing seemed to hover over my bed. Jane Doe didn't blink. She just waited, like she needed company and had no one else. An uncomfortable image, but not quite a nightmare. I wondered if Josh also saw her in his dreams.

When I woke, I woke tired. Even with concealer under my eyes, and airbrush makeup across my face, I hoped not to have to broadcast a live shot.

CHAPTER 16

All news employees were summoned via the loudspeaker for a station meeting the next morning. We stood in the center of the newsroom—apprehensive—because the announcements that came out of such gatherings were typically unpleasant, relating to staff layoffs and budget cuts.

Our old general manager and our new news director stood side by side on the assignment desk's elevated platform so we all had a clear view. A broad Cheshire-Cat grin stretched across Bryce's face, and I braced myself for what was about to be said.

But when the GM started to speak, his words made me think that perhaps the pattern of doom was breaking. "We all know these are tough times for the news business, but Channel 3 is through trying to wait out this cursed economy. We're going to be proactive."

His stump speech had our interest. "Now you've all had some time to get to know Bryce, and I want to tell you that together we have developed a strategy that will increase station revenue and allow us to devote our news resources in more creative ways to better compete with our rivals."

The elocution now had the sound of a snake-oil scam, but if Bryce knew some management secret to make Channel 3 the news leader of the market, I could get over my fear of snakes.

"I'm going to let our news director fill you in on this exciting next step for the station." Then he turned the floor over to Bryce, who thanked him for his enthusiasm and support.

"We're here to discuss three little words that will transform how Channel 3 covers news. Can anyone guess what they are?"

No one spoke. After all, we already had "high-definition cameras."

We already were network "owned and operated."

And we'd had "Doppler weather radar" for years.

Bryce waited to build suspense before yelling out the answer with an animated fist pump to emphasize each word. "ONE. MAN. BANDS."

If he was expecting cheers, he was disappointed. We were speechless.

One-man bands are the mark of small-market stations be-cause they're cheap. The term is used for reporters who have to shoot their own stories. Normally rookies, not veteran journal-ists. And certainly not in a major market like the Twin Cities where news employees specialize, whether their skill be anchor-ing, reporting, videotaping, or producing. We each like to think we excel at our particular jobs.

I'd seen one-man bands toil in the field when news events took me to small markets like Mankato or Duluth. And I'd always felt sorry for them.

"Come now, you must have questions," he said. "Think of it as Multi. Media. Journalism. Hey, that's three words, too."

I figured the whole session must be a trap to weed out those of us who weren't team players. I bit down on my lip, warning myself to keep quiet. The photographers looked nervous because they sensed job security at stake. If reporters were shooting their own video, what were they going to do?

"If the reporters will be working as photographers," camera-man Dave Chaney asked, "will photographers be going on the air?"

"An excellent question," Bryce said. "We will be deciding that on a case-by-case basis. Some of you may end up on camera, others will function as field producers conducting interviews as well as videotaping stories. I realize this can't happen overnight. Staff will require training."

One of the more recent hires, a reporter named Nicole Wilson, looked nervous, and I understood why. Carrying a camera and tripod is hard—especially in high heels. This was her first reporting job in a large market; she was probably still a probationary employee and had to do as ordered. But she was also young and blond, so I figured she'd wind up fine. I gave her a smile of encouragement, even though I myself wasn't encouraged. Nicole responded with a flash of gratitude, and I made a mental note to do a better job of welcoming her to Channel 3 and teaching her TV chick tricks.

I was old enough to know better than to run around in heels all day. High heels are not worth the pain in your feet. Your legs may look good, but your legs do not show on the air. I'd take Nicole shopping for pants and sensible shoes.

Shooting your own video meant static reporter standups, which are boring, to say the least. I waited for one of my colleagues to mention the obvious question, but no one stepped up.

So I did. "We're a major-market station, Bryce. How do you expect one-man bands, which typically result in poor-quality video, to increase ratings?"

Bryce seemed surprised by my question. "Who said anything about increasing ratings? Ratings are the least of our worries."

His answer stunned me. Almost every boss I ever worked for was so obsessed with ratings that the newsroom had a toxic vibe during the sweeps months of November, February, and May. Maybe Bryce would introduce a healthier atmosphere by taking the focus off ratings. Could this be a good thing?

But then he outlined how he had crunched the numbers and the station could be more profitable by settling for second or even third place rather than fighting to be first, and I got it.

"It's a numbers game," he said. "And for too long, Channel 3 has been focused on the wrong numbers."

It was clear our new boss was going to run us into the ground until we were dirt last among viewers. We would be the laughingstock among our news peers. The station would never land another Emmy again.

Bryce pulled a poster from behind the assignment desk with a pie chart labeled with topics like Salaries, Overtime, Equipment, Travel. "It doesn't matter if our viewership goes down as long as our costs go down more. Simple economics."

That's when we learned Bryce had graduated with a BA in business, not journalism.

Cost is definitely a factor in weighing which stories get covered. But to hear it embraced as a primary business strategy was sacrilege to our civic mission to seek truth and report objectively. Newsrooms should not be run the same as hardware stores.

Bryce concluded his lecture by insisting that the implementation of one-man bands would allow Channel 3 to actually cover more news by being in more places at the same time. I wanted to point out a flaw in that reasoning: the station would have to buy twice as many cameras. But in the interests of job preservation, I zipped my lip.

"Channel 3 is paving the way for a new brand of TV journalism," he said. "Working smart by doing more with less."

He and the GM high-fived each other, which sent a loud smack reverberating through the silent newsroom. And then Bryce moved among the employees handing out buttons that read WORK SMART. Unprompted, one reporter pinned the slogan to his jacket to demonstrate he was a team player.

Hypocrite.

Kiss-ass.

Suck-up.

Slowly I stepped back, away from Bryce.

But he headed toward me, wrapping his arm around my shoulder. "Riley, I think you're worried because you've been doing your job a certain way for a long time." He emphasized the word *long*. "You're filled with trepidation. That happens with change, but rest assured, I have confidence you can learn new tricks."

Then he called everyone else over. "I've decided Riley will be the first to kick off our one-man-band coverage. Today, you'll be trained on how to work a television camera. Tomorrow you'll shoot your first story."

Bryce started a round of applause that made me nauseous.

"I thought you said this wouldn't happen overnight," I said.

He leaned over and whispered in my ear. "A subpar job won't end this. What you shoot goes on the air, no matter what. Screw up and you'll be the one who looks bad—on air and on paper. You better cooperate. I wouldn't want to write up insubordination for your personnel file."

CHAPTER 17

Bryce sure meant what he said.

The next morning I was assigned to cover a news conference solo on the front steps of the State Capitol. The training he had promised consisted of showing me how to turn the camera on, and explaining the concept of point-and-shoot.

As I hauled a tripod and camera up the steps of the Capitol with my oversize purse slung over my shoulder, I longed for the golden days of television—just yesterday—when all I had to carry to a story was a pen and notebook.

I had been hoping for a less public arena where my competitors couldn't witness my inaugural shoot. Instead, Jenny Turrentine from Channel 8, clutching only a reporter's notebook, passed me effortlessly.

"What's going on?" She turned a couple of times to see if anyone was behind or in front of me. "Where's your photographer? Why are you lugging all that stuff?"

I mumbled something about us experimenting with shooting our own video.

"You mean one-man bands?" She rushed to tell the other stations the news. "Hey, everybody, Channel 3 is running one-man bands. Look at Riley Spartz."

They all looked at me, torn between savoring my disgrace and fearing their own newsrooms might emulate the move. But one of the other cameramen gave me a reassuring smile and helped me center the camera on my tripod head.

I was spared more razzing when a woman with gray braided hair arrived on the scene, shaking something yellow and pink in front of the cameras.

"Can everybody see this? Who can't see this?" she called.

We stayed silent and let her rant a couple minutes, waiting to learn where this was leading. I kept my eye glued to the viewfinder, afraid she would walk out of frame and I'd miss something essential.

We'd been called there for a news conference about protecting black bears.

Turns out, like Noreen, Bryce believed animal stories attracted the most viewers. Apparently, a news director manifesto. Unlike my previous boss, Bryce had no pets of his own and no personal love for furry creatures. To him, they were business tools, good for audience share and ratings numbers. And generally, animal features were cheap to produce. So when the assignment desk mentioned a possible bear story, Bryce ordered me out the door.

"My name is Teresa Neuzil." The woman worked for a non-profit center for black bear research in northern Minnesota. "Do we want people who can't see well enough to see this to be shooting guns?" She waved the colorful streamer again.

"What is that thing you're holding?" I finally asked. I felt more normal asking questions than aiming the lens. The rest of the media pack seemed relieved to cut to the chase.

She walked over to me and held the item in front of my camera lens. The other photographers shifted their gear so they could also get the shot. "This is a bear radio collar. We use it to track research animals."

Teresa drew our attention to the pink and yellow ribbons attached to the leather collar. "Even from a distance, these ribbons are quite noticeable." Then she pointed out a dark stain on the collar. "Can anyone tell what this is?"

None of us answered. So she told us. "Blood."

The word startled me. I found myself hoping news was near, even if an actual bear wasn't.

Teresa waved a large photo of a black bear in one hand, the collar in the other. Her voice sounded choked up. "This was Ginny. The bear who wore this collar. Now presumed dead by a hunter's bullet."

The collar had been left in a mailbox outside the research station. No note. "This creature was one of our windows into the bear world."

This wasn't the first time such a misfortune had happened in her line of work. She'd lost five research bears to hunters over the last several years. Yet state wildlife officials refused her pleas to make hunting radio-collared bears illegal.

"That's why I've driven hundreds of miles south to St. Paul to bring this recurring travesty to the attention of our state lawmakers," Teresa said. "These research bears are not mere trophies. Their worth is more than a bearskin rug. They provide valuable knowledge to schools as well as scientists. Such a death sets our study back years."

The North American Bear Center was familiar to me. Last year, a live online camera was placed in a den, letting viewers watch a hibernating bear give birth. The website had gone viral with Internet hits and the cub had become a cyberdarling.

"Is it possible that it's hard to see the ribbons in dim light or deep brush?" the newspaper outdoors reporter asked. "Do we need to give hunters some slack here?"

The woman shook her head. "By law, deer hunters in the southern part of the state are required to count the points on a buck's antlers before firing. This is much simpler."

She shook the ribbons again. Close up, I could see they were made of fluorescent duct tape, well suited to survive north woods winters.

"Also," Teresa continued, "most bear-hunting parties use bait to attract their prey, giving them ample opportunity to see the bears before pulling a trigger or releasing an arrow."

She described how the bear center was dedicated to clearing up misconceptions regarding scientific facts about bears.

"People are the number one cause of death of black bears, yet our bear center is not opposed to hunting. In fact, our work helps manage bear populations. And hunters benefit from that data. But there are more than twenty thousand black bears in Minnesota. Surely we can spare a dozen."

The closest I'd ever been to hunting animals was flushing pheasants out of cornfields as a child so my dad could shoot them. So while I'm not opposed to the sport, it made sense that the killing of these tagged bears should end.

"What is your next move?" I asked. "What do you hope to accomplish here today?"

"We've asked state wildlife officials for their support, but failed to get it," Teresa said. "Now I'm asking the citizens of Minnesota to implore their lawmakers to make killing research bears illegal."

All in all, her speech seemed like fine campaign rhetoric. I wondered why state wildlife officials rejected her proposal. So after the news conference ended, I drove about a mile to the Department of Natural Resources headquarters to find out.

I'm not a particularly outdoorsy news type, so the last time I'd spoken with the DNR was a year earlier after a burglary in one of their storage buildings. The break-in wouldn't have attracted any attention except the thieves stole twenty animal head mounts from a traveling Wall of Shame display designed to encourage the public to report poachers. The haul included trophy bucks, a large walleye, turkey tail feathers, even a bear head.

Their communications director, Zach Loecher, was miffed when he heard about the crusade at the Capitol minutes earlier. "This is an issue with a lot of public emotion behind it. Not nearly as clear cut as the bear center is making it seem." Then he wondered out loud why no other media were pressing him for answers.

"My guess is Channel 3 must be the only one that cares about getting both sides of the story," I said.

But it actually crossed my mind that the other reporters might be dismissing the event as nonnews. The dead-bear tale fell into the category of discretionary news. It certainly wasn't mandatory for coverage, except on a real slow news day. So the other newsrooms in town could be passing, simply phoning the DNR for a comment to include in the story tag, or have a much better story Channel 3 was missing.

But hunting research bears certainly could be made into an interesting *issue* story. That's what I was hoping for, so I wanted to interview Loecher on camera before it occurred to him that keeping quiet might make his problem go away.

He got back to the matter concerning the bear center. "It isn't that they love bears and we hate them. Our agency has to deal with a bigger picture."

"I have no doubt Mother Nature can be complicated," I said. "Let's put you on camera to make sure we get it right."

Loecher's office had nice natural light, so all I had to do was clip a microphone onto his shirt. I considered starting out smart alecky and asking what he had against black bears, but decided to simply play it straight so I could leave promptly with a usable sound bite.

"What's the downside of making it illegal to hunt research bears?" I asked.

He knew his material and made his argument. "While we believe such research to be popular and interesting, we do not believe it essential to managing bear populations."

He pointed out that the DNR also uses radio collars to study bears and also loses some of those animals each year to what he called "legal harvest" by hunters.

"Such is the circle of life," Loecher said. "Our policy is to request that hunters voluntarily refrain from shooting such bears, but in the case of such a kill, we do not believe it would be easy to prove the hunter could tell the bear was marked, especially since so many bears are taken at dawn or dusk."

On my way out, I stopped by a black bear display in the front lobby. The furry creature had been mounted on its hind feet, leaning against a tree stump. The head wasn't much taller than my own, which surprised me. We could almost see eye to eye.

It seemed the perfect place for a stand-up. With the toe of my shoe I marked a location on the floor that seemed the right position for me to speak. Then I set up the tripod and camera, hit Record, and rushed to that spot.

((STANDUP))
UNDER CURRENT STATE LAW,
RESEARCH BEARS ARE "FAIR
GAME" FOR HUNTERS AND COULD
END UP LIKE THIS TROPHY.

I rewound the tape to double-check my standup and found that my head cropped off at the nose. All that could be seen of my face was my mouth talking. The stuffed bear in the background was barely visible.

I tried again, pulling wider with the shot. This time I clipped one ear and arm, but at least the bear was discernible.

The news desk called then, ordering me back to the station because one of the evening shift photographers needed the camera.

"I really need to shoot another version of my standup," I said. "I'm having a hard time centering."

"Then write a set piece instead of a standup." Set pieces are used with limited video stories; the reporter sits on the news set for most of the story. They are often dull.

I used the standup anyway, the one with the clipped arm and

ear, because I thought the shot would demonstrate the futility of one-man bands. That wasn't the only video problem. When Teresa waved the bear color ribbons, the focus blurred. Her audio was a little scratchy because I'd forgotten to use the wireless mic. And the color on the DNR guy's face was washed out.

Instead of calling a halt to the trial, or at least giving me more training, Bryce dubbed the mistakes "artistic." He assured me that soon I'd be as comfortable behind the camera as I was in front of it.

As for the bear story: my boss loved it. "I see it as controversial, not complicated." And we both knew that while many institutions view controversy as a negative, newsrooms welcome brouhaha. We tell ourselves that it's proof of free speech, but we know it also breeds buzz.

The station ran a link to the bear center's website so members of the public could sign a cyberpetition supporting the legal protection of radio-collared bears.

CHAPTER 18

The morning sky was darker longer as we moved deeper into fall, so I couldn't count on the sun to wake me. After silencing my alarm, I reached for the TV remote and turned on the news before lifting my head from the pillow.

I liked making sure nothing wild had happened overnight before I faced the day. The morning anchors read the news on a set in front of a window overlooking the streets of downtown Minneapolis. Viewers could see weather and city buses in the background. But today, all you could see were protesters whose signs read Hunters Have Rights and Bears Are Fair Game.

I scrambled to turn up the volume. The anchor introduced one of the protesters for a live through-the-box interview about radio-collared bears.

((ANCHOR, DOUBLE BOX))
SEEMS LIKE THERE ARE MORE
THAN ENOUGH BEARS IN
MINNESOTA THAT WE COULD
SPARE SOME FOR RESEARCH . . .
WHY SUCH STRONG OPPOSITION?

((PROTESTER CU))
GETTING SHOT IS ONE WAY

ANIMALS DIE. IT'S A LEGITIMATE
PART OF THE BEAR RESEARCH
AND THEY NEED TO ACCEPT THAT
OUTCOME.

((ANCHOR DOUBLE BOX))
YOU SOUND QUITE PASSIONATE
ABOUT ALLOWING HUNTERS TO
KILL THESE MARKED ANIMALS.

((PROTESTER CU))
WE NEED TO PROTECT THE RIGHTS
OF HUNTERS. ANTIHUNTING
GROUPS ARE BEHIND THIS. AND IF
WE GIVE IN HERE, PRETTY SOON
THEY'LL BE PUTTING COLLARS AND
RIBBONS ON DEER AND WOLVES
AND ALL WILD ANIMALS JUST TO
END THE SPORT OF HUNTING.

The debate was provocative. And the story tagged out with a mention that this particular hunting group had started its own online petition to continue the "legal harvest" of radio-collared black bears. Channel 3, in the interests of fairness—and controversy—also made that link available to our viewers.

Husky needed a morning stretch. Or maybe I did. My newly acquired dog actually didn't like going out any longer than necessary to do his doggy business, but I enjoyed his company on the street and thought I looked less lonely with him on a leash. That didn't mean I wasn't lonely. Or that he wasn't lonely. We both had a lot of people missing from our lives—some dead, some behind bars, some just far away.

"Come on, boy." We both started running through the neighborhood. Husky was a hand-me-down dog. First he belonged to Toby Elness, an imprisoned animal activist. Then Noreen Banks, his ex-wife and my deceased boss, took custody. Now me.

Even in my current rough patch, my life was better than most—especially with a ball of fur by my side.

I dwelled again on how lucky I was to find a TV news job in a market near my childhood stomping ground. Old teachers tell me they watch me on the news. People come up to me on the street and tell me they know my parents or they used to baby-sit me.

I'd done some checking on Bryce through the TV news grapevine and Channel 3 was his fourth station. When journalists aren't chasing news, we're chasing gossip. But oddly, Bryce was the guy nobody wanted to talk about.

CHAPTER 19

The bear story ended up being one of those instances where covering news makes more news.

By midmorning, just over two hundred people had put their names on the petition supporting the hunting of radio-collared bears. But for the opposition, more than five thousand signatures sided with safeguarding research bears and two lawmakers were already vowing to sponsor such legislation.

Two major hunting organizations were distancing themselves from the morning extremists and taking a more mainstream political approach using lobbyists rather than protesters.

Dozens of viewer comments followed my story posted online. THE MADNESS MUST CEASE. I scrolled and read through them. HOW CAN HUMANS BE SO CRUEL? Predictably, most were from people against all forms of hunting. ALL GOD'S CREATURES HAVE A RIGHT TO LIFE. Yet some were even from hunters. I AM A HUNTER AND HUNTING COLLARED BEARS IS A DISGRACE. RESEARCH BEARS HAVE HAD CONTACT WITH HUMANS, REDUCING THEIR FEAR OF US. But others were from hunters who supported the status quo. DEATH BY HUNTING IS PART OF A BEAR'S LIFE.

One comment had a familiar, snarly tone. PROTECTING RESEARCH BEARS . . . I'M TORN BETWEEN POSING THE QUESTION, DOES A BEAR SHIT IN THE WOODS? OR

BRINGING UP A QUOTE FROM *ANCHORMAN: THE LEGEND OF RON BURGUNDY.*

I dismissed the first half of the comment because jerk clichés don't merit replies.

As for *Anchorman*—set in the 1970s happy-talk, Action News era—the movie includes a debate over whether women should be hired in TV newsrooms. I knew the quote in question: the weatherman and a reporter have a conversation about bears being attracted to women's menstrual periods, and how that meant that hiring a female would put the entire television station in jeopardy.

The film was a tongue-in-cheek comedy, but I still considered the dialogue crude and wasn't about to respond on Channel 3's website. Viewers weren't required to leave their real names on their comments, and this one didn't. But I had a feeling we'd watched *Anchorman* together, on DVD, curled up on my couch once upon a time. And we'd also developed a routine of incorporating famous movie quotes into our own conversations and guessing the actor, film, and year.

For Nick Garnett to comment on my story, he had to be missing me. Or stalking me. And I wasn't sure how either scenario made me feel. I'd spent the last couple of months trying not to look at the photo of us holding hands by the Lake Harriet band shell, even though a framed five-by-seven lay among other memorabilia in my bottom desk drawer.

We had been ready to spend the rest of our lives together. Our engagement was brief, yet intense. The breakup was complicated. On one level, his fault. On another, mine. To be mature, I was willing to share responsibility for our split. After all, if, like the song says, it takes two to tango, it must also take two to untangle.

Yet given time and distance, I could also make a strong case that neither of us was to blame. Call it circumstances beyond our control. We'd both seen it on the street: sometimes tragedy brings people together, other times heartache pushes them apart. Living through the newsroom nightmare apparently made it impossible for us to find happiness around any reminder of that day. Even each other. And if our love wasn't powerful enough to withstand such stress, maybe we were better off apart.

His phone number was still on my speed dial, but I wasn't bold enough to call. Neither was he, clearly. Texting would have been more direct. Even Facebook. Posting an anonymous comment on one of my stories was a long shot. But maybe "long shot" best described our destiny. I posted a line that seemed to fit our predicament. "What is it about love that makes us so stupid?"

If Garnett was behind the original comment, I would know soon enough. Our fondness for movie trivia had developed over the years into a competition of quizzing each other on film quotes. If he kept quiet, he would lose.

An hour later, I read a reply to my reply. "Diane Lane. *Under the Tuscan Sun*. 2003."

So it was Nick Garnett on the other end. I still wasn't bold enough to hit speed dial. Online exchanges felt safer.

Searching for a profound rejoinder, I posted: "Oh yes, the past can hurt. But the way I see it, you can either run from it, or learn from it."

If no answer followed, he was running and I would not chase. But seconds later, I read, "Rafiki. *The Lion King*. 1994." I resisted reminding him that Rafiki was a character, not an actor.

Instead I was focusing on what I had learned from the past and what that understanding might mean to us—if there was an "us"—when my cellphone rang and Garnett's number appeared on the screen.

One ring. Two rings. Seconds to weigh past versus future. I took a deep breath. Then, I answered.

"Riley, I'm not a smart man, but I know what love is."

He couldn't see me smile, but his words made mine easy. "Tom Hanks. *Forrest Gump*. 1994."

• • •

We caught up on the basics, discovering much of our lives remained unchanged. Washington was messed up; Channel 3 was messed up.

"I don't need you to tell me that," he said. "I saw that horrible bear story of yours. It looked like you shot it yourself."

I explained my new boss's approach to news.

"One-man bands?" Garnett said. "Sounds like the uproar over one-man patrols that police departments went through twenty-some years ago."

Most cities shifted from two-man squads to one-man squads to save money, despite opposition from police officers who feared for their personal safety.

"Now it's the norm," he said.

"I don't want it to ever be the newsroom norm," I replied.

"It may not be up to you. My experience is that decisions like those are made far above our pay grade."

He was probably right. Instead of arguing employment philosophy, I told him about my latest Jane Doe. Nude. Dumped. Unclaimed. Garnett had spent a career as a homicide detective, and I was interested on his take on my case.

"That's cold," he said. "Ditching a body in a pit. Too brutal a farewell to someone you cared about, so I'm going to make a guess the victim didn't know her killer."

"Random?" Too bad. "Those are tougher to solve."

"They can be."

"So even if the victim is identified," I said, "there may not be an obvious suspect."

"And even if there is, that doesn't necessarily close the case. Otherwise Agatha Christie would be out of print. Remember how she made the least likely suspect classic."

We chuckled over a few of those whodunits and I confided that I was trying not to get too attached to this murder because of the news director's desire to concentrate on crime closer to the Twin Cities.

"Nothing unusual in metro murders right now?" he asked.

"Mostly gang shootings." Those kind of homicides were never very interesting to the police or media. Often unsympathetic victims as well as killers.

"So you might be stuck on the bear beat," Garnett said. "Maybe I should fly in this weekend and give you a bear hug."

It wasn't just a bluff. He worked as an investigator for the Transportation Security Administration and could come up with a reason to fly anywhere, anytime.

I didn't want to rush our relationship from a phone call to a blanket brigade. "Sorry, Nick."

I made a special effort to call him by his first name. In the news biz, staffers often refer to people by their last names. To save time. And when Garnett was simply a source, that didn't bother him. But when that changed, he wanted a feeling of intimacy in our conversation as well as our relationship.

"Really, Nick, the only bear I'm hugging this weekend is named Teddy." That was my flirty, yet not phony, way of telling him I wanted to take things slow.

He got it. But we both knew this conversation wasn't over.

CHAPTER 20

Jane Doe became Sarah Yoder.

I was on my way to the station greenroom for a powder and blush touch-up when my cell phone rang again. I expected Garnett with a final line about not being able to *bear* being apart.

"I'm not *caving* on your demands." I hit the answer button and spoke without looking at the caller ID. Or even saying hello.

It was my mother. She didn't know the name, but said the talk around town was that the dead woman was Amish.

When she said the word, I got chills. That was one direction I hadn't anticipated regarding this sinkhole murder. If you go by police reports, Amish are seldom crime victims or perpetrators. Of course, the numbers could be skewed because Amish prefer to handle infractions within their own community and not involve outside law.

"Call me if you hear anything else, Mom. I'm going to try to get ahold of the sheriff."

Ed Eide was preparing a news release, but read me the details over the phone.

Sarah Yoder, age 18, Harmony, Minnesota. Definitely local.

"How come no one reported her missing?" I asked.

"We're trying to find that out," he said. "Her name is all I'm prepared to disclose right now at this stage of our investigation."

"How was she identified, Sheriff?"

"Somebody saw her picture on the news and contacted us. And no, I'm not releasing that name at this time. We've got our own questioning to do first."

"How about a camera interview, you and me?"

He declined, so I thanked him for the information and told him I'd check back later.

I phoned the farm and relayed to Mom what I knew about the victim.

"So young," she said.

"I know," I replied. "But this case has been unusual from the start. Now let me talk to Dad for a minute."

My dad had friends everywhere. And he never forgot a name. "Do you know any Yoders around Harmony?"

He didn't, but he said he wasn't in touch with the Amish so much anymore, not like when he was actively farming.

"There used to be an Amish family who lived just a few miles east of us, but they moved years ago. You were just a little girl and probably don't remember them."

I wished I did. "Do you know any leaders in the Amish community now?"

He replied that one of the bishops around Harmony used to be an Abram Stoltzfus. "Not sure if he's still around or not. My recollection is they serve for life." Then he expressed regrets that his bad knees kept him home more than he'd like or he'd come along with me.

I thanked him, and then rushed from my office to the newsroom, trying to figure out how to sell Bryce on this new Amish angle.

"This story is ours," I said. "We broke it first and we need to stay on top of it."

He responded that we already had the news of the day: Sarah Yoder's name. "What more do you expect to learn?"

"Who Sarah was, for starters. People around here are fascinated with the Amish. This murder is going to attract enormous interest. The network may even want our video. Do you want to be the one to tell them we don't have any?"

That argument had some impact. Bryce probably hoped to be running the news division at the network someday.

"This is a case where cold calling won't get us answers," I said. "The Amish don't answer phones. To find sources for this story, we need to door-knock and win their trust."

The new boss stared at my face until he was certain we had eye contact, then told me to get moving. "Remember, Riley, I did this for you. I expect your cooperation when I need it."

To my relief, he also let me bring a photographer for the trip— something I would never take for granted again. I made Malik drive so he would stay awake and I could brief him on what to expect.

"We're not going to be able to show faces of the Amish," I told him. "So much of the video is going to have to be generic—shot from behind. Backs of buggies are fine, too. Barns. Clotheslines. Faces shrouded by hats or bonnets. Men harvesting crops, again as long as we're careful about identifiable faces."

"No faces. Got it." He sounded a bit peeved, and I realized I was repeating myself.

"Sorry, Malik. I just don't want us locked out of the story over some misunderstanding about the camera. We may have to continually assure our Amish subjects that we're being respectful of their beliefs."

"If they don't watch TV, Riley, how are they going to tell whether we broadcast faces?"

"They might not know right away," I said. "But word usually gets out from others in the community. If we make them a promise, I want to be able to truthfully tell them we kept our word and keep them as sources."

My cameraman turned on the radio, tuning me out. I thought about offering to drive so he could sleep. Maybe a nap would improve his mood. I purposely didn't bring up the one-man-band issue because I didn't want to provoke more tension.

Malik was making a better transition to reporter than I was making to photographer. I had tried convincing him that if he was too successful, we'd be stuck with one-man bands. And that would hurt our news product.

"You need to start stammering or swear on air," I teased. "It's like throwing a game. Do it for the cause."

What I really meant was do it for me. But I wanted him to decide that on his own. Realizing there was no way for me to verbalize that thought without sounding selfish, I kept quiet. Trouble was, I could tell he liked being on camera. He was a good-looking guy. Plus, his Middle Eastern genes gave the station some much needed diversity.

An attractive young woman even recognized him yesterday while we were walking in downtown Minneapolis. "Aren't you Malik Rahman? I saw you on TV." He could hardly wait to get home and tell his wife. His real wife. Not his work spouse.

Because Malik had much more experience behind the camera than I did, the stories he reported looked better on all visual levels from standup to cutaway to straight video. And a station producer was helping him write scripts. So while he was on his way up professionally, I was on my way down.

CHAPTER 21

A sign on the outskirts of Harmony read Population 1,080. Make that 1,079, I thought.

Malik was more interested in a yellow road sign with a black silhouette of a horse and buggy—a common warning of slow-moving Amish traffic. He dropped me off at the Village Square restaurant on Main Street so he could get the shot, and I could get acquainted with townsfolk. When covering small towns, I'd found that local diners often made good starting points. The red-and-white awning on this one seemed inviting.

One slice of raspberry-peach pie later, and I had some leads scrawled on the back of a paper napkin. The waitress had already heard the news about Sarah's body being identified.

Yoder was a common Amish name, so she wasn't sure exactly where the dead woman lived but gave me general directions to a couple of farms owned by Yoder families. The bishop was easier. Apparently everyone knew his place. She drew a quick map with a star, pointing out the window which direction to turn.

"Everything's fairly close with a car." She suspected the word was out among the Amish about the murder because some plain customers often stopped at the restaurant for lunch. But today none occupied any of the booths, nor were any buggies parked on the side streets.

I thanked her with a nice tip and business card in case she

heard anything else. Malik was waiting in the van and disappointed I had not brought him any pie.

"This was a line-of-duty pie," I said. "I ate it too fast to enjoy."

I assured him there'd be plenty of chances to sample local cuisine when we bought food from the Amish as a means of gaining access and making friends. "Cashew crunch, here we come."

We drove through some lingering fog on gravel roads to reach the first Yoder farm and found a sturdy two-story white house of modest design. I told Malik to leave the camera inside the vehicle until we got an all clear from the inhabitants. A young man wearing suspenders walked toward us from the barn.

"I grew up on a farm the next county over and I'm looking for the family of Sarah Yoder," I said. "Did she live here?"

He seemed friendly enough until I identified my employer, then he headed for the house without looking back. We turned the van around, drove out onto the road, and Malik shot some general cover of the farm in case it ended up being Sarah's home.

"Maybe we can get the bishop on our side." I figured if the group's religious leader approved of me, others might cooperate.

At our next stop, I explained to an elderly bearded man standing by a woodpile that I was looking for Abram Stoltzfus.

"I am he," he said.

I handed him my card and said that I understood Sarah Yoder was a member of his church. "I'm hoping to learn a little about Sarah so she's not just a murder statistic. Publicizing this case might even help find her killer."

"What is this work you do?" He seemed puzzled that I sought word of Sarah.

"My name is Riley Spartz. I'm a television reporter from up in the Twin Cities."

"I cannot help you."

I tried to get him to reconsider, but he refused to look at me or speak further and went inside his house. We got the same cool reception at the next Yoder residence. A thin woman in a bonnet answered the door, but she too brushed me off hastily when I mentioned Sarah's name—like they were reverting to a prepared script.

We stopped at another homestead that posted a sign advertising baskets for sale. An older woman, carrying some baskets loaded with quilted pot holders and candy, displayed them on a table in the yard. While I counted out money for some cashew crunch, I mentioned being a TV reporter and wanting to tell Sarah Yoder's story. That was enough for her to close shop without further word.

Malik was discouraged. "Whatever you're doing isn't working."

I couldn't disagree. The buttery toffee candy improved his mood, though I knew that was only temporarily. Our Amish encounters puzzled me because I usually had better luck getting my foot in the door and getting people to open up, even those from other cultures. I suddenly felt cursed. I'd walked into this story knowing the Amish didn't particularly welcome outsiders, but for some reason, I thought playing up my farm girl past would insulate me from that attitude.

I also had a romantic, probably unrealistic, idea of their life that I envied. While theirs was simple, mine was complicated. Later I would learn that simple did not mean safe.

The next Amish residence a couple miles up posted a sign advertising "New Potatoes. Not on Sundays."

It was Wednesday, so we drove in and parked near the porch where a young woman and child rocked together. For two bucks, I got a brown bag of baby reds.

I admired her little boy—a smile under a straw hat—and deliberately made no mention of my line of work. As a covert customer, I chatted her up while purchasing a second bag of potatoes for Malik even though he seemed unenthusiastic about the produce.

"We were on our way to the Yoder farm to offer condolences for Sarah. But we got confused." I held out the makeshift map. "Was it this place or this one?"

She shook her head. "Neither. Their homestead is here."

She pointed toward the other side of town. I handed her a pen and she drew in a couple of roads. "This one."

I thanked her and we headed in that direction until we reached another mailbox reading Yoder. A handmade sign read Eggs, Crafts, Jelly.

A young Amish girl stood in the farmyard, holding a basket of various shades of brown eggs when we arrived. To avoid spooking her, Malik had decided to wait in the van with the cashew crunch.

I bent over and complimented her on her full basket, relating tales of hunting for eggs myself as a child, under sheds and behind woodpiles. Anywhere hens could hide. Back then when I was growing up, they were simply farm eggs, viewed as less desirable than the white dozen sold in stores; now they're billed as upscale free-range eggs and sell for a premium.

I asked the child her age and she replied nine. "What's your name, sweetie?"

"Hannah."

She glanced down at the ground as she answered, but I didn't take it personally because I'd found that habit common when mingling with children who'd been taught not to talk to outsiders. A white bonnet with side pleats framed her cheeks and shielded her eyes. Yet I could see they were red and suspected she'd been crying.

"I'm here to talk to someone about Sarah." I held out the forensic sketch. "Did you know her?"

"That's my sister." The girl reached for the illustration. Now we were getting somewhere. "She was in the bann."

"Excuse me, where did you say Sarah was? What barn?"

Just then the door to the house opened and an Amish woman

rushed over in a panic, calling Hannah's name. She grabbed the girl's arm and yanked her away, letting the drawing flutter to the ground. "Leave us."

"Are you Sarah's mother?" I followed behind them through the yard until we reached the porch. "I'm sorry for your loss, Mrs. Yoder." She pushed the girl inside and left me alone outside. "I'm here to tell Sarah's story." I hoped they were listening on the other side of the door. "I don't want this to just be about her death. I want to hear about her life. What made her special."

Families of victims often responded to that pitch. But here my words sounded flat and empty because they went unheard. At one of the upper floor windows, a curtain seemed to move, but no one looked down to weigh granting an interview. My goal of taking viewers inside the world of the Amish looked more distant than ever.

I picked up the drawing of Sarah and left.

CHAPTER 22

Upstairs, Miriam Yoder watched the news van drive away. If she weren't so devout, she'd have cursed. When the vehicle was far out of sight, she stared her youngest daughter in the eye and told her never to mention her older sister again.

"Sarah is gone. We may see her in the afterlife or we may not. You must not speak of her. Especially not to the English. More may come to ask questions, but you must walk away from them."

Sheriff Eide had been out earlier in the day with news of her death. Homicide was virtually unheard of in the Amish community. Sarah's murder was unprecedented.

The sheriff wondered why no one had reported her missing.

But in Miriam's mind, Sarah was never missing. She was simply gone. She had left her faith and home. And when she turned away from their church, they had turned their backs on her, placing her in the bann.

"What happened to my sister?" Hannah had been in school earlier in the day when the sheriff arrived with the sketch and questions. Now the girl had questions of her own for her mother. "How did Sarah die? Why won't anyone talk about her? And where did that woman get a picture of her?"

Miriam resisted the impulse to admonish her youngest. How

Sarah died was exactly why no one wanted to talk about her, especially to a child. "Pray Sarah is safe in the arms of Jesus. God called her to him. We must not fault anyone for His will. We must forgive."

"But who should I forgive?" Hannah asked.

"You might never have that answer." Miriam squeezed Hannah's hand and closed her eyes tight. "But for now, forgive Sarah."

The funeral would be held two days after tomorrow and many people would come. Miriam wasn't sure what kind of atmosphere to expect—their family tree was vast but spread wide across the Midwest.

A line of buggies had come for her husband's funeral several years ago in Ohio. Amish traveled far to offer their support following his accident on the farm.

Mark Yoder had been dragged by a team of horses after becoming entangled in the reins when a wagon tongue broke loose. She was never sure whether to blame the equipment or the animals. Even though she knew she wasn't supposed to place any blame at all, she sold the horses and burned the wagon.

Since then, they'd moved from Ohio back to Iowa, then to Minnesota. Even though they had kin everywhere, nowhere felt like home. Now they would probably move again to escape the scrutiny that was sure to follow.

In some ways, Sarah's death was easier to bear than her husband's. Because the child had been in the bann, she had already died in her mother's heart.

But her death was also harder because of all the prying from within and outside. She found herself anxious for the burial. She imagined, shovel by shovel, dirt filling Sarah's grave and ending speculation about her life and death. But nothing is so simple. Miriam even had unanswered questions of her own. Had her husband not died, might her daughter still be alive?

She heard someone downstairs and saw Gideon, done with chores. She welcomed her son and told him about the English woman. He was angry about the picture. Everybody in the Amish community was talking about the sketch of his sister.

Even in her passing, Sarah brought shame upon their family.

CHAPTER 23

The station decided we should remain in southern Minnesota for the 6:00 PM news and broadcast live with the latest development, whatever that ended up being. Then we'd transmit back a packaged version of the story from the satellite truck for the 10:00 before heading north.

Because the sky would be dark, we decided on using the Amish buggy traffic sign as a backdrop rather than the anonymous rural countryside by the dead woman's house.

About ten minutes before the newscast, just after I'd finished my audio check, someone started yelling at me in my ear to immediately feed a photograph of Sarah Yoder back to the station. "Not the sketch, a real-life photo, Riley. I want to run them side by side so viewers can see how closely they resemble each other."

I didn't recognize the voice. It didn't sound like any of the producers, directors, or assignment editors. "Who is this?"

"This is your boss speaking. Bryce Griffin." He sounded annoyed that I didn't know him without seeing him. "We still don't have a photo. And you're the lead."

"We aren't going to get one either." I reminded him the victim was Amish. "They don't allow their members to be photographed. It's against their faith because they believe the Bible bans graven images. By that they mean likenesses."

"Don't quote the Bible at me." His voice changed from annoyed to angry. "Channel 3 made a big commitment covering this homicide and you're telling me we don't even get an actual photograph of the murder victim? What kind of a reporter are you?"

I explained that I hadn't failed to find a real picture, but that none existed. "This woman has likely never had her picture taken in her life. Her family doesn't keep photo albums. They don't allow their faces to be shown."

"How about a school yearbook?"

"She's probably only had an eighth-grade education, Bryce. The Amish use one-room schoolhouses."

"How about a driver's license photo? Did you check with the state?"

"The Amish don't drive cars."

I realized that my news director had most likely never been exposed to any aspect of Amish culture. That, the fact that he could fire me, plus the reality that I was less than three minutes from air time, made me refrain from getting into a long-distance shouting match.

I promised to explain more about the Amish when I got back to the station.

"I know plenty about the Amish," he said. "I saw a movie about them once."

Him and millions of other people. "That would be *Witness* with Harrison Ford."

He paused like he was replaying the film, which had become a worldwide hit. "They showed faces in that movie. What do you mean we can't show faces?"

"Those were actors. They weren't real Amish."

"Well, if our competition leads with a real-life victim photo, you'll have plenty to answer for when you get back tonight."

I'd seen no other news crews all day, so that scenario of being scooped didn't scare me. But it should have.

CHAPTER 24

Because Malik and I weren't rushing back to the station for a late news deadline, we stopped off the freeway for dinner at a popular family restaurant.

Malik ordered a cheeseburger and fries. "That's what men like after a long day of work." Lugging all that camera gear seemed to keep the pounds off his waist. Maybe one-man banding would keep me slim.

I ordered a chicken salad from their list of Lite Entrees. "As women my age count years, we also count calories." I preferred places that posted those numbers along with fat grams on the menu.

While waiting for our plates, a text came up on my cell phone.

"You be careful out among them English."

Garnett must have checked the station website to see what my day was like. I could have texted back: Jan Rubes. *Witness*. 1985. But I didn't want to just then, with Malik across the table from me. So I left his message unanswered.

"Garnett and I talked this morning," I said.

"Really?" Malik replied. "Are you back together?"

"No. I don't know what we are."

Malik always had a front-row seat to our on-again-off-again relationship. He was still happily married to his college sweetheart and couldn't understand why my love life was always a wreck. I couldn't really either. Most of the time I blamed myself, but lately I'd started blaming God.

God was definitely a character in my Amish romance book. Continuing the read that evening, I learned that the heroine was resisting wild passion in favor of inner peace to please God and her family. If she followed this path, her reward would be obedient children.

It might be admirable, but was it realistic? The book was more spiritual than I could handle just then, so I guiltily put it down. Then I started thinking more about Sarah Yoder, and what fatal error might have caused her death.

Her eyes didn't watch me that night while I slept. Maybe having a name again had calmed her. But Sarah was still the first thing I thought of in the morning.

Moving from rental to rental the last couple years, something happened I had vowed never would: my newspaper subscription lapsed.

I love the feel of paper and ink on my fingers, but the customer service desk put me on hold so long I finally hung up and decided getting my news online wasn't so bad.

Of course, when you read unwelcome news in an actual newspaper, you can rip the article to pieces. Or burn the pages. Or throw the whole thing in the garbage along with pizza boxes and coffee grounds. The physical act of destruction can be cathartic.

But when you read bad news on the Internet, clicking to another site or turning off the computer screen doesn't make the bad news disappear. Online is eternal.

As far as journalism went in previous years, once I'd filed my story, I was done. Whether the news changed or not. Now on-line means my work is never finished. And my competition is younger and hungrier. I may have more news experience, but their phones are smarter than me.

Even though I wanted to smash my fist against my computer when I read the Minneapolis newspaper's lead story, I knew that wouldn't change the fact that I'd been beat on the job. Badly.

"Exclusive." Newspaper reporters used to mock TV news for using that word so liberally, but recently they'd adopted the term themselves. Usually as an exaggeration for mediocre content. But not today.

The headline taunted me.

Murder Gives Glimpse Inside Amish World

The story killed me.

> A cloistered Amish community in southeastern Minnesota reacted with shock at the discovery that one of their own had been murdered. But a strict moral code that values forgiveness over anger is apparently impeding the criminal investigation into an Amish woman's homicide.
>
> The body of a woman discovered a few days ago has been identified as eighteen-year-old Sarah Yoder of Harmony, MN.
>
> Law enforcement officials are frustrated. "If any of the group witnessed anything useful, they're keeping quiet," said Sheriff Ed Eide. "But that's the norm for them. If a buggy is vandalized, they never press charges. Same if property is stolen from a homestead. And we've respected that. But this is murder. So we are going to continue to ask questions."
>
> For Amish bishop Abram Stoltzfus the rules of the church trump the laws of the court.

> "We must not think evil of this perpetrator," he said.
> "We must forgive him in our hearts. This deed is not
> something we can change. We must accept this course
> as God's will."

The story went on to quote an Amish neighbor of the Yoders
who seemed to echo the bishop's philosophy of hate the sin, not
the sinner. The article also recapped the Amish schoolhouse
shooting in Pennsylvania five years earlier, after which the victim's families forgave the killer and even donated money to his
surviving family.

The reporter gave good perspective on tourism in Harmony
benefiting both the Amish and English, but the accuracy wasn't
what bothered me.

Sources are everything in news. One of my top news-gathering
skills has always been in getting people to talk to me, scooping
the competition. Sure, there are news events in which people
revel in their fifteen minutes of fame and insist on talking to
every reporter who wants an interview. In other cases, people
hide from public view and refuse to be interviewed by anybody.

But there are enough times when people choose to talk to me—
and only me—that have made my reputation as a top journalist.

But that didn't happen this time. Bishop Stoltzfus spoke to the
newspaper instead of me. When I introduced myself, he turned
away like I was the plague. Yet he found time to give print reporter Jack Rhodes quite a sermon.

I'd have some explaining to do at the station, where I was due
in two hours. The only way to avoid a whole lot of yelling was
to not go into work. Or to wear earplugs. I considered calling in
sick. Instead, I called my mom for support. Something I hadn't
done since high school when I ended up as salutatorian rather
than valedictorian.

"Mom, the Amish talked to the newspaper and not me. I got
scooped."

A few seconds passed before my mother processed my words over the phone and realized her daughter was a loser. "Oh Riley, I'm so sorry. You'll get them next time."

"You don't understand. My new boss is going to flip over this. This was not a story that was dumped on me. I campaigned for this story. And I didn't deliver."

She made some soothing "now-now" noises before saying something that put the whole mess in a different perspective.

"You couldn't have actually expected the Amish, if given a choice, to talk to you instead of a newspaper reporter?"

"What do you mean?"

"The Amish think TV is evil."

"Why? Because it uses electricity?"

"More likely because it represents the corruption of the modern world. They fear the messages on television will entice family members to leave the Amish fold." She went on to explain that Amish consider rooftop TV antennas the "devil's tail," and the box inside the house his "tongue."

I loved the vivid metaphors. But I was certain Bryce would never accept that the newspaper had an unfair edge over us for this story and that their scoop was the devil's fault, not mine.

"Maybe learning a little more about the Amish faith might help you better relate to them," my mother said. "You might have more luck in another round."

"Where can I get a crash course?"

That's when she told me that Father Mountain, my childhood priest, knew a lot about Amish religion from earlier days in his rural parish. Looking at the clock I realized I might have time to dash over to his church in St. Paul for a quick lesson and still make the morning news meeting.

And while in the vicinity of holy turf, I vowed to whisper a prayer for some breaking news—nonfatal—to divert my boss from my failings.

CHAPTER 25

Miriam Yoder's favorite memories of Sarah came when she was a happy girl, catching sleepy pigeons in the barn.

Another time she remembered her child bringing in the sheets off the clothesline as part of her chores, running with them draped over her body as if flying herself.

"Fly here, young bird," she laughed with her. "Show me your wings."

She never imagined, years later, her daughter would fly away from their family nest and land in dangerous hands. Other Amish would now warn their children, this is what happens when you join the English. The scandal of Sarah would be whispered about in Amish circles afar.

Hannah was off to school and Gideon was in the barn, so for the first time since the English lawman delivered the news of her daughter's body cast off in a pit, Miriam wept.

She wiped her eyes with the shirt she'd been mending. Sewing a tear or fixing a loose button required less concentration than cooking on the woodstove. And in her rattled state of mind she'd rather prick a finger than burn down the house.

The English had offered Miriam the sketch of Sarah, not understanding his affront. She tried not to think about her daughter, focusing instead on the funeral plans which lay ahead. But her mind kept dwelling on the past. And the past left her heartsick.

As Sarah grew older and headstrong, their relationship became strained. Most of their conversations ended in arguments like "Why are you always so stubborn?"

Raising her family alone, Miriam moved from spank to strap to teach her daughter. The bishops always supported her, as did the Bible. She urged Sarah to pray harder to end her troubles. At first the girl tried to obey, but then fell back to her old habits.

When Sarah finished eighth grade, she did not want to stop schooling, but no compromise existed. Soon after, Miriam found a diary under Sarah's mattress. The early pages talked of enjoying her time as a scholar and hoping to teach school herself one day.

Miriam recalled smiling at an entry where her daughter wrote about playing kickball during recess.

I was the first girl picked because I am the fastest. Once I even caught a brown rabbit. That's how fast I am.

Another day, Sarah wrote of a boy in class smiling at her during a history lesson.

I thought Caleb to be looking at Anna, then understood it to be me, and I smiled back.

But the later pages of the diary shocked Miriam, jeopardizing Sarah and even their entire family standing. She had begun to think her future more important than her brother's.

Miriam confronted the girl with her discovery. "Look, my child, I found your guilty secret."

Sarah swallowed nervously and asked for her journal back. "Please, Mamm, it is my life."

"Your words are unclean," Miriam said. "You must never utter such things again. No more journals for you."

She burned the book in the kitchen stove and waited until all the pages were destroyed so Sarah could not reclaim her life story. Then she handed her daughter a Bible and instructed her to turn to the book of Deuteronomy. She pointed to a verse. "Read this."

So Sarah read aloud, "'The secret things belong unto the Lord our God: but those things which are revealed belong unto us and to our children for ever, that we may do all the words of this law.'"

"Do you understand your sin?" Miriam asked.

Whether she did or not, Sarah quickly apologized for her writings. "Please, Mamm, forgive me for my misdeeds."

And as was the Amish way, Miriam forgave Sarah. But she was never convinced her daughter forgave her.

Over time, she suspected Sarah might be keeping other journals, but though she checked her room when the girl was outside, she found nothing.

CHAPTER 26

Father Mountain was finishing breakfast at the rectory when I pounded on his door. His ability to sense unspoken despair was a job requirement for clergy, so he poured me a bowl of cold cereal and offered to take my confession.

"Unless you'd prefer accompanying me to daily Mass." He glanced at the clock on the stove. "I have to be changing into my vestments in half an hour."

"I'm all confessed out, Father." My last confession was epic. He should know. He was there for it. "And I need to be at the station just about when you'd be saying opening prayer. What I really require is a quick class in Thinking Amish."

"Is this what brings you?" He held up the newspaper front page and I swatted the Amish article away defensively.

"Yeah. I didn't do so well covering that story."

I gave him my mother's theory that my hot TV job got me the Amish cold shoulder. "I want to cover this murder investigation without feeling humiliated by my competition. To do that I need to convince those folks that talking to me is not flirting with the devil."

"Well, Riley, to truly understand the Amish you have to start with their religion. Their life choices stem from their spiritual beliefs. Let's test your knowledge. How many Amish does it take to change a light bulb?"

Father Mountain enjoyed using religious humor to illustrate serious issues. When I was a little girl, his jokes delighted me. With each jest, he would remind me that God gave humans the gift of laughter. But today I was low on patience.

"None," I answered his joke about the Amish and light bulbs. "Amish don't believe in electricity."

"That's right. They believe God will provide light unto the world."

"I'm more familiar with their self-reliant lifestyle than their piety, Father. I'm hoping to get a deeper sense of their faith at Sarah Yoder's funeral. Providing my boss gives me another chance with the story."

Funerals often reveal secrets about murder victims and their lives. Who showed up and who didn't says a lot. Sometimes the police even videotape the attendees, looking for clues, even suspects masquerading as mourners.

"That's not going to happen this time," Father Mountain said.

"I know, no cameras for this funeral, but I'd be content just to sit quietly in the back of the church and assimilate."

"That's not going to happen either," he said. "Amish services are held in homes, not chapels. They believe in simplicity. They would consider our formal churches to be opulent and a deterrent to true worship. The same with dressing up in fancy 'Sunday best' attire. Believe me, none of them are going to let you hide in a corner and watch them pray."

Father Mountain was right about one thing. In order to stand a chance of mingling with the Amish, I needed to learn more about their religion.

"So how do Amish differ from Catholics?" I asked. "Are they a Protestant sect?"

"Heavens, no," Father Mountain said.

As I crunched cornflakes, he took me through the history of the Amish church, starting with the sixteenth century. But as his lecture became engaging, I traded spoon for pen and made some scribbles in my reporter's notebook.

He explained that while Martin Luther was leading the Protestant Reformation, another significant movement was also attempting to change the Roman Catholic Church.

"Anabaptist reformers rejected what they considered the corruption of both the Catholic and Protestant religions," he said. "From this, Amish tradition grew."

"So what are their core beliefs?" I asked.

"Back then, Riley, adult baptism was considered a crime." He spelled out that among their prime tenets was that *only* adults should be baptized—hence the name Anabaptists. "They also believe lay people are just as capable of interpreting scripture as clergy. And that forgiveness of sins can be attainable by faith alone."

"Personally, I like those last two ideas," I said.

"Those messages resonated with the peasant class, which alarmed status-quo theologians. So almost from the start, Amish brethren were persecuted by mainstream religion.

"In fact," he continued, "considering the Amish and their reclusiveness, many scholars believe their withdrawal from society came from having to worship in secret because of this oppression."

"So much for religious tolerance," I said.

"That's a fairly recent concept, Riley. And why the Bill of Rights assuring freedom of religion was so novel. Note what our forefathers put up at the very top in the First Amendment: 'Congress shall make no law respecting an establishment of religion . . .'"

I gave a short laugh. "This is a new twist, Father. I'm used to you quoting the Bible at me, but not the Constitution. Maybe there's a little bit of politician as well as priest in you."

"Running a parish requires some degree of political skill, Riley."

"So does working in a newsroom, Father."

He told me the Amish residents in southern Minnesota were Old Order Amish, the most conservative, allowing the least technology and other frills. Their clothing sported hooks and eyes rather than buttons. And while they could ride in automobiles, they could not own one. No telephones in their homes, either, but they could use an English neighbor's phone or even share a community phone with other Amish.

"I don't understand the distinction between using versus owning," I said. "That seems sort of lame to me."

"It can be difficult for us, as outsiders, to appreciate their rules, but it's where they choose to draw the line. They feel such practices help preserve their cultural identity. The rules—called their *Ordnung*—vary between Amish communities. A less conservative sect may be more tolerant about modern devices."

"So is Mom right? Do the Amish consider TV evil? Is my paycheck cursed?"

"More likely they think television represents a connection with the rest of the world and the Bible tells them they are not to be 'conformed to the world.' They fear watching TV can lead to temptation and the deterioration of family life."

"There might be some truth to that," I said. "But I'm starting to think the next time I venture to Harmony, I'll just describe myself as a writer, not a TV reporter."

At the same time, we both glanced at our watches, realizing we needed to end our discussion. So he left to work for God, while I left to work for the devil.

CHAPTER 27

Backed up in rush-hour traffic between St. Paul and Minneapolis, I put my cell phone on speaker and called Sheriff Eide to get an update on Sarah's homicide. He didn't offer much beyond the fact that they were continuing the investigation.

"I wish you'd mentioned to me that the Amish were being less than cooperative," I said.

"Oh, you mean the newspaper?"

"Yeah, Sheriff, the newspaper. I would have appreciated knowing that fact yesterday instead of reading it sprawled across the front page today."

"Well, their reporter just happened to come by as the whole thing was heating up." Just then either my cell got glitchy or his voice got muffled. All I could make out was a few words that sounded like "forgot about."

"Excuse me, Sheriff? Did you just say you forgot about me?"

His pause was his admission.

Barely a few hours old, this day kept getting more depressing. And I wasn't even at Channel 3 yet.

"Sheriff Eide, I've been covering this story since Josh was rescued from the sinkhole. I thought you and I had an understanding."

An insincere apology followed and some bland excuses. I

had to acknowledge that the sheriff and I weren't as tight as I'd hoped. I decided to be blunt about what the media could do for him.

"Besides news coverage helping solve crimes," I said. "I see from your campaign signs that you're up for reelection. Murder can keep you in the news—almost like free advertising—and voters become familiar with your name."

But the sheriff had another take on the situation. "Every story you air reminds voters that I haven't done my job. Not solving this case could cost me the election."

"Stop thinking you won't find the killer," I said. "Voters don't go to the polls for another month. By then they might be marveling over your law-enforcement skills. Why don't you tell me who identified Sarah and we'll start fresh."

I had a suspicion that knowing whether the ID came from inside or outside the Amish community might yield a clue.

After a slight pause, he told me that the owner of Everything Amish called them with the name Sarah Yoder after seeing her picture in the media.

"Everything Amish?" I asked. "What's that?"

He explained that the store was a large warehouse outside of Harmony that stocked Amish merchandise. "Sort of like the middleman."

"Sounds like the Walmartization of the Amish to me," I said.

I was distracted briefly from our conversation by a truck trying to merge in front of me to make a last-minute exit. Just then Sheriff Eide made some remark about also being busy with a family lost in the corn maze.

"What about corn mazes?" I asked.

"Some out-of-towners became confused in the maze last night. They ended up calling 9-1-1," the sheriff said.

Mazes can be traced back to Greek mythology, when Theseus fought the Minotaur in the Labyrinth. Hedge mazes can also be found in the history of Belgium, England, and France. Recently, cornstalk mazes had become a popular autumn activity in rural Minnesota. There was one not far from Harmony.

"Someone called the police?" This needed clarification. "Because they were lost in a corn maze?"

I remembered being lost in a cornfield once when I was young, having to tough it out and walk till the corn turned to soybeans and I could see the farm silos. Of course, that was before the age of cell phones and 911.

"The couple had a baby along and it got dark and they got scared," the sheriff said. "So we had to send a K-9 unit over. Turns out, they were only twenty-five feet from the exit."

That wasn't a half-bad news story. Except the corn maze was outside the Channel 3 viewing area. But then I had an idea. "Where was this family from?" I asked.

"Edina," he replied.

Excellent demographics. An affluent Twin Cities suburb. The kind of narrative people would watch and chat about with their coworkers the next day. Viewers liked stories about stupid rich people. Bryce might buy the corn-maze pitch and forget about the Amish debacle.

And it worked. After yelling at me loads, he sent me off to land an interview with the directionally challenged urban family. If they were good talkers, the story would merit a trip south for scenes of the actual maze. The dark corners. The dead ends. And an interview with the rescue team.

My penalty was that I had to shoot the video myself.

Bryce's office door was shut when I went to double-check that he wasn't expecting a live shot. Times like this I missed Noreen's glass walls, when her business was our business. I was nervous about interrupting him. Just as I had decided to march over and knock, his door opened.

Nicole, the new reporter, came out and something about her face made me reluctant to enter. So I left the newsroom to hit the road behind the wheel, figuring Bryce could always call me.

Once again, I promised myself I'd invite Nicole out for a drink after work and officially congratulate her on joining the Channel 3 news team.

Since I was traveling solo, I stopped by my house to pick up Husky for company. He curled his tail around his nose in the backseat and I left him there in the thick of a dog nap. He reminded me of Malik, asleep while I drove.

I taped an interview with the lost maze mother, complete with cute shots of her newborn baby Barlow in his luxury nursery. She was feeling a little silly about the whole corn-maze episode, but was a good sport about being on TV.

"Maybe I did overreact," she said, "and maybe someday we'll look back on this bit of family history and laugh. But suddenly it was dark and I started worrying about the baby."

She planted a kiss on his forehead. "I guess the corn panicked me."

City slicker talk.

I texted the assignment desk: we have the mom.

Maze of Mystery had long been a popular local tourist attraction near Harmony. The kind of entertainment three generations could enjoy together on a pleasant autumn outing. Visitors were greeted by displays of antique tractors, pumpkins, and scarecrows holding scythes that looked too sharp to be mere props. They reminded me of the horror film *Children of the Corn*.

If Garnett had been with me, he would certainly have recited, "I spy, with my little eye, something that starts with C."

I would have answered, "Corn." But instead of cluttering my mind with movie trivia, I needed to reap a story. So I went to work.

The owner had never dealt with a lost-customer situation in all his years operating the corn maze. "I always thought the whole point was to get lost." The only other time the cops had been called was when an elderly man had a heart attack inside the maze and needed to be transported to the hospital.

The labyrinth wasn't open for guests for a couple more hours. Some liked to wander during broad daylight, all the better to see the corn; others preferred the drama of darkness. He agreed to take me and Husky on a tour through the twists and turns, even though dogs weren't technically allowed. He pointed out posted maps along the way that appeared clear enough for most folks to find their way out.

"The maze is old-fashioned family fun," he said. "Even Amish families come by to meander through."

He also showed me a covert shortcut that employees used to escape when they were in a hurry. Husky and I made our way from start to finish, where I framed an acceptable standup, eight-foot-tall cornfields on either side of me.

I fingered the stalks. They were extremely dry tinder because of a lack of rain during the end of the growing season. Peeling back the husks on one ear revealed hard, ripe kernels.

"No smoking allowed," the owner teased.

All the corn would be harvested after Halloween and fed to their cattle.

I missed having Malik along as photographer because he'd be able to use special stick equipment he kept in the back of the van to shoot a challenging overhead point of view shot of the maze. Not as good as a helicopter aerial, but certainly better than what I'd accomplished.

((RILEY STANDUP))
MOST VISITORS SEEM TO FIND
THEIR WAY OUT OF THE MAZE
FROM START TO FINISH IN ABOUT
AN HOUR. NONE HAVE EVER
REPORTED BEING LOST BEFORE.

When I stopped at the Fillmore County Law Enforcement Office for the 911 call, Sheriff Eide was out, but I heard a news bonanza in the form of an agitated woman's voice on the tape.

> ((911 AUDIO))
> HELP! WE'RE LOST IN THE CORN.
> WE CAN'T FIND THE END.

The dispatcher—more accustomed to dispatching paramedics and fire crews—seemed taken aback by the nature of the call and asked the woman to confirm her location.

> ((911 AUDIO))
> WE DON'T KNOW WHERE WE
> ARE. DON'T YOU GET IT? WE'RE
> SOMEWHERE IN THE CORN MAZE
> AND CAN'T GET OUT. OUR BABY IS
> SO LITTLE! PLEASE SEND HELP!

"You're lost in Maze of Mystery?" the dispatcher asked. Everybody in the area apparently knew of that place. "I'll stay on the line with you until help arrives."

For the next eight minutes I heard a reassuring radio voice say that assistance was near, amid baby cries, heavy breathing, and the rustling noise of cornstalks in the wind. The audio cut out when barking from a K-9 team seemed to signal rescue was under way.

I had enough sound for a hilarious story, so I was satisfied.

Husky expressed more interest in the dog on the 911 tape than previously during our corn-maze visit, but seemed disappointed that the other mutt remained in hiding. I thought about how lonely he must be living with me; then I thought about how lonely I was living with him.

"Too bad neither of us can meet the right man or dog." I

scratched his ears and he settled for that affection. But I craved more than dog approval.

While I toyed with the idea of what to say if I phoned Garnett and if he answered, my cell buzzed. I thought karma was on the line, until I realized the area code was from southern Minnesota, not Washington, DC.

"Hello, this is Riley Spartz." No voice on the other end. "Can I help you?" I persisted.

"I hope so," a woman's voice finally said. "I'd like to discuss the murder of the Amish woman. Can we try again?"

"Who is this?" I asked.

The caller was Josh's mom.

CHAPTER 28

When Michelle Kueppers heard we were both in the same county, she urged me to stop by her place before Josh got home from school. That detour didn't give me much time to swing by Everything Amish, but I could tell something had changed since my last visit with her, so this became top priority.

Husky and Bowser did a playful dance in the farmyard, during which Husky wisely recognized the other dog's dominance. Bowser seemed to remember me as nondangerous, and at least didn't growl at my heels as I walked to the porch.

Michelle invited me inside this time, and apologized for the last time. I complimented her on her house, decorated in an upscale Norman Rockwell style.

"Let's talk about why I'm here," I said, curious how our balance of power had shifted since her son was pulled from the sinkhole.

"I want you to find who really killed Sarah Yoder," she said.

"I want nothing more. Same with the police, I'm sure. Why? Do you have any information?"

"I believe the police are settling for a quick and easy suspect."

I had no idea what she was talking about. "Do they think Josh did this?"

"No, his father."

Her husband, Brian, was overseas in the armed forces. She even showed me a picture of him in uniform displayed on a superb walnut end table next to a small American flag. He was a good-looking man, but then again, a military uniform can make almost any man appear attractive.

"If he's serving abroad, why are the cops even looking at him? Seems like that would be a sufficient alibi."

She picked up some dried flowers from the table and started arranging them in a brick-colored vase. She fidgeted with the stems and that made her seem even more nervous about my question.

"He shipped out about five days before her body was found," she said.

I did the math. According to the medical examiner report, he was still here when she was killed. But numerous others also had opportunity. There had to be more to Brian Kueppers to interest the cops.

"Other than that, why are they looking at him?" I asked.

Location, location, location. Sheriff Eide apparently thought only area farmers would know about the sinkhole. He'd ordered them all interviewed in case they saw something or did something.

As authorities took Michelle down the investigative play-by-play of who was where when, she had unwittingly confirmed Brian was unaccounted for during what they apparently believed was the critical time of Sarah's death. In fact, he'd been gone for nearly four hours. Out driving is what he'd told her the night they'd argued.

Even that wasn't nearly enough evidence to suspect him, I thought. There had to be more.

"I checked you out, Ms. Spartz, and you know what it's like to be wrongly accused."

She had checked me out. I had briefly been charged with murder once. But I wasn't convinced of Brian Kueppers's innocence. He might be plenty guilty of killing Sarah Yoder. And apparently, military police had conducted an inquiry with him wherever he was in the Middle East at the request of Fillmore County law enforcement. He'd given them the same "out driving" alibi.

"It seems to me this isn't enough for the law to get excited over." I dropped my voice to a whisper. "They must know something else about your husband. The question is, do you know what it is?"

She crushed a brown flower in her palm and rubbed the dust between her fingers. I was reminded of Father Mountain delivering that traditional Ash Wednesday line about being dust and returning to dust.

Michelle wiped her hands on her jeans and looked up at me. "A couple times a few years back, he scared me."

That was something. "Did he hurt you?" That was something else.

"Not badly. But I was frightened."

"Did you ever call the authorities for help?" I asked.

She nodded.

That meant they had paperwork on her husband. "That's why they're interested in him."

"But he changed. He got help. I know that sounds feeble, but we have a strong marriage even six thousand miles apart."

I wasn't convinced, but let her argument pass unchallenged by changing the subject. "How's Josh doing?"

"He's good. Proud of his role in helping to identify Sarah. Now that she has a name, he doesn't seem afraid anymore."

"He did important work," I said. "I'm glad he's coping."

At the mention of Josh, she glanced at the clock in the kitchen. I realized she wanted me to leave before the school bus brought her son home.

"Let's stay in touch," I suggested, and she readily agreed. "Do you and your husband ever do webcam conversations?"

She said they'd had one frantic cybertalk after Josh fell in the pit, and were hoping for less urgent ones.

"I might like to chat with him myself," I said.

I didn't press the issue, just planted the idea of a face-to-face encounter with this possible suspect. But first, I'd want to see what the sheriff might cough up about Brian Kueppers. Because I sensed there had to be something else that Michelle either didn't know or wasn't telling.

CHAPTER 29

The highway route back to the Twin Cities took me through the other end of Harmony, where I passed a large warehouse building with an enormous banner that read Everything Amish: Furniture Quilts Crafts.

I drove around the store and noticed a truck backed up against a loading dock. The cab was empty and the cargo had been unloaded.

I parked near the front door, next to a fast-looking Chevy Camaro. The sports car caught my eye because it was the type of vehicle that my deceased husband would have loved to test drive. I ran my hand over the shiny black fender. The rest of the lot was ordinary. Several cars had out-of-state license plates and seemed to belong to tourists, shopping for a piece of Amish culture.

Since the autumn day was cool, Husky waited in the car while I explored. The professional setup contrasted with the occasional handwritten signs along dirt roads professing to sell New Potatoes or Baskets. Those all cautioned Not on Sundays.

What this sprawling enterprise lacked in country charm it made up for in selection. And hours. I noted it was open Sunday afternoons. And at the cash register, a modest sign indicated they took credit cards. A convenience not found on the Amish farms I visited.

A young woman greeted us, but immediately retreated to a

corner room when I mentioned I'd like to talk to someone about Sarah Yoder.

I was admiring an oak dining-room table when a handsome man approached me. He wore designer jeans and a black turtleneck under a fashionable blazer. He looked good enough to be on air, or in *GQ* magazine. But something about him seemed different, perhaps his manner of speech or way of walking.

"We deliver," he said.

I was tempted. If Malik had been along, he wouldn't have left empty handed. After all, our station van has plenty of room in back. Usually during ratings months my cameraman saved his overtime money to buy a new household appliance for his wife. But lately, overtime was virtually nil. So were any real prospects of new furniture.

"Maybe another time," I answered. "The set is stunning, but space is an issue."

I was renting another furnished house in south Minneapolis and until I knew I was settled somewhere to stay, I didn't want to acquire anything large or heavy.

"Then maybe the quilts are calling you." He walked me over to a full wall display of color and design hanging from rails across the ceiling.

A vivid geometric one attracted my attention, but when I saw the prices, I warned myself not to become too attached. The cheapest was marked $750, the most expensive $1,195. Buying cashew crunch, potatoes, and pie in the line of duty was one thing. A quilt, at that price, was something else.

"If the Amish are such simple folk," I asked, "how come their goods are so pricey?"

"Because Amish must make a living, too," he replied. "And because in this manufactured world of ours, finding something so beautiful that is truly made by hand is difficult. Each of these quilts is as unique as a fingerprint."

His answer seemed obvious and made me want one even

more. Clearly he couldn't charge those prices if customers weren't paying up.

"But you haven't come here to talk about quilts, have you?" he said. "I understand you have questions about Sarah Yoder." He introduced himself as Isaac Hochstetler, the owner of Everything Amish. "But you can call me Ike."

I handed him a business card that read Riley Spartz, news reporter, but assured him he could call me Riley.

"Are you Amish, Ike?" Hardly seemed possible. His clothing far from plain. But he appeared to be running a thriving business selling Amish merchandise.

"Once," he said, "but we should talk about Sarah, not me."

Ike's past sounded fascinating, and he might be a more interesting tutor than Father Mountain. But time was tight. Channel 3 would be expecting the corn-maze story soon.

I told Ike that I understood he had contacted the police after seeing the artist sketch of the murdered woman and had identified her as Sarah Yoder.

"How did you know her?" I asked.

"She worked for me for a few days. And then she stopped showing up." He walked over to a desk calendar and flipped the pages back. "This was her last shift."

The day was five days before her body was discovered in the pit.

"What was Sarah's last day at work like?" I asked.

"I missed most of it." He had to drive to the Mayo Clinic in Rochester midafternoon to visit a sick friend, so he left Sarah to close up the store. "All she had to do was shut the door and the place would lock. And she apparently did. Whatever trouble befell her, it happened after she left here."

"Seems sort of trusting to leave her in charge after only being on the job a matter of days," I remarked. "You certainly have valuable inventory."

"She was Amish," Ike said. "I didn't worry."

"So you might have been the last person to see Sarah alive?"

"No, that earmark goes to her killer."

Ike said he had already gone over these details and his whereabouts with investigators. They had examined the store for fingerprints, but so many customers had come and gone since Sarah that no such clues were possible. They were also checking phone records, but found nothing suspicious during her final afternoon at work.

"And there was money in the till," he continued, "so you can rule out robbery."

"What about surveillance cameras?" I glanced around the ceiling and corners.

He shook his head, caressing another gorgeous wooden dining table, this one maple. His hands appeared strong and I wondered if he made some of the furniture himself.

"Never bothered with cameras," he said. "Always figured most of the merchandise was too heavy for shoplifters. Anything else wasn't worth stealing. Maybe that was a mistake."

"When she didn't show up for work the next day, did you consider reporting Sarah Yoder as missing to the police?" I asked.

"I never considered her missing. I thought she had returned to the Amish. And I respected her decision."

"Sarah left the Amish?"

He nodded. "She was temporarily staying in a bed-and-breakfast across town. Sometimes I get a call from them to hire Amish who are starting over. I agreed to give her some hours provided she wore her Amish garb. The tourists appreciate the authenticity."

"Why was she leaving the Amish?"

"An issue with the church." He shrugged. "I didn't go into the details with her because I didn't want to know the details. Sometimes that type of sharing muddies the employer/employee relationship."

I sympathized. My Channel 3 relationships were often muddy. But his next words changed everything. According to Ike, Sarah was being shunned.

CHAPTER 30

Confusing scenarios flashed through my mind on the drive back north to Minneapolis. I wished Malik had been along instead of Husky so someone would talk back to me over the miles and help me make sense of this situation.

"What do you mean shunned?" I had asked Ike.

In the Amish world, he explained, being shunned meant being avoided until the member repented of their infraction. "It keeps Amish for the Amish."

Ike speculated Sarah might have been caught drinking, smoking, or even listening to the radio. "If the church was shunning her, it means, in their eyes, she brought some form of disapproval on herself." He didn't think she was keeping company with English, or she wouldn't have ended up working for him.

I wanted to learn more, but if I missed my corn-maze deadline, I'd be shunned as far as my boss was concerned. So to be polite, I bought a couple quilted patchwork pot holders and left.

Father Mountain answered my call from the car, and I put him on speaker. He described what he knew about the Amish custom of shunning. It was similar to excommunication, but not just from the church but from the entire community. "It's the ultimate social rejection."

"Worse than unfriending someone on Facebook?" I asked.

"Much worse."

Shunning, known as *Meidung*, apparently involved some shaming rituals, such as not eating at the same table as the offending individual.

"While to you and me," he said, "the practice might not sound arduous, to the shunned individual, it can be brutal to be in the bann."

"In what?" Suddenly I heard the echo of a little Amish girl speaking of her dead sister and realized "barn" was not the word she used.

"The bann," Father Mountain repeated. "That's another term for being shunned. Placed in the bann."

Shunned, I thought. A silent ban.

"The bann is harsh business," my priest pal continued. "Spouses cannot sleep together. Parents must eschew grown children. It can tear families apart unless the sinner asks forgiveness."

"What about children? Are they shunned?"

"Only adults. Once a member has been baptized into the Amish faith—and remember, Riley, for the Amish, only adults can be baptized—they must adhere to the *Ordnung*, church rules, or else. They must stay true to their vows, whether pertaining to religion, electricity, automobiles, clothing, even companionship."

"Can Amish marry non-Amish?"

"No. They must both be of the faith. But prior to baptism, Amish teens are allowed a *Rumspringa*, a time of experimenting with English vices such as forbidden technology, cigarettes, or alcohol. Sometimes even sex."

That sounded like the Amish romance I'd started reading the other night. But I'd written such escapades off as fiction.

"Father Mountain, that seems like inviting serious trouble into the Amish church."

"The hope is by facing and rejecting sin, the next generation will be even stronger in their faith. How old was your victim?"

"Sarah was eighteen."

"If she was being shunned, that means she had been baptized. If she was only eighteen, she couldn't have taken her vows very long ago. What happened between then and now that made her leave?"

My childhood priest might have just hit on the pivotal question in this homicide. "Their reason for shunning Sarah could be a motive for murder," I said.

We were discussing that possibility when I hit a dead-cell zone north of Rochester on Highway 52 and lost him. A half a mile later I was glad not to be on the phone because an SUV pulled out at a notoriously dangerous exit and a truck in front of me swerved to avoid a collision.

The close call made me once again miss Malik and a second set of eyes on the road. As far as brushes with death, this one was minor. Not like some of the scrapes I'd endured, such as the day of the newsroom shoot-out.

Since then, I'd been thinking of asking Father Mountain to anoint me, just in case. But that strategy made me feel a little like a quitter. And when it came to sacraments, he was a by-the-book priest. Without me being close to death, or even sick, he might be reluctant to administer what the Catholic Church used to call last rites. Soldiers going off to battle could be anointed, and while I was prepared to argue that news was fundamentally a war of words, I could imagine Father Mountain telling me to pray more if I sought peace.

CHAPTER 31

When I sent Bryce my corn-maze story, instead of reading the script, he merely asked me the length. When I told him a minute twenty, he replied, "Good job."

If I'd told him two minutes, he'd probably have ordered thirty seconds chopped. To him, the math of a story seemed to mean more than the words. I'd heard him telling one of the newscast producers earlier to increase story count. So bringing Lost Corn Maze in tight was my way of showing him I could be a team player.

Sort of like a cyber high five. The best part being I didn't have to touch him.

Channel 3 ran the 911 audio during all the network prime-time crime shows that evening as a tease.

((TEASE))
HELP! WE'RE LOST IN
THE CORN.

Even the techs in the news control booth were chuckling at the hysteria. And not too much amused them these days as automation took over their jobs.

Once I'd voiced my audio track, my mind left the corn maze and became engrossed with questions about the Amish murder:

Why had Sarah left the fold? Had her departure put her in danger? Or could her attack simply have been random?

I started to arrange a murder wall in my office with a map of the area and Sarah's sketch. Then I paged through my notebook, looking at names and listing how they related to the homicide case.

Sarah Yoder—victim.

Kueppers family—Josh, Michelle, Brian. Found body—Rescued—Possible suspect.

Ike Hochstetler—identified Sarah's picture/employer.

Yoder family—Mother, sister, others?

Abram Stoltzfus—Amish bishop.

Ed Eide—Fillmore County sheriff.

More people would certainly yield more clues. Like the owner of the bed-and-breakfast where Sarah spent her final nights. How best to approach? While I hated the idea of driving back south, a phone conversation would go bust.

I decided to ask Bryce if the station would pay for me to stay there overnight—undercover. Maybe I could strike up a conversation over breakfast.

He said no, and didn't even hesitate.

"We're trying to keep costs down. That would be an unnecessary expense on an unnecessary story in an undesirable location."

"But I thought we wanted to own this story."

"You had your chance, Riley. If authorities make an arrest, we'll cover that development. Otherwise this story seems like it will be difficult for us to nail. For lots of reasons. So let it go."

From a purely dollars-and-cents position, his decision was logical. But in journalism, story selection is not all about money. Or at least shouldn't be. The cheapest news shouldn't rule.

I still wanted to tell Sarah's story, but when I tried filling Bryce in on shunning, and what I had learned about our victim leaving her faith and meeting murder—he didn't want to listen.

"I think you're more enamored with this Amish story than the viewers are," he said. "Maybe this weekend you need to give some thought to how we can work better together. Just because you've spent your career at Channel 3 does not mean your job is guaranteed."

He paused, like he was giving me a moment to weigh his words. And he was the boss.

So I nodded like I agreed with him. "Some of these answers may not come instinctively to me, like they do to you, Bryce. But I think I'm trainable and I think I proved that with the corn-maze story."

"I think you are, too, Riley. And I'm looking forward to us working closely together to turn Channel 3 around. And your work on the corn-maze story deserves congratulations."

He walked around his desk toward me and I prepared for another uncomfortable high five. But that didn't happen. Instead he rested his hands on my shoulders and kissed me. On the forehead. It was more insulting than sexual.

I wanted to tell him that better not happen again. But I also wanted to keep my job. The news business is full of strong, assertive women who are supervised by pigs and after weighing their options, chose to let it go. I didn't know Bryce well enough to know where this situation was headed, and didn't want to overreact. At least I hadn't had to worry about that with Noreen.

CHAPTER 32

A wild animal out of its territory can be newsworthy. Viewers perceive them as underdogs, even if they're wolves or mountain lions. Sightings of a black bear had started to circulate in southeastern Minnesota, more than two hundred miles from the real bear country up north.

A couple of kids waiting for a school bus cried bear first. Then a lady collecting autumn leaves for a scrapbook claimed to have surprised one in the bushes. The most believable sighting came from a farmer atop a corn harvester who insisted a bear ran out of his field. A few naysayers insisted the creature was a large dog. But my parents started keeping their canine buddies, Blackie and Max, inside at night, and my dad began carrying a rifle when he walked to the mailbox.

I had tried reassuring them that night after work that they were safe. But safe was dull. So even while no one actually wanted to face a bear, they still liked the allure of one lurking.

"The closest sighting to the farm was a good forty miles away. Dad, even if there is a real bear, you've got plenty of distance."

"Not risking any trouble," he said. "Just glad we don't have any cattle around."

For more than 135 years, my family had farmed corn and raised cattle. Now my parents rented out the land to neighbors and tried to relax in retirement. Despite all their bravado, this bear talk was making them tense. And they weren't the only ones. Local parents were encouraging kids to play video games on the couch rather than run outside in fresh air.

State wildlife officials had downplayed the odds that a bear had wandered into that geographical area. While some creatures may have been migrating from the deeply forested areas of northern Minnesota, those bears were heading west toward North Dakota, not south toward Iowa.

"They'd have to move through the Twin Cities to reach southeastern Minnesota," one of them said during a radio interview. "And that's not likely."

Yet earlier in the year, DNR officials had shot a bear spotted running through suburban neighborhoods east of St. Paul. Authorities had speculated that any bear in that location probably swam across the Mississippi River from Wisconsin. Forested valleys were intermingled with farmland in that corner of the state. So while there were no endless woods like in northern Minnesota, plenty of nooks existed for bears to hide. And if nuts and berries were scarce, farm grains beckoned, as did the potential for a dangerous run-in with humans.

I told my parents I'd bring Husky down to the farm the next morning and spend the weekend disproving their bear theory. What I didn't tell them was that I was also going to be investigating Sarah Yoder's murder. I didn't tell Bryce my plans either. What I did on my time was my business.

What I didn't know then was that Amish out of their culture could also be like wild animals.

CHAPTER 33

I stopped by my parents' farm early to reunite Husky with his canine brethren, Blackie and Max. They raced between barn and silos, never giving me a second sniff.

Mom and Dad were abuzz with the news that the nearby Taopi Post Office—the second smallest in the country—had closed.

"It's the end of an era," he said.

"Maybe that could be a news story for you," she said.

Taopi was far outside the Channel 3 DMA and had only reached a population of fifty-eight in the last census. If Bryce wasn't interested in small-town murder, there was little chance he'd care about small-town mail.

I told them I needed to run over to Harmony and poke around the Amish for information. "Keep the dogs away from bears while I'm gone."

The old house had a wooden sign advertising the Lamplight Inn. I knocked on the door and told the owner I'd heard she'd been a friend to Sarah Yoder.

She invited me inside. "The word is out that I allow Amish to stay here for free while they sort their lives out," Linda Kloeckner said. "Sarah brought very little with her. Not even a change of clothes. Just a small bag."

She opened a closet door in a rear bedroom and showed me a row of Amish garb for men and women. "They leave these behind when they move on. I told her to help herself if anything fit. She was going to use her first paycheck to buy English clothes."

While she might not have known Sarah long, I could tell she was shaken by the nature of her death. Knowing someone who has died violently makes us all feel more vulnerable. After all, what if Sarah's killer had watched her through this very bedroom window? To switch the mood, I grabbed a hanger from the closet, and held a modest black dress in front of me and imagined I was Amish.

Linda pointed me toward a full-length mirror on the back of the door. "If you want to play dress-up, go ahead." She was serious. So I was tempted in the name of research. The hooks and eyes were tricky and she helped me tie the apron in back.

"My hair isn't long enough." Just past my shoulders. A knot at the nape of my neck would be more convincing.

"Pinned up under your bonnet, who can tell?" she said. "If it wasn't for your makeup and lipstick, you'd blend right in at her funeral."

"Sarah's funeral?" I asked. "When and where?"

"About a half hour. At her family's house."

"Are you going, Linda?"

"No, I'm English. And not one the Amish especially appreciate. Best I stay away."

But ten minutes later, I had scrubbed my face and talked her into dropping me off down the road from the funeral. And when she crowned me with a white pleated cap, we were both surprised at how realistic I appeared.

"I won't say anything at the service," I promised. "I just want to observe."

Linda liked the idea that somebody cared about Sarah's story.

She felt some guilt that she'd done nothing. But the first night Sarah didn't show up after work, she too had assumed that the young woman had gone back to her Amish family.

"I was disappointed she didn't even stop by to say goodbye or thank you," Linda said. "Then I learned she was murdered and felt terrible for my thoughts."

When I arrived at Sarah's home farm, an interesting line of buggies were parked along the gravel road. Each had a chalk number on the side, presumably their order to drive to the cemetery. Or maybe so their owners could tell them apart. The largest number I noticed was thirty-eight.

The sight was unusual enough that I shot some video with my cell phone through the windshield. Then I fastened the device under my skirt to my leg with duct tape so I could call my ride later to be picked up.

Linda reminded me to act quiet and shy. "If anyone asks where you're from, say 'Ohio.'"

A few other cars also were dropping off Amish men and women for the funeral service. With them, I walked the last hundred yards or so to Sarah's house. The other women also wore black dresses; the men, black pants and vests over white shirts.

I saw no tears. Only stoic expressions that I tried to mimic.

Inside the barn, a simple pine casket sat on a table at one end. Closed to viewing. No surprise, considering the description I'd heard of her mangled face. Under English circumstances, a photograph of the deceased in happier times would be prominently displayed next to the coffin. But not among the Amish. No flowers either.

Hay was strewn on the floor. Rows of benches filled the building. I took a seat on an end by other women, in case I needed to leave quickly should my impostor role be discerned. I noticed the men kept their hats on while they sat. The duct tape holding my phone to my leg started to itch.

My observation of the ceremony didn't yield much insight be-

cause the service was in Pennsylvania Dutch—the Amish tongue.
I chimed in for Amen, but didn't volunteer anything else. Oc-
casionally, a word reminded me of high-school German. The
prayers and preachers went on for hours.

A jug of water and glasses were passed around and I had a
drink. A kitten in a corner started to meow. Later, I heard cows
mooing and a horse whinny.

Toward the end, I heard the name "Sarah Yoder" called out.
Some more scripture was read, then most of the folks knelt for a
final prayer and the service appeared over.

All present lined to file past the casket, and I noticed a girl
with her hand outstretched, touching the wooden box. I pegged
her as the sister I'd briefly met in the yard the other day. Near
her, her mother and a young beardless man I presumed could be
a brother mingled with mourners. I wasn't sure who among the
men might be her father, but thought I heard someone refer to
Sarah's mother as Miriam.

I steered clear of anyone who looked like family, while con-
templating my next move. Some sort of protocol seemed under
way, with the bereaved separating in groups, possibly by age.

An Amish man without a beard came up beside me, took me
by the elbow, whispering in my ear. "You need to follow me outside."

It was Ike—the Everything Amish owner.

He didn't give me away to anyone else. So I left without a
tussle.

CHAPTER 34

Ike led me to a two-seater buggy hitched to a pleasant brown horse and told me to climb in. I kept tripping inefficiently over my long skirt, so he hoisted me up.

"You're lucky to be getting out now," he said. "What were you going to do when everybody headed to the cemetery? How about when they gathered for the meal?"

"I hadn't thought that far ahead," I admitted.

"You were attracting curiosity already. This could have ended badly if they found out you worked for TV. Now they'll simply think you were with me and dismiss us both as odd."

"I thought you weren't Amish anymore, Ike. Why are you here?"

"I can still attend funerals, providing I respect their dress and customs. And that's never been a problem."

While he didn't call himself Amish anymore, he was related to many in the congregation, including Sarah. Apparently half of the Amish population shared six surnames—Miller, Stoltzfus, Schrock, Hershberger, Hochstetler, and Yoder.

"Particularly, since I briefly employed the deceased," he continued, "my presence was not questioned. Yours, however, would have caused trouble."

I could certainly understand, but attending Sarah's funeral raised more questions for me than it answered. "If Sarah left the faith, how come she had an Amish funeral?"

"I guess the church decided to value forgiveness rather than punishment," Ike said. "After all, once she was identified, there was no one else to claim her body."

"I'm still trying to understand this shunned business. Are you also being shunned?"

"Technically, yes. That's why I didn't mind leaving the funeral early."

I thought about how hard finding balance between two worlds might be, and wasn't sure what to say next. That was okay, because Ike kept talking. Maybe his denial of faith was always on his mind and he didn't have anyone else to listen.

He'd left the Amish life after *Rumspringa* to embrace modern society. "I decided I enjoyed the benefits of electricity and automobiles too much to go back to kerosene lamps and buggy harnesses on a regular basis. Now I'm a techno nut. I even watched you on the news the other night."

The thought of him clicking a TV remote and stopping at my face kept me quiet even longer. But as I became accustomed to the gait of the horse, I began to enjoy the ride.

"Can I drive, Ike?"

"No," he replied, as we headed back to town. "The buggy is not a toy."

"Why do you even have a buggy?"

"Sometimes I have need of primitive wheels."

During nice weather, he liked to park the buggy in front of the store as part of the rustic decor. The rest of the time he kept it in a large shed with a collection of other vehicles. When he needed a horse, he borrowed a neighbor's. That's when I learned he owned the sports car I was admiring the other day outside the store.

To pass the time, I asked him how sales were going at Everything Amish. He talked about making his monthly trip to Ohio soon to pick up fresh merchandise. He even had some special orders that would be ready.

"Seems like a long drive," I remarked. "Can't you just carry stock from Amish around here?"

Drily, he explained that he used a truck, not a buggy, for those over-the-road trips. And while he stocked some Minnesota Amish products, there simply wasn't enough available. Also, because he'd left the faith, many local Amish declined to trade with him. Not wanting to touch money he'd touched. And others simply preferred to sell directly to the public.

"They're businessmen as well, and see the benefit in eliminating the middleman. Me? I make shopping easy for the tourists. Everything Amish under one roof."

His store name was catchy. "Is there any resentment that you're taking money from area Amish?" I asked.

"Well, I'm local, too. And if there's bad feelings, it's not just them toward me."

Evidently, many English around town had mixed sentiments about the Amish contributions to the economy. As one example, he said, English stores selling food have to comply with health codes. The Amish don't.

"More than once I've heard the owner of the town bakery complain about all the government regulations she has to follow before she can open her shop, but the Amish can cook and can next to where horses crap."

"I guess you could call that rustic atmosphere." I laughed, enjoying both the vision and Ike's candid demeanor. "Yet when tourists come to see the Amish, they spend cash here in town."

"Absolutely, Riley, but it's still an uneasy alliance."

"Sounds like marriage."

This time he chuckled and I found myself pleased at making him laugh. I was just appreciating what a fun connection we'd developed on our ride when he spoiled the mood by turning our talk to more serious matters.

"I suppose your career doesn't leave time for a personal life or family?" he asked.

I felt like I'd been put on the spot too much lately for not rushing home to kids or a spouse. I had been first to mention the M word, so perhaps the fault was mine. But I'd only said it in jest.

"Actually, I'm a widow." I told him that my husband, Hugh Boyer, was killed a few years ago in an explosion in northern Minnesota. I avoided the law enforcement line-of-duty details and Ike didn't pry. It wasn't that I wasn't proud of Hugh. But it was still too grievous to relive his hero's death as the bodyguard for a governor who didn't deserve to be saved from a terrorist blast.

"He was kind of a car freak like you," I said. "Loved to rent and drive all sorts of vehicles—especially muscle cars. I would have liked to see him behind the wheel of a buggy."

Hugh was a city boy. The thought of him and a steed made me chuckle.

"They are two very different types of horsepower," Ike said. This time we both laughed.

"How about you? I don't see a ring on your finger. Or is lack of jewelry one of those Amish customs you've kept close?"

"I don't like being alone, but I haven't found a good fit. The English I've met weren't Amish enough and the Amish weren't English enough."

"Sounds like a hard match."

After leaving the church years ago, he had simply showed up at the local hardware store and been hired. He'd saved his paychecks for modern purchases, like computer and television, which reaffirmed his life course. So rather than concentrate on the empty house awaiting him at the end of his work shift, he kept his mind focused on his techno toys.

Then one day he envisioned Everything Amish.

"I realized when it came to Amish goods," he said, "demand was greater than supply. And I had a certain expertise. Now, I'm running a booming business and thinking of expanding nationally."

"So you probably don't have time for a personal life, either."

"I'd consider making time if I met the right person." Then he turned the topic back on me and invited me out to dinner.

"You mean like a date?"

I hadn't gone on a date in a long time. Garnett and I had evolved well past the dating stage. And since Hugh's death, I had developed a policy against dating anyone I couldn't imagine spending a lifetime with because that seemed a good way to weed out time wasters.

Lots of reasons came to mind for not dating Ike. Distance. Education. Religion. But maybe I was being too fussy. Maybe I needed to let myself date for the moment, not the future.

I realized I liked Ike. So I said yes.

"But I can't guarantee when or where. My job is a little unpredictable. You'll have to call me and drive to Minneapolis."

He replied that transportation and communication would not be a problem. Unlike traditional Amish, he had a telephone and plenty of cars.

CHAPTER 35

The Lamplight owner was glad to see I'd found my way back from the funeral and helped me climb out of Ike's buggy. "I was starting to worry when I didn't hear from you about a ride back."

I understood Linda's concern and apologized for not calling. After all, the last woman who came to her place had ended up dead.

She took a picture of me in my Amish garb on my cell phone for a souvenir. Then I changed back to my English clothes and thanked her for all her help. We agreed to stay in touch in case either of us heard anything break about Sarah Yoder.

I almost missed the Amish cemetery on my way back to my parents' farm. Because I had no notebook with me, Ike had drawn a map on the palm of my hand. Since the graveside service would be over, this seemed like a good time to see Sarah's final resting place.

When covering homicides, viewing the victim's grave was a routine of mine. I'd give a silent prayer for God to help me report the truth, and for the family to find peace despite their pain.

In this case, the cemetery looked even smaller because it sat in the middle of a large pasture. In the distance, an Amish barn bordered one side, a grove of trees the other. Backing up the car,

I parked on the side of the road and climbed down into the ditch for a close-up.

The grave markers were small and white. Plain. Many of the older ones were overgrown.

None of the tombstones indicated status or wealth. No fancy angels or crosses, only a listing of name and date of birth and death. Nothing to reflect personality.

Sarah's headstone was easy to find by following the trampled path to the fresh dirt of her hand-dug grave. SARAH YODER. I knew nothing of the years of her life, only the day of her death. And that's unsatisfying to any reporter.

I found an extra copy of her forensic sketch, still in a side pocket of my purse. Even though I knew the Amish disapproved of graven images, I spread Sarah's face flat over her burial plot and placed a small rock in each corner because I wanted to do something personal for her. If the rest of the cemetery was any indication, I didn't think she'd get many visitors.

CHAPTER 36

As my parents grew older, their fascination with funerals also seemed to grow. The newspaper obituaries were the first items they'd read each day. To me, their captivation with death seemed unhealthy. But they felt strongly that those of their generation still alive owed it to those now departed to note their passing.

My parents, having never been to an Amish funeral, had more questions than I had answers. All our conversation netted was a dialogue of clichés.

"Why didn't you bring us along?" my mom asked. "You never take us anywhere."

"I didn't know I was even going," I said. "And besides, you wouldn't have had a thing to wear."

I showed them the picture of me dressed plain and my mom wanted a copy. "We might use it for Christmas cards." I lied and told her it was only viewable on phones.

The three of us spent the evening dining on steak from one of the neighbor's steers, and brainstorming directions the Amish murder might go.

"My boss is still not crazy about the case," I said. "So keep your ears open if there's something that makes for irresistible news."

I had little hope that would happen. But my folks liked to

stay involved in my life, and were pleased whenever their rural grapevine of eclectic sources yielded a story harvest for Channel 3. I'd tell them when the story would run and they'd watch the news on satellite TV, pointing proudly to the screen in ownership.

That night at the farm, silhouettes of distant wind turbines danced outside my bedroom window. I tried counting the red flashing lights to put myself to sleep.

While lying there, I thought about what Ike had said about a possible date and realized that the prospect of being desired by a stranger sounded enticing.

Reporters aren't supposed to date sources. That's one of those ethical rules we embrace along with not doing puff pieces on advertisers. But Ike had been a source for only about thirty seconds. He really wasn't involved in the case anymore, although I could see using him as an Amish consultant. I wondered if he really would call me, but decided to stop worrying about whether we had rapport.

That's when I realized I hadn't called Garnett. And he'd left two messages. My cell phone reception was lousy in bed, so I moved to an opposite upstairs corner and crouched in the hallway until the signal improved.

"I'm at the farm," I told him when he answered.

"I'd rather you were here," he replied.

I told him the latest about Sarah Yoder's murder, and that I'd even attended her funeral incognito. I didn't mention Ike. He'd started to feel like one of the characters in my Amish romance, struggling for goodwill amid a secret society.

"You dressed up Amish?" Garnett said. "I'd like to see that up close. If I fly out there this week, will you play dress-up with me?"

I told him this week looked busy, and texted him the photo

instead. "To work this case, I'm trying to think Amish, Nick, and not so much about sex."

"Why do you think the Amish aren't into sex? Each family has a pack of kids. They have sex all the time."

"Well, for them it's probably more an obligation than an urge."

"Don't go assuming, Riley. You know what you always say about that."

He had me there. But he wanted more.

"If we can't have hot sex," he said, "at least let me leave you with hot dialogue."

"That's what phones and friends are for," I replied. "Start talking, Nick."

"I believe in long, slow, deep, soft, wet kisses that last three days." He said the words convincingly—just like the star who made them notorious.

"Kevin Costner. *Bull Durham*. 1988."

And then, to heighten the drama of distance, I hung up.

I woke early the next morning to drive from the farm back to the Twin Cities before work. "Do you hear anything about the Fillmore County sheriff's race?" I asked my parents. "I see a woman is running against Ed Eide."

"I think there's some flap about the sheriff handing out gun permits," Dad said. "I hear he gave one to the town drunk."

"Why would he do that?" I asked.

"Probably for money," Mom said.

"Do you know that or are you guessing?" I said.

"It's as good a guess as any," she answered.

Minnesota has a controversial conceal-and-carry gun permit law that allows sheriffs to decide who carries firepower. There's no statewide standard, except that violent felons can't pack heat. Whether citizens can or can't depends a lot on the county where they live. Some sheriffs are strict, others have never turned down any applicant.

"Granting the permit is really at the sheriff's discretion," I explained. "Experience tells me that any time an elected official has that kind of clout, politics are always in play."

I decided to make some calls later and see what I could learn. In the meantime, because Husky seemed so content running around with the other pooches, I left him behind. And because we'd seen no sign of bear, I worried not.

What a difference twenty-four hours makes.

CHAPTER 37

The mysterious black bear of southern Minnesota was in the news again—this time with corroboration.

A couple of hikers surprised the creature as it stood on its rear feet marking a tree in a state park near Harmony.

"We froze. It froze. Then it disappeared into the woods," one was quoted as saying in the *Rochester Post-Bulletin*.

The other hiker snapped two photos. The first showed a hairy butt in some weeds; but in the second, the animal had turned as if mugging for the camera, thus ending the debate over bear vs. dog. The picture, the size of the tracks, and the height of the claw marks definitely established it as an American black bear.

"By the size, I'd guess a male. And a big one," a state wildlife official estimated. "At least a six-foot reach. For sure, three hundred pounds. Maybe more. Plenty of bear."

Every news agency in Minnesota had apparently linked to the story on their website. And it was now among the top viewed stories in the state. As a courtesy, I'd called in to the assignment desk to tell them I was in southern Minnesota, but would be back in time for the morning news huddle.

"Stay where you are." Ozzie filled me in on the bear story. "Bryce is interested in it. I'll let him talk to you."

"Keep an eye on this," Bryce said. "A bear out of his territory could be news."

While I lived to chase news, I had no interest in chasing bears. Bryce was sounding more and more like my old boss, Noreen, crazed with the animal beat. "But isn't this story out of our Channel 3 territory?" I asked, playing his designated market area game against him. That proved unwise. Immediately I was driving east under orders to shoot a standup next to the bear claw tree. I tried to argue against being my own photographer because who wants to hike alone in the woods with a bear loose?

But when I arrived in town, I discovered bear hunting season was still under way, and anyone within fifty miles who owned a gun was also out looking for the bear. The woods were a dangerous place.

I got a quickie lesson in bear hunting. Hunters can only actually fire during the day between a half hour before sunrise to a half hour after sunset. The rule wasn't designed so much to give wildlife a chance at survival as to keep people from shooting each other.

I recorded some sound bites from hunters on the prowl.

((HUNTER1 SOT))
THIS IS MY CHANCE TO
LAND A TROPHY.

Signs with names and addresses showed up in the woods, and were described to me as "stands" where hunters reserve their spots. I considered putting up a sign myself to reserve safe space for the station even though our form of shooting was not fatal.

((HUNTER2 SOT))
HUNTING IS WHAT I DO AND IF
THAT BEAR'S AROUND, HE'S MINE.

Southern Minnesota is not considered prime bear-hunting territory. In fact, few hunters bother trying. They go after deer and waterfowl. The knowledge that an American black bear was somewhere close changed the hunting dynamics.

((HUNTER3 SOT))

WAHOO!

One hunter expressed confidence that his bait station would do the job, and showed me donuts and jelly designed to lure the mammoth beast to his sight line.

"Isn't that cheating?" I asked.

Sure seemed like cheating to me. But a DNR official defended the practice on the grounds that bears are so elusive, few of the beasts would fall prey to man without baiting. He guided me to the parkland and showed me the tree bark clawed deep by our celebrity bear.

((WILDLIFE SOT))

SEE THE STRENGTH BEHIND

THAT REACH. NO WONDER

EVERYBODY'S AFTER THAT BRUTE.

I found myself feeling sorry for the bear. And I was starting to think Channel 3's viewers would, too.

Once I had enough bear material for a news package, I drove down the dirt road toward Sarah Yoder's grave. During my walk in the woods, I'd picked a couple stems of red autumn foliage to lay on her plot in lieu of a flashy floral bouquet.

The first thing I noticed was that the sketch I'd left of her face was gone. But I wasn't actually surprised, knowing that Amish faith rejected pictures as vain. Leaving Sarah's picture might have been selfish of me. But I didn't see any shredded paper or burnt ashes. Any destruction must have happened off site.

I decided to be bold and drive by Sarah's house in case anything looked different postfuneral. As I got closer, I saw a small figure carrying a lunch pail in the driveway. It was her sister, probably coming home from the Amish country school.

I pulled alongside her and rolled down the car window. I didn't make any mention about Sarah, because I didn't want to ruin our second encounter.

"Hi there, I could use some eggs. Are you open for customers today?"

She glanced around as if checking to see whether I might be talking to someone else, but she was the only one on the road. I smiled at her like my presence was a blessing.

"Maybe you could tell your folks you have a customer."

While she went in the house, I parked the car down the road so that my ultimate departure would take longer in case her mother chased me away again. The girl's lunch bucket sat on the porch steps. Bored, I plopped down and peeked inside it, under the cloth dishrag.

The drawing of Sarah Yoder stared up at me from the bottom of the pail. I dropped the fabric quickly to keep the secret covered and scrambled to my feet as mother and daughter came outside.

I knew now who had beat me to the cemetery.

I said nothing beyond requesting a dozen eggs from Mrs. Yoder, who startled me by agreeing. She sent the child back to bring them out and told me that would be a dollar. I handed her the bill and asked what crafts she sold, making sure I flashed the cash in my wallet.

"Just a moment," she said. "I'll be back."

I knew she recognized me from my other visit, but was certain she had no idea I'd been to her daughter's funeral.

The child returned with the eggs first. "Your name was Hannah, wasn't it?" I asked.

She nodded, and I handed her the bucket. "Best you take this away." She knew I knew. And so she left.

Her mother brought a key and led me to a shed between the house and barn. Shelves lined the walls and crafts filled the shelves. Quilted table runners. Numerous handmade baskets. Jars of jams. But most unnerving, a row of rag dolls, dressed like Amish men and women. Without faces.

CHAPTER 38

The empty faces wore hats and bonnets along with their aprons and suspenders. They lacked eyes, noses, and mouths. I was both fascinated and repelled.

I picked one up, but couldn't understand how a child could embrace such a blank slate. Yet even without eyes, the dolls seemed to be watching me. Their expressions covert.

Somehow, I couldn't shake the feeling we'd met before. I set a pair—boy and girl—on the counter to purchase with some cash.

"Why don't they have faces?"

My question didn't seem unexpected. Tourists probably asked it all the time because the Amish woman had a practiced, ready answer. "That is our way. No images or likenesses."

The image of Sarah as a faceless Amish doll came to my mind. And until the forensic artist gave her back her identity, that's what she was, another Jane Doe lacking a proper burial.

Just then the little girl stuck her head in the door to check on us. Her mother made a sharp comment in Pennsylvania Dutch and left me alone at the counter while it sounded like she was scolding her daughter. Reaching to put my change back in my purse, my fingers found a marker. On impulse, I added facial features to my handmade doll to make her more human. Eyes. Nose. Mouth. I smiled at my creation just as Hannah was leaving the shed.

The Amish woman gasped when she saw the blemished toy. Before I could react she'd grabbed my rag doll away from me and ripped its head off. But holding each piece of doll in a different hand, the woman seemed even more shocked than me. She, embarrassed for displaying temper. Me, impressed by the strength necessary for the damage.

As we considered each other, the doll's head and body dropped from her hands to the floor. I picked up the torn head and flashed back to a childhood moment of dismay, finding another doll head facedown in a ditch by my family's farm.

"I suspect we might have met before." I described two little girls having tea with their dolls decades earlier while our fathers talked business. "Perhaps you are that other child?"

She nodded without hesitation. The long-ago afternoon had apparently made a bigger impression on her than me.

"My father tore my doll," she said. "He told me the face you drew was prideful."

"My name is Riley Spartz. And you are Miriam Yoder?"

Another nod.

"Sarah's mother?"

Again, a nod.

"Can we talk about Sarah?"

She shook her head. "God's will."

"God also wills justice," I replied. "I know your daughter lost her Amish faith. I'd like to try to understand why."

Sometimes a victim's family appreciates being able to talk about a loved one. Not the case here. Miriam seemed a by-the-Bible Amish.

"I'm sorry for what happened to her," I said. "And I'm sorry for you, too. Nobody deserves to lose a child like that."

Her mouth tensed, before once again she replied, "God's will."

"Why was Sarah being shunned?" I asked.

I sensed her struggle. How best to explain such an esoteric concept to an outsider?

Miriam Yoder paused. "Sarah was rejecting the Amish way. Things most important to our people."

I talked about all teens struggling to find their path. "Sports cars can be habit-forming."

Miriam did not look amused. She justified the shunning because in her words, Sarah had her chance to test the English world, but chose to be a baptized member of their church.

"She should have respected the *Ordnung*," Miriam said. "But she refused. We couldn't look away."

"Did she tell you she was leaving? Or was it a surprise?"

She shook her head. "She was gone one morning without a word."

"How about the rest of the family?" I asked. "Her father? Her siblings? Was she close to them?"

Miriam was a widow. I shared that I also had lost my spouse. Neither of us said anything right away after that. Miriam started stacking baskets methodically.

"Sometimes I think having a child would have helped me better cope with my loss," I told her. I hadn't ever said that to anyone else before. "I envy that you have a family to raise."

"My son is everything to me."

I was puzzled she didn't mention Hannah. But I saw her remark as another indication that men have higher standing among the Amish. If Miriam was grieving, she was keeping specific feelings private. Considering I was a stranger, that seemed normal. But I doubted she was sharing them with anyone since Sarah's burial.

I remarked that she and her youngest both wore black dresses. "Is there a certain length of time you will keep the black?"

"One year," she answered.

Maybe she thought by getting me to understand their manners, our conversation would end. But it just made me more curious. The journalist in me focused on the one question her story seemed to hinge on. "What rule did she break?"

Miriam squirmed, clearly not wanting to say more. "That is our concern, but Sarah knew the outcome for obstinance. The bann."

Then I asked again about how Sarah's brother and sister coped after she left. "Did she tell either of them goodbye? Or where she was headed?"

Miriam shook her head. "Hannah was upset. And her brother knew nothing about her plans either." She mentioned how a neighbor reported later that Sarah had been seen in town. But because of the shunning, her family did not seek her out.

When investigators arrived with questions, she did not imagine Sarah had come to harm. She suspected her daughter was in trouble with the law. Maybe drugs and sex. Or theft. She had heard disturbing tales of other runaway Amish youth.

"The sheriff carried the same drawing you did the first time you came," she said. "I told him, yes, it was Sarah. He told me she was dead."

"That must have been horrible," I said. "But surely you can understand how using the sketch—and the media—might help their investigation."

Before she could answer, an unmarried Amish man entered the shed. I concluded he was single because he was clean shaven. Miriam called him Gideon. Hannah had apparently told him I had returned as a customer. He was her brother. The head of the family.

He ordered me to leave. "You don't belong in our world." Then he scolded his mother. "This is the television woman I warned you about."

The nickname wasn't especially flattering, so I tried to tell him my real name. But he wasn't interested in that or a business card. My phone number, email, or station address meant even less to him than my moniker.

"Why was your sister being shunned, Gideon?" I hoped his answer might yield more detail than his mother's.

It didn't. "That's no business of the English."

I noticed one of the fingers on his left hand was missing, but didn't pry because he didn't seem the chatty type.

I thanked Sarah's mother for her time and didn't let on to her son that we'd been visiting before he interrupted us. At the car, I realized I only had half a doll in hand. The boy doll was still on the counter, the girl doll body presumably still on the floor. I was afraid to go back for either souvenir, instead settling for my doll head with a smudged face.

CHAPTER 39

A woman with a hammer was pounding orange campaign signs in the ground near Chatfield, another town up the highway en route to Minneapolis. When I saw the notices were for Sheriff Eide's rival, I pulled over.

Turns out, she was Laura Schaefer—his opponent—currently a deputy sheriff.

"So why are you running against your boss?"

I introduced myself as a TV reporter covering the murder of Sarah Yoder. I figured their race was too local for Twin Cities media, but I was still curious about their rivalry.

"Give me your campaign spiel, Deputy."

"I'm running to make a point, and you can call me Laura."

Her issue was that the sheriff was too free in handing out gun permits. One had gone to a buddy of his who had been convicted twice of drunk driving, and had been inebriated at the high school football game.

"A blatant example of public intoxication," she said. "He ran out on the field and tried to stop the game when a call went against his team. He had to be dragged off so play could resume. No telling what would have happened if he'd been armed."

After she outlined that story, I wish I hadn't stopped to meet her. Now the newsroom spree shooting would torment me the entire drive back. I tried to shake it from my mind and instead saw visions of bloody referee uniforms and fallen cheerleaders on the twenty-yard line while a coach tackled the drunken gunman.

"Certainly sounds like an issue worth raising, Laura. How did the sheriff react when you announced your candidacy?"

"Transferred me to the night shift."

I believed her. Sheriffs generally don't take it well when subordinates challenge them for their job. Besides being dark and lonely, the night shift is full of crazy calls.

"But working nights gives me time for this." And she gave the sign a final pound, then stepped back to admire her work.

"What makes you think this guy and the sheriff are pals?"

"They're more than friends. Roger Alton's his biggest fundraiser. He hosts an annual party for campaign contributors."

"How much does he raise?"

"More than five grand in an afternoon," she said. "Certainly enough that no one's wanted to run against him."

"So how about you, Laura? Do you have any supporters?"

"Not nearly enough." She showed me, in the backseat of her car, campaign signs with her name blacked out. "That's why I'm out here today."

CHAPTER 40

The six o'clock newscast was still half an hour away while I waited for my set piece about the rogue bear. Then the desk got word that firefighters, with lights flashing and sirens blaring, were racing to a restaurant in south Minneapolis.

Malik was on his way home, not far from the blaze, so Ozzie ordered him to meet a live truck and broadcast from the scene. This week was Channel 3's political reporter's chance to audition for the anchor slot. After the standard good-evening greeting, he informed viewers of the two-alarm fire, promising a live report within minutes.

I watched the early action from the control booth, because I was the second story, after the lead about school referendums. After my wrap, the producer cut away to the fire, which by now, had been upgraded to a three alarm.

((ANCHOR CU))
NOW FOR BREAKING NEWS—
MINNEAPOLIS FIREFIGHTERS
ARE RESPONDING TO A BLAZE
THAT HAS ENGULFED GRETA'S—A
NEIGHBORHOOD RESTAURANT
THAT IS CONNECTED TO SEVERAL
BOUTIQUE SHOPS IN THE SAME
COMPLEX.

            ((DOUBLE BOX))
            MALIK RAHMAN IS STANDING BY
            AT THE SCENE WITH DETAILS
            IN THIS LIVE REPORT.

Malik stood across the street from dramatic smoke and flames. Truck engineers manned the live-shot cameras to forestall technical difficulties. But Malik, despite wearing a mic and an earpiece, was silent.

"You're hot," the producer yelled in both his ear and the camera operator's.

The anchor also stepped up to fill time. He didn't have any facts about the fire but used questions.

            ((ANCHOR DOUBLE BOX))
            WHAT'S THE SITUATION THERE,
            MALIK? ANY REPORTS ON
            WHETHER THE RESTAURANT
            WAS EVACUATED?

Malik just stood there.

His lips weren't even moving, so we knew it wasn't that kind of an audio problem. The anchor referenced technical difficulties to the viewers. Then those of us in the control booth realized at the same time that the problem was Malik.

"He's frozen."

Sometimes the pressure of a live shot—knowing there's no do-over—freaks rookies. By the time reporters reach a market the size of Minneapolis–St. Paul, they've worked through those issues or left the business. But Malik had never reported live before. He'd been able to re-record himself over and over until his lines were perfect. The same difference between acting onscreen and onstage.

"Camera off Malik." The producer instructed the photographer to pan to the burning building itself. The assignment desk ran over with a written page of details about the blaze which the producer rushed to the anchor to ad-lib under pictures of a row of firefighters aiming hoses of water at broken windows.

> ((ANCHOR NAT))
> WE'RE ALSO GETTING WORD THAT
> THE BLAZE HAS SPREAD TO THE
> NEIGHBORING SUNFISH CAFE.

Then the producer gave a wrap and signaled him back to the comfort of the teleprompter and the original newscast lineup.

> ((ANCHOR CU))
> WE'LL BE BACK IN A MOMENT WITH
> THE DAY'S WEATHER.

> ((ANCHOR NAT))
> AND YOU'LL HEAR FROM A
> WOMAN WHO HAS SPENT HER
> LIFETIME COLLECTING SALT
> AND PEPPER SHAKERS . . . WHAT
> DOES SHE INTEND TO DO WITH
> THEM WHEN SHE DIES?

The newscast was crippled, but this week's anchor sub showed he could adapt to the pressure of breaking news. I figured this now made him the leading internal candidate for the job. Normally the anchor would tease that more on the restaurant fire was coming after the break. But no such promise was made here.

My cell phone rang. It was Malik calling. I rushed back to my office before picking up.

"How bad was I?" he asked.

"Pretty bad." Then I pretended to believe he had thrown the live shot on purpose to end one-man bands and return us to our specialized skills and the newsroom to normal. "But I know you did it for me."

He rejected the out I was giving him. "No, I didn't, Riley. I froze. Over the years, I've seen reporters freeze going live. And that's what happened to me." He drew a deep breath of discouragement. "I'm through with reporting."

I urged him not to make any sudden decisions. That all he needed was some more training and he'd nail a live shot with the best of us. I reminded him live TV was unpredictable, and a poor appraisal of reporting skill.

"No matter how good you are, Malik, you can have a bad live shot. No matter how bad you are, you can have a good one."

Then he told me Bryce had texted him to return to the station immediately.

"Malik, you need to point out to him you've never received adequate training for a live shot."

I wished for the glass walls back so I could watch how their discussion went down. My answer came from Malik's hunched shoulders as he left the news director's office. At least Bryce didn't tear his head off like the Amish doll sitting on my desk.

I offered to take Malik out for a comrade drink, but going home where people loved him sounded a whole lot better than being with someone who reminded him of his job.

Home had no particular appeal for me, though, so when I saw Nicole just finishing her shift, I invited her out for a drink and she eagerly accepted.

CHAPTER 41

I'd been trying to avoid my boss lately. And apparently I wasn't alone.

Nicole and I headed across the street to Brit's Pub. We were too late for the regular happy hour and too early for the late happy hour. So we both ordered fish-and-chips and a beer. I got an ale, she a lager. I tried to put the calories out of my mind.

I didn't normally have much time for gal-pal socializing. But I rationalized that this was work-related.

I asked Nicole how she was enjoying the Channel 3 newsroom. Her story was unusual. She'd accepted an entry-level reporting job from Noreen a week before the shoot-out. So she'd never actually worked for the boss who hired her. Instead, Bryce was her taskmaster.

"It'll be up to him whether I make probation or not," Nicole said.

"At least he hasn't made you be a one-man band."

"I told him I'd give it a try. I have some experience shooting my own video because I come from a smaller market. But he says they will get around to me eventually."

"Lucky you."

"I'm worried. That makes me think he's going to dump me."

"No. You're safe because you're cheap. He'd like to hire more of you. I'm expensive, but he can't dump me because I'm under contract. So he's doing everything he can to make me quit."

She seemed to mull over my words. "What kind of things is he doing?"

"Well, you've seen how he's thrown me out on stories without a photographer and without any camera training. My next job review will score something like 'fails to meet expectations.' This is all about getting rid of the high-salary people."

"Is he doing anything else?" She asked the question like the answer really mattered. Not just small talk.

I weighed just how far I wanted to take our conversation. After all, she and I had sort of just met. I was a senior reporter, she a rookie. But, at the same time, newswomen need to stick together.

"He's a little more touchy-feely than I like in a news director," I said.

Relief swept across her face. "Me too."

Sexual harassment used to be a bigger problem in the early days of women in news. There was still talk about an old cameraman who used to crank the air conditioning in the news cruisers to better see women reporters' nipples. He was long retired, but I always wore a jacket on the job, just in case. Men were supposed to know better now.

Over the next ten minutes we developed a plan to try to alert each other if Bryce ordered either of us to come to his office. We'd text a * to the other as the signal.

"Then we'll interrupt the other's meeting," I said. "The goal is that neither of us is ever alone with him."

"Let's leave his office door open, too," Nicole said.

"Right, if he wants the door shut he has to say so. Even better, make him shut it himself."

A lot could go wrong, and probably would. But it seemed worth trying.

Lacking the energy to cry myself to sleep that night, I reminded myself that the average news director's tenure was only eighteen months. I breathed slowly and deeply into my pillow, repeating over and over, "I can outlast this jerk."

The only flaw in that logic: my contract was up in a year.

CHAPTER 42

As if deep in a cloudy dream, a voice sounded familiar. A couple seconds passed before I realized my cell phone was ringing, and Michelle Kueppers was on the other end. The clock read just past three in the morning. Unless Josh was missing again, I wasn't sure I needed to have this conversation now.

"Sorry to wake you." Michelle explained that she and her husband had just had an online video chat. "You said you'd like to talk to him, and he doesn't get too many chances to call. He's game if you are."

That news woke me in a hurry. "What's the time difference between us and him?"

"Nine hours."

She gave me the website and user name as I scrambled for my laptop. Within minutes the three of us were staring at me through video boxes on my computer monitor.

Michelle handled the Internet introductions. She looked stunning, even on low resolution. Because she'd set up this cyberdate, she had time to prepare. Blush, mascara, a low-cut shirt with enough cleavage to make a man homesick. She also mentioned that Josh and his father had schmoozed a few minutes earlier about school and sports before Josh had crawled back to bed.

Brian Kueppers seemed understandably uncomfortable. Me, I looked like I'd just woken up. I'd have preferred the talk was just between Brian and me, so I could be more candid. But I conceded that without Michelle present, he might not say a word. Agreeing to talk to me might be his way of convincing her that he had nothing to hide.

"What's the temperature in the desert these days?" I didn't ask for specifics of where he was stationed, because I knew military guys were closemouthed about location.

"About a hundred degrees," he replied.

I also wished I'd had some notice so I could have recorded our exchange. But maybe they figured ambushing me gave them the interview advantage.

"Tell her what you told the police," his wife said.

I waited to see if he would, glad that Michelle had brought up that awkward issue about law enforcement, but feeling like the whole thing seemed staged.

"I don't know anything about this body Josh found," he said.

True or not, I had a hunch the cops might want more than just his declaration. "Why do you think they're looking at you?"

"I'm not taking it personally," he said. "We've all got jobs to do. This is just a case of simple elimination. I'm doing everything I can to cooperate."

"Like what?"

"Like a DNA test."

That was the last thing I expected him to say. "When are they taking your sample?"

"Hours ago. Now we wait."

My gut told me anyone with enough confidence to volunteer their DNA must be innocent. But then Michelle started talking about how the whole case against her husband was a pile of coincidences.

And I remembered that I don't believe in coincidences.

"You're talking about the location of the body being near your farm, right? And Brian not having an alibi for Sarah's time of death, right?"

"Right," she answered. "And us being at the Amish store earlier that day."

"You were at Everything Amish the day she was killed? Both of you?" I hoped my voice didn't reflect my incredulity.

"Yes, that's where Brian bought my going-away present. The entryway table you admired at my house."

I recalled running my hand over the graceful piece of furniture.

While talking to Brian was a coup, Michelle's bombshell was bigger. When Josh finished his work with the forensic artist, and Michelle first saw the sketch of Sarah, she sensed something about the dead girl's face that seemed familiar.

"Like maybe we'd met. Then when I heard on the news that she'd worked at the Amish store, I realized she'd waited on us."

"You met Sarah Yoder just before she died?"

"Strange, huh?" Michelle said. "That's probably the biggest coincidence of all."

During this dialogue, Brian stayed quiet.

During the brief time Sarah worked at Everything Amish, investigators ran all the credit numbers for purchases. So Brian's name popped up on two lists connected to the murder victim: as a customer and as a property owner. And he also had a police file indicating that he had a temper and might be capable of violence.

I was beginning to better understand why the cops were looking at him.

I decided ending the questions for now was the best interview strategy. We were all on good terms, and I wanted to keep things that way. So I thanked him for fitting me in his overseas schedule and asked him to keep in touch regarding the results of the DNA test. Then we all signed off.

I don't know how soon sleep came to Michelle, but once again, every time I closed my eyes, Sarah's face popped up and robbed me of any rest.

CHAPTER 43

A few hours later, another phone call woke me. This time it was my mom, calling to say that a local billboard had been defaced. "Everyone around here's talking about it, Riley."

Trying to be nice, I clarified that unless the vandals had scrawled neo-Nazi propaganda over a red, white, and blue billboard supporting our troops, minor vandalism just wasn't major-market news.

Bryce would go ballistic if I even pitched such a story. He would probably write up a note for my personnel file, using this as an example of my poor news judgment.

"Nobody wrote anything on the billboard," Mom said. "They just painted over it."

"What do you mean?"

She explained that a large billboard had gone up outside Harmony a couple days earlier with the Sarah sketch, a headline reading "Call Fillmore County Sheriff's Office with information about Sarah Yoder's murder," and the phone number.

"And someone painted over it?" I asked. "Why?"

"Talk is the Amish did it because they didn't want her face up there for everyone to see," she said.

"They don't like pictures," I heard my dad yell in the background, trying to be helpful. "So they gave it a good whitewashing."

The theory made sense. Especially after meeting the rest of Sarah's family.

If I could pick one Yoder to spend some alone time with, I'd go for Sarah's younger sister. *Out of the mouths of babes.* Hannah seemed curious about her sister's fate, perhaps not old enough to have bought into the "God's Will" philosophy of her mother. She might even have seen or heard something that made her uneasy, that she needed to share with someone.

But such an encounter seemed unlikely. It's not like I could dial a number and hope a little girl answered the phone. These were Amish.

Yet our paths had crossed twice. Perhaps the third time could be the charm.

The news staff was settling down for the morning huddle. Word on the Minneapolis blaze was that a kitchen grease fire destroyed two popular dining spots as well as a shopping complex.

"The fact that restaurants burned down is more interesting than residential homes," Bryce said. "Viewers only care if it's their house. Or maybe their neighbor's. But thousands of people probably dined at those places. Everybody cares about food."

He got no arguments from any of us on that theory.

"We need to be airing more food stories," he continued. "Within the next week I want everyone here to suggest a story about food. Some we'll air immediately, some we'll hold till next month's sweeps."

"Food news or food features?" I asked.

"Just food," he said. "I'll know it when I hear it."

I had no objection to covering the food beat. That's the kind of research underpaid journalists love. Before I became recognizable, the newspaper food critic used to let me tag along during her reviews.

We were back to discussing further coverage of the restaurant fire when Ozzie yelled over from the assignment desk that he had a live one. "The bear's been collared!"

Apparently the southern Minnesota bear was being tracked, not just by hunters but by scientists. A private donor—curious about bears moving out of forested areas into farmland—was funding research to learn how animals adapted to new habitat.

A researcher from the Bear Center had hit the animal with a tranquilizer gun and banded its neck with a radio collar. No details on the location would be forthcoming because they didn't want to give clues to hunters.

Especially since today was the last day of hunting season.

Ozzie printed out an emailed photo of a large black bear sporting colorful streamers around its head. Awfully darn cute. He sort of looked like a circus bear, except for trees in the background instead of trapezes.

"They're naming the bear Walden," he said, "meaning 'from the woods.'"

"'Walden' sounds adorable," I said. "Any hunter who shoots him is going to get death threats."

We discussed how naming animals personalizes them for the public. Bryce told me I owned the bear beat and better deliver a follow-up story.

"You know there's no chance I'm going to get any video of this bear," I said. "Especially doing the camera work myself. You realize that, right?"

"I dislike such a negative attitude, Riley," Bryce said. "I'm seeing that in story after story. You were certain you wouldn't find a photo of the Amish woman, and you didn't. Now you're convinced you won't find the bear. Try thinking positive."

I wasn't sure how to answer him. So I merely nodded my head, to show I got his message. And deep down I started worrying maybe he was right about me and negative energy.

Then I decided not to let him beat me down. Maybe he needed a message.

"Speaking of Sarah Yoder," I said, "and I like to use murder victims' names to personalize them—well, there's been some interesting developments in that case."

I explained about the vandalized billboard and the apparent feud going on between the Yoder family and the law.

"Plus, Sarah was being shunned."

That announcement brought a round of questions ranging from "what" to "why." Bryce was the only one not talking over everyone else at the news table. I pretended not to notice he was caught in a management sulk.

"Sarah had turned away from the Amish so the Amish were turning away from her," I said. "Whether her departure from the community relates to her murder, we don't know."

"I'd sure like to know," Nicole said. "And I bet viewers would, too."

I smiled at her for the support. She was taking a risk, backing me.

A couple of the producers also seemed interested in the story. As the new boss, Bryce was in a management pickle. Without control, he'd lose respect. But if he dismissed an intriguing story, he might lose more respect.

I needed to give him an out. "I realize my top priority has to be this bear. That's the story I need to come back with. But how about if the opportunity is there, I poke around on Sarah's homicide?"

He opted for public peace. "As long as you understand your primary assignment."

But when I asked if a photographer could come with me to help with all the ping-pong driving, Bryce shook his head. "Those resources are needed here on other stories within our viewing area."

I had hoped Malik and I might team up in the field again, but I also grasped that Bryce needed to slap a firm "no" my way as a warning to the rest of the staff to fear him.

CHAPTER 44

A fatal accident on the highway between the Twin Cities and Rochester changed our news plans. Lanes were closed and traffic backed up just south of Cannon Falls, the same stretch where I'd encountered the near miss the other night.

Walden the bear was put on hold. So was Sarah Yoder.

Talk of turning the highway into a freeway came up every time a motorist died. But lawmakers insisted no money existed for such a permanent solution. Dead people can't (or at least aren't supposed to) vote. So driving south on that road was like a round of roulette.

The state was experimenting with high-tech signs at the intersection to alert drivers when it was safe to cross, but elevation differences in the lanes created blind spots.

The accident happened within the designated market area—the magic circle of news—so Channel 3 cared enough about the story to send a satellite truck and photographer to join me for a live shot.

((ANCHOR CU))
TWO VEHICLES CRASHED AT ONE
OF THE STATE'S MOST PERILOUS
INTERSECTIONS JUST SOUTH OF
THE TWIN CITIES. NOW A WOMAN

IS DEAD AND A FAMILY INJURED.
RILEY SPARTZ IS STANDING BY AT
THE SCENE.

((RILEY LIVE))
MORE THAN A HUNDRED
ACCIDENTS HAVE OCCURRED AT
THIS SAME LOCATION BEHIND ME
IN THE LAST DECADE.

((NAT SOT))
RESIDENTS WANT ACTION BUT THE
STATE HAS NO MONEY BEYOND
PUTTING UP WARNING SIGNS.

((RESIDENT SOT))
THOSE OF US WHO LIVE AROUND
HERE LIVE IN FEAR WE OR
SOMEONE WE LOVE WILL BE NEXT.

After also voicing a track and shooting a standup, I could have called it a news day and headed back to the Twin Cities. But because I keep an extra set of socks and underwear tucked in my shoulder bag, I suggested continuing south that night and returning the next day.

"I could bring back a Walden story," I said. "By then we might know his fate. I can at least get some fresh video and sound from hunters."

Bryce agreed, provided I do a phoner—a live telephone report covered with video. Not the most interesting means of storytelling, but a cheap way to transmit information.

These were the final hours of bear hunting season and the woods would be full of blaze orange. Radio collar or not, Walden was an attractive target.

So was I. So was anybody tromping in the dark thicket.

With hunting fever at a frenzy, I vetoed any idea of going undercover in the underbrush. I figured folks with guns on deadline would shoot anything that moved. I decided instead to interview hunters as they gassed up their pickups or filled their thermoses with coffee. I even attempted an artistic shot down the barrel of a gun.

I feared for this one bear against masses of camouflage.

But Walden had supporters. Protesters had arrived in town with signs and chants to oppose the hunting of research bears.

If Walden was shot in the waning minutes of bear hunting season, the hunter who landed him would be required to report his trophy to the state. I'd then report that as news. And such a controversial kill would absolutely mean the lead, especially since Bryce was bullish on this bear story.

And if Walden survived the night, that would also be news. But certainly not the lead. Even so, I was rooting for the bear.

CHAPTER 45

I meant to chase Walden more to please my boss. But outside of town, a white billboard with no message caught my attention. No doubt this was the one in the buzz. I pulled over, then walked closer to inspect. The paint looked dry, but the work fresh. Spatters covered brown grass below.

I stretched upward to try to touch my palm against the lower edge of the sign just to feel closer to Sarah, but fell short. "I will keep your picture in the news," I silently vowed.

The surface was cold and bumpy in places. Sloppy whitewash work got the job done fast. The goal was to obliterate the message completely, not to create art.

Whoever did the deed must have used a very long paint roller to reach the top. And waited until late at night when traffic was sparse. Could one person have worked alone? Probably. But the chore would have been easier with a lookout.

I checked my watch and saw less than twenty minutes stood between me and my phoner about bear season. The beauty of a phoner was that it could be done anywhere—provided you had cell service. I checked and had four bars. I ran across the road and took a picture of the blank billboard with my cell phone, then unpacked the station camera and tripod to get a wide moving video pan of the billboard. Through the viewfinder I saw a law enforcement vehicle drive into screen. Technically I shouldn't have stopped there.

Sheriff Eide rolled down the window. "What's new in news?" he asked.

I was relieved to see him behind the wheel, figuring I had just avoided a ticket. "You might know better than me, Sheriff. What can you tell me about the situation here?" I waved my hand at the blank sign.

He explained that because advertising was slow, the billboard company agreed to donate space for a public-service sign asking for clues about Sarah. "It was barely up forty-eight hours."

"Do you have a picture of what it looked like prior to the vandalism?" I asked.

He showed me one on his cell phone and emailed it to me so I could give viewers a before and after.

The weather was chilly, and he noticed I wasn't wearing a coat. He invited me to sit in the car with him and chat. Backseat of course. The invite gave me a sense we might be getting along better, and I decided to capitalize on that in the hopes of obtaining more facts about the case. I climbed in, hearing the auto lock behind me as I shut the door.

"I hope folks driving by don't think I'm under arrest, Sheriff."

"That's a risk you'll have to take," he said.

The back of the squad car was certainly warmer, and I voiced my appreciation. He opened a Plexiglas window in the security divider so we could talk more easily. I told him I actually was in town to cover the bear hunt and would probably stay at the bed-and-breakfast that night to await the fate of Walden.

"I just hope all the hunters don't end up shooting each other," he said. "We have enough work."

The billboard was surrounded by farm fields and highway. Nothing to distract from the contracted message. Not a gas station or convenience store around, so there was no hope of surveillance camera footage of the vandalism.

"Any witnesses, Sheriff?"

"Nope."

"So how are you going to prove who did this?"

"Oh, we know who did it," he said.

"Amish?" I asked.

"Definitely."

"But you can't charge a whole community for the actions of one."

"We have all the proof we need which one," he said.

"Really?" I said. "I'm impressed. How did you come by this information?"

"The Amish aren't into lying, Riley. When we asked Gideon Yoder who might have done such a thing, he came right out and admitted he had."

"Are you going to charge him with anything?"

"We're going to give him a pass this time." But the sheriff said he stressed to Gideon that Sarah's picture was going back up on the billboard as their top clue and it better stay there.

"I told him if we had another round of whitewash, his mug shot would be the next graven image he'd have to worry about."

He agreed to let me shoot a brief interview with him about Sarah's murder. For interest (and to stay warm) I framed his face from the backseat of the squad.

We discussed the overnight billboard paint-a-thon and he gave me a couple useful lines about how this homicide presented certain challenges because of the Amish angle.

"When do you expect the DNA results from Brian Kueppers?"

The sheriff seemed surprised. "How did you hear about that?"

"I'm a reporter," I reminded him. "It's my job."

"We're not going to be talking about any DNA business."

"That doesn't mean I'm not going to be reporting it. What kind of DNA did you find on the victim's body?"

"Who have you been talking to?" he said.

"My sources are my business, Sheriff. Was it blood, saliva, semen?"

He wasn't answering so I pulled an old investigative reporter trick and startled him with an unanticipated question.

"Instead, how about we talk about the brouhaha over the gun permit for your buddy, Roger Alton? Would you have granted one to him if he wasn't a campaign contributor?"

The sheriff scowled. "Turn the camera off."

When elected officials say things like that, journalists just push harder. Sort of a reflex move.

"Do you think someone who has a problem with alcohol should be allowed to carry a gun in public?"

He ordered me to hand over the videotape. He even tried to reach through the divider and grab the camera.

"I'm not giving you my video, Sheriff. Are you crazy?"

I turned to protect the camera, but kept it rolling as I scrambled to escape the squad car. I went for the door handles but no luck. Locked was locked. "Sheriff, let me out." I tried to sound like I was warning him.

Instead, he slid the middle security window shut, signaling that our conversation was over. Then he put the vehicle in gear and started driving.

"Let me out." I banged on the Plexiglas, but he ignored me. I tried screaming louder in case he couldn't hear because of the partition. "Where are you taking me?"

"Headquarters." He kept his eyes on the road and didn't look back at me.

"Headquarters? Do you mean jail?"

Jail was ten miles away, in Preston, the next town over. I didn't have time for jail. I had a phoner due in about six minutes.

"Sheriff Eide, I'm scheduled for a live phone report on the bear hunt any minute. So stop this craziness."

I could see part of his face in the rearview mirror and he looked amused. "Maybe a little cell time will help you think more clearly."

"You can't put me in jail for asking questions, Sheriff. That's what reporters do. And you can't just leave my car on the side of the road like that."

"Don't worry. We'll have it towed."

That threat was enough to get me on the phone to Miles Lewis, Channel 3's media attorney. Our connection was scratchy.

"Where did you say you were?" he asked.

When he finally understood I was locked in the back of a squad car being hauled to the Fillmore County Jail at high speed, he said he'd find Bryce and call me right back.

This was the first time I'd dealt with Miles on business since the newsroom bloodbath. He was off work for a while, healing from a bullet wound to the stomach and the trauma of seeing Noreen take a bullet in the head. I wanted to ask how he was feeling, but in case the spree killing wasn't on his mind just then, I didn't want to remind him of it.

Even though I escaped the gunfire, I couldn't escape the memories and doubted he could either. Talking about that day with Miles might help us both, but not over the phone. That kind of dialogue seemed best face to face.

I banged my fist against the plastic wall again. "Sheriff Eide, let's talk!"

Just then my phone vibrated. It was Miles and Bryce. On speakerphone in the news director's office.

"Riley, aren't you supposed to be doing a phoner on bear hunting in a couple minutes?" Bryce asked.

"Yes, but instead of talking about bears, I think the anchor should tell viewers I'm reporting live en route to jail. Then toss to me, and I'll take it from there."

I summarized the current situation. Difficult, because I had to compromise between being heard over the road noise and not letting the sheriff overhear us. I decided to opt for speaking up, figuring there was nothing I could say that the lawman didn't already know.

In the background, Bryce was filling the control booth in on the changes and telling them to kill the bear video set to run under my phone report. "Naked audio."

"The tape contains no real smoking gun," I told them. "The sheriff comes across as unprofessional in the interview, especially when he tries grabbing for the camera, but this campaign is probably too small-town for us to air a story anyway."

"Doesn't matter. Don't give up the tape," Miles said. "They have no legal right to it. And we need to stay consistent."

When Sheriff Eide realized I had someone on the other end of the line, he turned the siren on full blast to try to drown out our conversation, then accelerated.

"What if they try to take it by force?" I was yelling now to be heard.

"Can you substitute a different video?" Miles suggested. "Bait and switch?"

I explained the other camera disc was in an equipment bag in my car. "This is all I have."

Then Bryce chirped in with an idea. "Put it somewhere they can't find it. Put it in your bra."

I didn't have a better idea, so I took Bryce's advice, even if it was a little creepy coming from my boss.

"Thirty seconds to air." The control booth was giving me my countdown. "Stand by, Riley."

Just then the sheriff drove into the law enforcement parking lot and started down a ramp under the building. My cell signal died. And with it, my live phoner died, too.

CHAPTER 46

Sheriff Eide unlocked the squad's rear door and motioned for me to climb out. "Hand me the videotape. And this can all be over."

The videodisc poked me from where I had stuffed it into my bra. He asked for the tape one more time, and again I refused, giving him a brief lesson about freedom of the press and the public's right to know that he seemed to tune out.

My worry was that he would make me trade the backseat for a jail cell, my camera for handcuffs. Just then, an office worker rushed in and motioned that the sheriff had a phone call upstairs. I hoped Miles had just finished screaming at the Fillmore County Attorney, demanding my release.

Before leaving, Sheriff Eide instructed a young female jailer in a tan uniform to pat me down and keep watch. She didn't feel the disc, luckily. That reminded me of the plus-sized Minneapolis woman who had hidden a stolen fur coat in her underwear for three days in jail while being questioned by police for the theft. Since no one had tried to fingerprint me or take a mug shot, I figured I wasn't technically under arrest. But not wanting to be accused of fleeing law enforcement, I stayed put, still clutching my controversial camera.

I glanced at my watch, hoping within the next few minutes Sheriff Eide would learn that taking me into custody was a real bad idea. Thirty seconds later, the door opened and the young jailer was telling me I was free to go.

Eleven minutes was all it took. Apparently the sheriff and I weren't on goodbye terms. She didn't mention anything about a camera or videotape, so neither did I. Instead I asked about my car.

"What car?" she responded.

I told her the road where I'd last seen my vehicle. She shrugged and told me to check there. The keys were in my pocket and I hoped I'd remembered to lock the doors. By now the sky was dark. Fillmore County was too rural for taxi service, and the Fillmore County Sheriff's Department too busy to give rides to media troublemakers.

I had only one transportation option, and hated using it.

My parents said they'd leave immediately.

When Bryce and Miles finally heard me play the sheriff's audio over the phone, they couldn't believe the flap. Bryce had hoped Channel 3 might air a news story about my time in custody, making me seem heroic. But the whole thing, even me, sounded silly. And as the top elected law enforcement official in the county, the sheriff answered only to the public.

"The county attorney pretty much dismissed it all as a misunderstanding," Miles said. "And we really have no one to complain to formally. So we might not want to make a fuss over this just now."

I agreed. As a journalist, I had to be careful not to come across as a crybaby in cop circles, as that could affect future sources and stories.

For now, Miles and Bryce had decided our best move was to pretend the fuss never happened—although Bryce admitted the whitewashed billboard had created some intrigue.

"We can always report this video skirmish later, in the context of the murder investigation, if the DNA becomes newsworthy," Bryce said. "As for this election, just because it's nasty doesn't make it news."

"I wouldn't mind doing a story saying authorities have found DNA and already one suspect is being tested voluntarily," I said. "Of course, unless he was charged we couldn't name him."

Well, legally we could, but most news organizations had an ethical rule about waiting for charges to be filed before reporting a suspect's name.

But right now, my boss still wanted me in position in southeast Minnesota to report on our bear's fate the next day. When it came to firepower versus fur, the odds were against Walden. If he died wearing his research collar, he'd become a bear martyr. If he lived, he'd become a bear legend.

CHAPTER 47

My car was still sitting on the side of the road—looking abandoned under the moonlight. My parents pulled behind so their headlights illuminated the scene. A parking ticket was stuck under the wipers and someone had stolen the tripod from the side of the road.

The entire drive over, my mom and dad ranted about the indignity of me being hauled to jail in the back of a squad car.

"That's treating you like a criminal," she said. "Then he has the nerve to try to take your video. That's stealing!"

"So much for protect and serve," my father said.

"Mom and Dad, it was a mix-up." The last thing I needed was them spreading this gossip around. "Let's just keep this between us."

When they heard I was on the bear beat and not driving back to the Twin Cities right away, they wanted me to sleep overnight at the farm. "Then you can see Husky."

I wanted to, but needed to snoop around town a bit longer before turning in, so it made more sense to stay there. "But maybe leave the front door open in case I can't get a room."

Sans tripod, I shot some night video of the billboard, using a flashlight for mystery effect. Then I went dark and leaned against the hood of the car trying to imagine the tension Gideon must have felt splashing paint over his dead sister's face.

Was Sarah watching from Amish heaven? Did she want him to stop painting over her face? Or was she relieved not to have her image displayed to the world in the place where she died?

For a minute the wind blew softly and I soaked up the quiet night. But then a faint sound caught my attention. A nostalgic clip-clop that I recognized as horses' hooves. A buggy approached, visible only by a hanging kerosene lantern—the most conservative (and dangerous) of all lighting for Amish travel.

I turned the car headlights on, so my car would be visible. And when the buggy drew close, I discovered my murder victim's brother holding the reins of the horse.

"Hello, Gideon." I figured he must be checking to see if her picture had been replaced yet. A paint can on the floor of the buggy convinced me I was right.

I reached over and petted his horse's neck, wishing I had an apple or sugar cube in my pocket.

"Sheriff Eide tells me you were our nocturnal artist. I was having an internal debate whether your sister would have approved or disapproved. What do you think?"

I didn't expect much of an answer from him, so I was surprised when I got one. "Pictures are sins of pride. We Amish prefer to be remembered by the lives we lived, and not the way we looked."

His reasoning was admirable.

"You'd get no argument from me," I said, "except your sister was murdered in cold blood and our society believes we need to do everything we can to find her killer. For me, that means telling her story."

"Our society believes forgiveness makes a safer world than punishment," he said.

"We believe in forgiveness, but we also believe in justice." And I told him I intended to keep Sarah's face in the news until her case was solved. "To us, her sketch is not an insult, but an important element in the search for her murderer."

"My church and I have buried Sarah and forgiven all. We do not need you to tell her story or find her killer."

"It was a beautiful service," I said. "Even though I couldn't understand much."

He looked at me, perplexed.

"Yes, Gideon. I was there. I watched and prayed along with the rest of your community. The service was enlightening."

"Stay away from us." Now he sounded harsh, where before he'd sounded instructive.

I told him I'd be at the Lamplight Inn in town in case he or his family reconsidered and wanted to discuss his sister. "Putting a homicide victim's face on television is a way of honoring them. Showing that their life mattered, as did their death."

"No. TV is the devil's tongue." He cracked the reins and I dodged the metal wheels just as the horse started to bolt.

"Tell me why you were shunning Sarah." This time I was yelling, sort of like when Tom Cruise wanted the truth in *A Few Good Men.*

"Sarah could not forgive."

Those were Gideon's final words before the buggy disappeared into the night. I could still hear the clip-clop echoing long after I lost sight of him.

CHAPTER 48

Sleep did not come easily to me in the same bed where Sarah Yoder had spent her last night alive.

A thick yellow chenille spread covered me with old-fashioned warmth in the front bedroom of the Lamplight Inn. A gray cat curled on a corner chair, purring. But still, my mind could not relax.

I had finished reading my Amish love story. As foreshadowed, the heroine had resigned herself to a simple life with her reliable suitor, rejecting the flashy outside world. It was a comfortable conclusion that made me envious of her happily ever after.

It's just fiction, I reminded myself. Real life is never so easy. Neither is true love.

Hours later, in a confusing dream about forgiveness and damnation, I woke to a crashing noise.

Two intruders barged inside, kicking the door to my room open. They both wore wide-brimmed hats. A clean-shaven man grabbed me by the arms with one hand and held my head with the other. His bearded companion turned on a flashlight and advanced toward me. He was careful to keep the light focused on the ground so I couldn't see their faces.

I tried kicking, but the second attacker caught my ankle and dropped down on the mattress next to me. We all were breathing fast, but only I feared for my life. My nightgown bunched up at my waist, and I felt both terrified and exposed.

"Let me go." I was too shaken to scream. They might not have even heard me; my voice was low and strained.

They said little, and I understood none of their language, but certain guttural noises reminded me of the Pennsylvania Dutch speech at Sarah Yoder's funeral.

I was certain my assailants were Amish.

I twisted my body. Someone yanked my hair. The mattress started to slide off the bed frame and the flashlight fell between the pillows. I tried rolling to the floor to escape, but strong hands held me tight.

I braced myself for rape.

I'd interviewed enough sexual assault victims to know this was going to be ugly. And even when my attack ended, it wouldn't ever be over for me. While these men might disappear into the night, forgetting me as memories of that night blurred with their other victims, I would never forget what they did.

But my assailants had other ideas. One seemed to flash the light under the bed and around the corners of the room, as if searching for something. Could they merely be robbers? Were they looking for money?

My optimism died in seconds, and I feared I was next to go. Enough light still shone to reveal a pair of scissors coming toward my throat.

"Please," I cried. "Don't."

I shut my eyes because the blades scared me, and all I could imagine was cold metal against warm flesh.

In the background, the owner of the inn was screaming for them to leave. I hoped she had already dialed 911. I didn't want to die minutes from rescue.

Then I heard snipping sounds.

They released me so abruptly, I fell off the bed. Then I realizing my hair had been sheared and scattered across the room.

Linda found the flashlight and helped me to the bathroom. The power and phone lines to the house had also been cut. When she heard my screams and tried to turn on the lights, they wouldn't work. Neither would the telephone.

I looked in the mirror, but didn't recognize my reflection. What used to be a fashionable shoulder-length bob was now an ear-length disaster.

CHAPTER 49

Linda kept apologizing because the attack happened on her turf. I reassured her that this wasn't her fault.

I couldn't understand the motivation of my assailants. While I didn't get a clear enough look to identify them, I was sure that the one with the scissors had to be Gideon Yoder.

So much for Amish pacifism.

"Why would they do this?"

She had neither answer nor advice, but to better assess the damage, carefully lit a kerosene lamp she kept to impress tourists.

My first reaction was to call the sheriff. Breaking and entering, assault and battery, trespassing—I wanted the pair arrested and jailed. I wanted their mug shots on the news coast to coast. But after today's wild squad-car ride, Sheriff Eide would obviously not be sympathetic to my plight, so that wasn't possible.

My second reaction was that I didn't want to make news this way. I'd be a laughingstock. The other media would pull file tape of me from old stories and run before-and-after pictures of my new 'do. They would make jokes about how I was losing my hair over my job.

I snapped a picture of my head with my phone camera and texted it to Garnett, because I didn't know who else might care or even be awake.

He texted back, "Is the station making you cut your own hair now?"

I couldn't bear his sarcasm, so I didn't answer.

Linda offered to contact Ike, the owner of Everything Amish. She had his home number from a local business directory and apparently thought we were closer than we actually were. I noted that she didn't suggest calling 911, probably because she didn't want her place known as a crime scene.

I didn't want Ike seeing me like this, because I still hoped to go on a date with him. But I needed some personal counsel and some Amish perspective. So I handed her my phone and let her make the call.

It all made sense to Ike.

"Hair, for the Amish, symbolizes their commitment to a pure and simple life," he said. "Women never cut their hair; men never trim their beard. To have them hacked off is shameful to the individual and indicates a lack of respect by the attackers."

And cutting the power lines could be interpreted as a statement of their opposition to modern conveniences.

"If they have a problem with my reporting," I said, "can't they just complain to my boss?" I dreaded having to explain my haircut to Bryce. "I thought Amish violence was rare. I'm starting to wonder if one of them killed Sarah."

Ike explained that a splinter group of Amish in Ohio recently broke into the house of a bishop in the middle of the night and cut off his beard and his wife's hair. He was surprised I hadn't heard the news.

"I don't follow Amish gossip," I said. "Was everyone talking about that attack the last time you were in Ohio picking up merchandise?"

He looked puzzled, then suddenly said, "Oh no, it's been on

the networks, Riley. And now Amish communities consider such an ambush the ultimate insult."

"So you think that's where these guys got the idea to come after me?"

"No doubt."

"And they're trying to send me a message that I need to stop putting Sarah's picture on the air?"

"After your confrontation with her brother, that's a good guess."

"But how did word of this Ohio haircutting news even get out?" I asked. "I thought Amish handled things internally and never involved the cops. That's sure the line they've been giving me. Forgive and be forgiven."

"That case is odd." He speculated that the anger of the Old Order Amish toward the renegades must have been grave for them to call in outside law enforcement.

"What about me? What should I do?"

"Only you can decide."

I decided to pack up and leave.

Minutes later, my plans changed. I'd lost something besides my hair, but gained even more.

My belongings had been scattered across the room during the break-in. Gathering them, I realized my camera was missing. I had purposely brought all the equipment inside, figuring it was safer at night with me than outside in the car. Then I remembered how the men seemed to be searching the room for something.

I was more convinced than ever that the Amish were punishing me for keeping Sarah in the news. Their culture appreciated symbolism, and to show their disrespect for TV, they'd also taken my camera in addition to my hair. Probably to use in some antielectricity ritual denigrating the "devil's tongue."

Bryce would be furious about the camera. Channel 3 would be out at least fifteen grand. There was no way I could get out of filing a police report for the theft or he'd think I sold the camera on Craigslist.

"Any chance you could call in the assault yourself?" I asked Linda.

"I'd rather not," she said, "but will if you want me to."

I didn't want my name going out over the county scanners. The sheriff might decide to respond himself and charge me with filing a false report. But Linda didn't want the name of her inn associated with crime.

"Could you not mention me on the phone?" I asked. "I'll explain the specifics when they get here, but just say there's been a break-in."

A county deputy showed up soon after. It was Laura Schaefer, still working the rotten night shift as her punishment for challenging the sheriff in the election.

In my nightgown and minus my hair, she didn't recognize me from our encounter by her lawn sign the other day. To convince her I was who I claimed, I had to show her my laminated Channel 3 ID. Even then she looked dubious.

"Really, Laura, it's me." Her hair was different, too. All pulled back like a ballerina's. But I still knew her, although her name on a badge certainly made recognition easier.

"That's Deputy Schaefer to you," she said.

She wanted to do everything by the book. As I described my attack, she grew even more skeptical, but took down the report.

"Let me make sure I have this straight, Ms. Spartz. They cut your hair?"

"Yes." I pointed to strands scattered across the floor.

"And stole your camera?"

"Yes."

"And you think they were Amish?"

"I'm certain of it."

"Do you have any better description?"

"No, the room was dark."

The landlady had no more to offer: the men were leaving as she was arriving.

I told Deputy Schaefer about my suspicions of Gideon Yoder and she took down his name. But if not for the broken door hinges and Linda vouching for me, she wouldn't have believed any of my tale. I couldn't really blame her. It sounded wild.

"I'll call later, Deputy, to add the camera's serial number to my report," I said.

"That would be helpful," she replied.

When she left, I left. But I didn't just leave with a bad haircut. I also left with a secret Sarah had hidden under her mattress at the B and B that had fallen to the floor during the scuffle.

I wasn't sure what it meant, but I was certain the answer would point to her killer.

CHAPTER 50

My parents had left the door open but didn't actually expect me to show up, especially not at that time of morning. If the dogs hadn't barked, they might have slept through my arrival.

My mom was in a fleecy pink bathrobe. My dad was in flannel pajamas with holes in the knees.

I regretted not taking an Amish bonnet along from the Lamplight closet to cover my hair, because that was the first thing my parents noticed even though they were half asleep. And boy, were they mad when they heard the details.

"Tell me about it," I said. "I have to be on TV today."

My mom reassured me that everything would be fine. "Remember who used to cut your hair when you were little? When I'm through with you, honey, you'll look like Halle Berry."

I didn't look like a movie star, but I did look better.

My mother had a haircut trick from my childhood called Scotch Tape Bangs. She put tape across my forehead and cut once. The result was as crooked as I remembered, but with a little gel and a blow-dryer, who could tell?

I thanked my mom for her snipping ability. Then I told her I needed a nap. "Wake me in an hour." By then, I hoped to know if Walden had survived the night.

When I crawled under the blankets, Husky followed me. I told him I'd bring him home soon, but today's assignment was dangerous and might involve bears and guns.

"You'll be safer here on the farm with the other dogs."

Then I started wondering if I'd be safer with him beside me. I willed myself to fall asleep, but no slumber came. I tried counting backward to the last night I slept well, but gave up.

I reached for my purse and Sarah Yoder's secret, pulling out a notebook. Only about a dozen pages contained writing. The language looked German. My hope was that this was a hidden journal of her final days. September translated the same in German and English. So I could see that the writing began about two weeks before what investigators determined to be Sarah's time of death.

I paged through the diary backward, because as a newsie, I wanted the most current look at Sarah's life.

Ich habe beschlossen, dass ich morgen zur Polizei gehe.

I had no idea what the sentence meant.

My last thought before dozing off was that Sarah's name wasn't actually on the notebook. I hoped conjecture wasn't giving me false confidence.

CHAPTER 51

I understood rearview mirrors are essential in automobiles, but I was trying to avoid my new look as much as possible. Just as I turned the key to head back to southeastern Minnesota's bear country the next morning, I received a text.

* appeared on my screen. It was Nicole signaling that Bryce was calling her into his office. She must not have known I was out of town.

I brainstormed about thirty seconds, then dialed Bryce. "Good morning, boss. There's something we need to talk about."

"I'm in a meeting, Riley. Can you call back in fifteen minutes?"

Sure he was in a meeting. "Believe me, I'd love to delay this, Bryce, but it's pretty urgent."

"What's it about?"

"It's about the camera. It's missing."

I heard him telling someone—probably Nicole—he had to take this call and would get back to them.

"What do you mean, missing?" he asked.

"It's been stolen."

Our back-and-forth dialogue was similar to the deputy interview all over again. Bryce seemed certain I was making up the entire scenario to avoid being a one-man band.

"If you think losing the camera is going to make me send photographers out on stories with you, Riley, you are much mistaken. I'm more likely to suspend you for misconduct."

He was serious. To TV stations, gear was everything. Some broadcast cameras cost more than a shooter might make in a year.

"It happened just like I said it did," I replied. "Here, I can prove it to you. Check your computer."

I shot a photo of my new haircut and emailed it to him. "So what do you think of my new haircut?"

There was a long pause. "I'll have to get used to it. But this debacle is still going in your file. Call me when you know if our bear is dead or alive."

Bryce didn't sound convinced I'd been robbed. And I knew he didn't really care one way or another about Walden's fate. He liked the idea of animal stories, but not animals themselves.

When I hung up, I saw I had another text from Nicole: "thnx."

Bear hunting season was officially over in Minnesota. During the final hours, one hunter in Fillmore County had shot himself and another had injured a friend.

But Walden was still very much alive, at least according to the North American Bear Center. Teresa'd gone from lobbying at the state capitol for the protection of research bears to taking her message to the people of Minnesota.

"How can you be sure?" I asked Teresa. "Is it possible someone just didn't report the kill?"

Teresa reminded me that Walden was wearing a radio collar with GPS technology. "We know exactly where Walden is at all times. It's our Big Bear version of Big Brother."

"How about we track him and get some video proving to viewers that he survived the night?" I asked.

Without a camera, I'd have little to report on post–hunting season that would get Bryce excited. Guaranteed video of the

VIP bear would be enough for him to send Malik down to join me.

But Teresa said no. "The fewer people who know where Walden is, the safer he'll be."

"Don't you think viewers will want to see him? What if I promise not to report his location?"

"Patience," she said. "Soon the entire world will be able to watch Walden."

"What do you mean?" I asked.

"When the time is right, we will show viewers where Walden is hibernating. He will have his own webcam."

She said the words quite casually, but I realized the overnight interest his webcam would draw. Walden might be just a bear, but online, he'd be a star. Even bigger than a circus bear. The only bears to outrank him on the Internet would be from Chicago.

She stressed the benefits studying hibernating bears could yield for mankind. "Putting humans in a hibernation-like state could help people survive heart attacks, or even travel in space."

Those were all future news stories. I needed to focus on the present. "How soon before Walden will be dormant?"

Teresa confided that he was hitting that lethargic stage, probably because temperatures had been unseasonably cold. "He's found a secure den and is sticking close." She agreed to call me first before the webcam went live.

I was right that without fresh bear video Bryce was busting the story from live shot to set piece. I was also ordered to head back to the station prepared to pitch a winning story idea about food.

CHAPTER 52

Thinking about food made me hungry. Because of my hair disaster, morning was a rush at the farm. Mom sent me out the door with only an apple and a piece of bread. I was now on a stretch of road without any restaurant exits.

I tried to remember food stories I'd once done. My favorite involved testing fortified juices and finding they didn't contain the amount of vitamin C their labels claimed.

Bryce probably favored stories that were easier to produce, like ones about food trends such as insects on Minnesota menus. If I could find an eatery that served crickets and worms, he'd probably promote that all day long.

And if hunting season hadn't been over, I'd look for a story angle on bear meat. Combining food and unusual animals would likely score high with my new boss. The only downside was I'd probably have to eat the cuisine during a standup. Or live on set, with whoever was auditioning for anchor.

Even though bears and bugs were spoiling my appetite, a fast-food restaurant beckoned from the highway and I ended up ordering a chicken wrap off their healthy menu. While waiting for my meal, I scanned a wall poster that bragged about the low fat and calorie content of their nutritious choices.

For many diners, those numbers count more than dollars

and cents. And then the idea for my food pitch hit me. A consumer investigation on whether menu claims matched actual numbers.

"We'll put 'em to the test," I said to myself.

In person, Bryce really hated my hair. He called me into his office and ran his fingers through the bangs, pulling on the ends.

"That's not going to make my hair grow any faster," I said, shrugging him away. I'd forgotten to text Nicole for backup, but at least the door was still open.

"To keep our story straight, Riley, when viewers call to complain about your hair, we'll tell them you donated it to that cancer kids group."

"I don't think lying is a good idea, Bryce."

Luckily, my food-testing concept distracted him from my locks, but now he shut the door. "I like the sound of your food idea. I don't want any interruptions."

I considered complaining that the air in his office felt stuffy, but decided just to keep focused on the story. "It's important we hire a respected lab, Bryce. They need to be certified. And we need to repeat the test to show a pattern."

"How much is this going to cost?" he asked.

"Depends on how many restaurants we check. The tests run at least seventy dollars each, multiply that by two, multiply that by the number of restaurants or entrees . . ."

"Sounds expensive." A predictable response from a boss who calculated a story's value by its cost. I convinced him a lawsuit over sloppy reporting would be even more expensive.

To help him feel ownership over the project, I had him help brainstorm a list of ten popular chains that viewers would find familiar.

"We do all this work, and you're sure we have a story, Riley?"

"Well, no, I'm not."

That was the risk news organizations took with investigative reporting. Journalists can invest time and money and not always find what they expected. And if you can't prove it, you can't air it.

More than once I'd had to tell a boss that I thought my story might be falling through. "Not all stories turn into Watergate."

"You mean we could spend more than a thousand bucks, plus all the time this will take, and wind up with nothing?" he asked. "This is starting to feel like your other stories. No bear and no killer."

"Bryce, I'm not a hunter and I'm not a homicide detective. I'm just a reporter."

He brought up the weaknesses of the Amish story being outside the viewing area again, but did admit the overnight ratings had showed a small spike instead of our normal drop-off.

I told him we'd use hidden cameras inside the restaurants so we could promote the story as Channel 3 going "undercover." Bryce ended up approving the food-testing story mainly because nobody else in the newsroom had come up with a better idea since his mandate.

That was my cue to escape his office. So I told him I needed a few minutes to fix my makeup before the newscast.

"Not a bad idea, Riley." As I turned to leave his office, he leaned over his desk and gave me a quick pat on the tush. "And counting a few calories might be good for you, too."

Right then I missed my old news director, Noreen. I'd always considered her a bully boss, but compared to Bryce, she was the big sister I never had.

((RILEY CU))
AND SO . . . HAVING SURVIVED
HUNTING SEASON, WALDEN
WILL BE THE SUBJECT OF BEAR
RESEARCH ALL WINTER LONG.

Literally seconds after the director gave me the all-clear signal for my bear debrief and gestured for me to leave the news set, my phone vibrated. This was the call I really dreaded answering. Not my boss, but my hairdresser. She called whenever her critical eye determined I needed a trim or highlighting. My hair was her canvas.

"How could you go to such an amateur?" she said. "Besides, people know you're a client of mine. They will think I styled that disaster."

I didn't want to tell her the truth, so I blamed my mother.

CHAPTER 53

The next day was like a scavenger hunt. I started out researching menus for places that specifically listed calorie and fat content. Luckily, most had the info posted on their websites. If they didn't, I called posing as a customer interested in bringing her book club to dine on healthy food while discussing fine literature.

"Please let this lead to news," I said to myself.

I narrowed the list to six chains, and picked two meals from each menu. Because the restaurants were all in the Twin Cities, Bryce let me use Malik to help with the hidden camera. Four of the places had take-out menus, which made those trips easy. I dumped the entrees in plastic ziplock bags and put them in a cooler on ice in the back of the van.

At the other two stops, we were seated at a table and ordered the meals we wanted to test. Me, a garlic chicken dish. Malik, tilapia, a popular fish.

He was happy to catch up on our lives and insisted he was finished going on air himself. He was quite interested when I told him of the webcam the bear center was preparing for Walden's hibernation and hoped he could shoot the story.

"That would be great," I said. "But Bryce might just make us take it straight off the web to save money. He's already sweating the bill on this food story."

After hearing of all the happenings in Amish land, my photographer was no longer so eager to return to that corner of Minnesota for our timeless feature. "Sounds treacherous."

I disagreed. "Normally they are a quiet and spiritual people. This murder, this whole thing, is so uncommon among them."

"That camera they stole was one of my favorites, Riley. The lens was simply incredible."

"For that, I'm sorry."

Then our food arrived. Malik was hungry, and wanted to taste just a bite of his dish.

"No," I insisted. "We need the entire serving, otherwise that will throw off the calculations. I'll have them bring us bread sticks."

Since bread wasn't included in the advertised healthy meal section, we wouldn't test them. I assured my work spouse he could order an appetizer at our next stop.

The lab we were using for our testing had instructed me to get every last drop of the serving, so I'd tucked a rubber spatula in my purse.

Malik shot video from his cell phone and kept an eye out for the waitress while I bagged the food. When she returned to check if we needed more water, she seemed startled to see our plates sparkling clean. She probably wondered if we had licked them.

"It was delicious," I told her, declining dessert. Malik glared at me, but after all, I was on a diet.

By the end of the day, I felt more like a food gatherer than a news gatherer. We were hauling the cooler across town to a certified food testing lab when I got a call from Bryce. I put him on speaker so Malik could hear, too.

"Are you at the lab yet?" our boss asked.

"No, but don't worry," I said. "We're close. We'll make the drop before it closes."

But Bryce had changed his mind. The calorie/fat testing story was dead. "I'm looking at the budget and can't justify gambling this much money on something that might not yield news."

"But we've already invested time and money," I protested. "And it's sure to be a ratings hit. Remember what you said about viewers and food."

I'd already started working on the script.

> ((RILEY SOT))
> RESTAURANTS ARE APPEALING TO
> DIETERS BY SERVING HEALTHY
> ENTREES LABELED WITH FAT AND
> CALORIE CONTENT. BUT ARE THE
> MEALS WHAT THE MENUS CLAIM?

It didn't matter. He ordered me to come up with a cheaper, no-risk food story. Then he hung up.

I had to scramble and call the lab to tell them our plans had changed and we wouldn't be needing their services after all. A technician had been on standby to blenderize one of the meals when we arrived so Malik could get video of her pouring puree into a test tube. They sounded disappointed they weren't going to be on TV.

"So what are we going to do with all this food?" Malik asked.

I told him he could take it home.

CHAPTER 54

Riley, Riley!" Someone was banging on my office door while I was trying to catch up on my emails and brainstorm another food story.

"Come in," I called.

Nicole was breathing hard. "It's getting worse."

I knew what she was talking about, but was torn between curiosity and disgust. Did I want details? I decided not. After all, I'd just had my hair and butt touched by my boss.

"Whatever it is, Nicole, I hope you're documenting it. Date. Time. Offense. Keep a record."

She started biting her lip, and it seemed to be bleeding. I handed her a box of tissues and some lip gloss.

Softening a little, I said, "I'm on your side, Nicole. I'll teach you how to use a hidden camera. We'll prove he's a jerk."

She blushed, even under her layers of makeup.

"Why didn't you text me?" I asked. "I would have barged into his office to help you."

"It didn't happen in his office."

I hoped she hadn't gone to his house. That would be most unwise. "What do you mean, Nicole?"

"Riley, it's too embarrassing to talk about."

"Talk anyway."

She took a deep breath and I cleared some files off a chair, and motioned her to sit down.

"He's sexting me," she said.

"Oh, ick."

"It was a picture of—" she paused to find the right word, "him. It was disgusting."

I called it the Anthony Weiner trickle-down effect. Men in power, be they politicians, executives, athletes, even apparently news directors, liked to show off their vigor.

I tried to console her, though I was cringing myself. "You poor thing, Nicole. But now at least you have proof."

She shook her head. "I deleted it."

"You what?"

"It was gross. My first reaction was to get rid of it."

"It was evidence."

"I know." She looked bleak. "Do you think we can get it back? I heard emails are never really gone. Maybe texts are the same way."

"It's quite possible," I said, "but we might have to ask Xiong for help." Lee Xiong was Channel 3's computer expert, whom I affectionately called my "alpha geek."

"Xiong would probably wonder why you wanted porn retrieved from your phone," I continued. "He might consider it a form of harassment himself and if you told him the photo was Bryce, because you're on air, gossip might get out. I think I know an easier way."

"What?" She didn't sound very hopeful.

"Wait. If he did it once, he'll do it again."

That was my theory after a decade of investigative reporting. Very seldom did I find a culprit who only cheated one person once. Most of my most memorable stories centered on repeat offenders— whether they be fraud artists, serial killers, or sex creeps.

That night I slept horribly. Visions of Bryce danced through my head.

CHAPTER 55

My cell phone buzzed in my pocket the next morning as I was going out the door. Teresa from the bear center was calling. "Today we're going to unveil Walden's den." She emailed me the webcam link so I could get a preview. "We're finalizing the technical support."

A camera had been mounted inside what looked like a snug cave where a plump black bear curled comfortably in a pile of dirt. A light was mounted on the roof of the den to make the scene visible twenty-four hours a day for global fans.

I saw no movement. Walden resembled a bear corpse. "He looks dead. Are you sure he wasn't shot?"

But then I heard the animal inhale before becoming quiet again.

"He's fine," she said. "The metabolism and heart rate slow down significantly for hibernating bears. Of course if something disturbed him, he could be alert within a couple of minutes and in a bad mood."

I asked what research might be gained from keeping him under surveillance.

"Walden will be the first radio-collared bear in southern Minnesota," she said. "By tracking this bear, we can learn how far south the species can roam and whether the milder temperature impacts the bear's habits, including diet and hibernation. He may not sleep as long as his northern cousins."

Viewers were going to love seeing Walden snooze. Animals and sleep—two highly rated topics.

"This cave camera is terrific," I said. "But if I drive down, is there any way I could get up close to the actual den for a story?"

"Afraid not." She said they wanted to keep the location private. "Best for Walden and best for humans. We don't need any incidents."

"But I promise to behave," I said. "And I'll even promise to be vague about the site. Please? We could simply say 'southeastern Minnesota.'"

I also swore not to broadcast any live shot anywhere near Walden's locale, and she finally agreed to take me on a personal tour. Bryce wanted a bear—well, I'd give him one. No time to wait for the news huddle—I called the desk and got the go-ahead for the story.

A forested area outside of town surrounded another old sink-hole, this one home to a bear. The den wasn't all that far from the road, which surprised me. I expected a middle-of-nowhere location. A large maple tree served as a useful marker. Most of the leaves had fallen, but enough gold and red still clung to the low-hanging branches to make the giant limbs pop against the snow.

Bryce had given me another camera, but no photographer. He figured that would have been rewarding me for my carelessness.

Teresa and I crouched low to get inside the den. She reminded me to keep quiet. The hanging light allowed me to shoot some video of her pointing at Walden.

"Thanks," I whispered, "this is good perspective."

She described researchers putting their heads against the silent chests of hibernating bears for kicks. "The skinnier ones sleep deepest." Once, with her ear against a bear, she heard a loud heartbeat and realized the beast was waking. "The blood flow to a bear's legs slows down considerably, so the head is the first thing to move. Usually a couple of minutes pass before the rest of the bear is ready for action."

Then I got bold and asked if I could touch Walden. This was a form of stunt journalism—like being tasered on camera or driving a car into a lake to show television viewers how to escape a submerged vehicle.

I figured describing the feel of his fur would make for a good anchor-tag question/answer. Channel 3 would have it alone. None of our competition could match our fur frenzy. And it was just the kind of feat to impress a new boss.

Recognizing a gimmick when she heard one, Teresa rolled her eyes and nodded yes. "Softly," she warned.

I held the camera back as far as my arm would reach and watched through my camera monitor to see my face with a bear in the background. Then I shot a close-up of my hand stroking his fur. It was coarse. Walden was no teddy bear.

We backed out slowly and softly to avoid tripping over each other and the bear.

"Funny," I said once we were outside, "in real life, even up close, he didn't look particularly fierce."

"Could be a whole different boy if he woke up."

Teresa decided to let Channel 3 make the webcam announcement. Bryce liked my bear encounter so much he sent the satellite truck to broadcast and shoot my live shot from Harmony.

"Let me get this straight," Bryce said, "you actually touched the bear? And have video of your hand on bear fur."

"Yes, and his name is Walden." I didn't mention that the shot could have showed my entire body next to Walden if I'd had a photographer along. And that that would have made a prime promotion picture.

Malik would have loved this assignment. I felt guilty without him sharing the glory. The desk was probably making him shoot boring old weather video in Minneapolis to keep him handy in case spot news hit.

Since I vowed to keep my distance from Walden's den as part of our broadcast deal, I had time to kill before the newscast. I didn't have the nerve to return to the Yoder farm after my haircut, so I decided to drive around the Amish countryside. A one-horse carriage in the distance prompted me to practice shooting rural atmosphere.

I did my best to hold the camera steady, watching the buggy come over a hill in a romantic scene of black against white. When the wheels were close enough for me to distinguish passengers, I turned the camera off and held it down, facing the ground, to be clear they weren't being photographed.

Children coming home from class were crowded inside the two-seater. I remembered their schoolhouse was across a couple of farm fields to the west. As they drew closer I could hear singing, an outdoor a cappella choir of young voices. As they came closer and saw me, their singing stopped.

When the buggy passed, I started videotaping the back and didn't notice a little girl behind me until she said, "Hallo."

It was Hannah. She hadn't been anywhere in sight a minute ago and must have cut through the fields on her way home. Our other encounters had all been initiated by me. This was different: she had made contact. I wondered if the child had something she wanted to discuss.

"Hello, Hannah," I said. "How was school?"

"Better."

Not exactly an overwhelming endorsement. "Some days is it not so good?"

"Sarah was going to be my teacher."

Now we were getting somewhere. I hadn't wanted to always be the one to bring up her sister.

"Really? I bet that would have been fun. For you and for her."

Hannah nodded, then started swinging her lunch pail nervously.

"I'm sorry Sarah died," I said. "This must be a hard time for you. But just like school was better today, life will get better, too."

"She was in the bann, so she could not teach us."

I had thought Sarah wasn't teaching because she was dead. "Teachers can't be in the bann?"

She nodded her head.

That rule sort of made sense, if you bought into the whole shunning matter. Teachers probably had to be above reproach.

"Why was your sister in the bann, Hannah?"

She started walking down the road. I wondered why she always walked alone and never rode the buggy. I supposed she lived closer than the others and the buggy was the Amish version of the school bus for those who lived farther out.

"I wasn't supposed to talk to Sarah in the bann, but sometimes I did."

"What did you like to talk about?" I asked.

She didn't answer that question. So I tried another. "Do you still look at Sarah's picture?"

"Neh. Gideon took it," she replied even though she stared straight ahead and didn't look back at me. "He found it in my room."

Darn, I didn't have any more copies on me. "I'll bring another for you, Hannah, the next time we see each other."

She stopped and this time turned around to face me. *"Danke,"* she said.

CHAPTER 56

I invited Ike to watch my bear-cam live shot in person from the satellite truck. He'd rushed over and immediately complimented me on my hair. "It sure looks better than it did last night." He may not have been sincere, but his flattery improved my mood.

Afterward the truck engineer even let him climb up on the roof for a close-up look at the satellite dish. While he was getting a television tutorial, I got another phone call about my hairstyle change. This one was from my former fiancé.

When Garnett heard that two men had held me down in the dark and chopped my hair off, he wanted to hop on the next plane for revenge. "Cutting off their hair is too good for them."

He was upset I hadn't filled him in sooner about the attack, instead of simply texting him a confusing photo. "I thought it was some kind of joke."

I saw his point, but also thought that if he really loved me, his first reaction should not have been to make fun of me.

Two other reasons weighed on me for convincing him to stay out east. One I shared with him, the other I kept quiet.

First, I couldn't positively identify the men, so retribution would be difficult.

Second, I sort of had a date with Ike.

We didn't actually have the details worked out, but we had

agreed on dinner together after my shift. And I rationalized that an evening out with another man might help me better decide where my relationship with Nick Garnett was headed.

Dinner was full of good food and conversation. The menu made no claims about fat and calorie testing, so I was able to ignore work.

I learned more about Ike's past, and he learned more about my television life. We each found the other's background fascinating. As we were leaving the QUARTER/quarter Restaurant & Wine Bar, Harmony's fanciest dining spot, he suggested an evening drive in his fast car.

"Enticing." I could sense the ghost of Hugh Boyer urging me to climb aboard. "But here's where I sound like I'm still in high school, Ike. I promised my parents I'd spend the night at the farm. So I have a curfew."

He laughed and promised not to keep me out too late. "Maybe someday I can meet them."

"They would like that," I assured him.

I didn't tell him they would insist on it.

I didn't want to kiss Ike unless I thought we had a chance for something more. But I also didn't want to kiss him and be committed to something more. If our liaison was doomed, I wanted to halt any courtship now and save time and anguish.

Such is the pessimism of love.

We were parked on a bluff overlooking the Root River, admiring the moon through the trees. A dreamlike mist rose from the partially frozen water. Like teenagers, we danced around our desires to kiss, while we watched the curfew clock.

His arm was around me, and in my mind I listed all of the potential complications that might doom our relationship. His Amish roots loomed large.

"What about me working for TV, Ike? Is that going to be trouble for us?"

Apparently he was also tired of being stuck in the flirting stage of dating. "Maybe the only way to know for certain is for me to taste the devil's tongue." Then Ike pulled me close and kissed me long and hard, his tongue dancing against mine. His unfamiliar lips were tantalizing. When he pulled away, I wanted more.

"The devil's tongue poses no problem for me," he assured me as his lips traveled down my neck.

Unbuttoning his shirt, I was glad I didn't have to mess with hooks and eyes or suspenders. His chest was smooth, and TV she-devil that I had become, I spread my hands across his muscles.

"As for the devil's tail . . . perhaps I should check." His hand slid down and caressed the back of my jeans. "No difficulty here."

By now our bodies were as close as two bodies can be with clothing on. I understood the blessings of spontaneity, but even though I wanted him, I also wanted romance.

Candlelight. And love under an Amish quilt. Not in a sports car, even with leather seats.

Ike understood that I wanted our first night to be memorable. So while we buttoned and zipped, he promised that when he returned from Ohio, he would bring back a virgin Bargello heart quilt just for us.

"A beautiful, complicated pattern. Like you, Riley."

Softly, in my ear, he whispered those words—possibly the most tender compliment any man has ever given me—and they lingered in my mind long after we drove off in separate directions.

I could feel myself falling for him hard, aching for our reunion.

In some ways, I was like the heroine in my Amish melodrama, torn between two men from very different worlds. Except I didn't feel so divided anymore. Maybe the reason Garnett and I never worked out was because we were never meant to stay together.

CHAPTER 57

When I walked into the kitchen the next morning, my parents had prepared a hearty farm breakfast spread of eggs, hash browns, and pancakes. I told them I was dieting.

"TV adds ten pounds, Mom, and your meals double that."

"Oh, Riley, you're lovely," my mom assured me. "Don't you worry about how you look. You probably weigh less with that haircut."

I decided to end the food debate by simply digging in with a fork now and being glad I wasn't served Amish specialties like sausage and tomato gravy. I could always skip lunch later.

I didn't tell my parents about Ike because I wasn't sure what to say. My love life was certainly more complex than it had been twenty-four hours earlier, but I was committed to seeing where our liaison might lead. Should my mom and dad learn I was possibly falling for a man who lived near them, they would become giddy with visions of grandchildren.

I pushed Ike out of mind and concentrated on pancakes. I showed my parents the notebook from Sarah's room, but didn't have much hope they'd be able to help interpret it.

My ancestors spoke German as well as English on the farm, until the world wars came and that language was considered unpatriotic. Those who knew *Deutsch* stopped speaking it, even at home, to demonstrate their allegiance to America. My father was the first generation of his kin not to learn German.

While Amish speak Pennsylvania Dutch, my mother believed they wrote English, just from watching them jot down her holiday pie orders. "But they do speak German during church, so maybe they can write it."

"Maybe Sarah didn't want her innermost thoughts easily comprehended by others," I said. "I have to find someone who can translate the diary. Someone I trust."

I had been thinking of asking Ike to look at the pages. He had told me he'd call in a few days when he got back from Ohio. While I relished the thought of his return, I didn't want to wait that long for an interpreter.

"How about Father Mountain?" my mom asked.

I dialed him immediately, but he had his own problems. The Catholic Church was changing some of the words for Mass. He gave me one example. Instead of responding "and also with you," the congregation was supposed to say, "and with your spirit."

"And the list of changes is long," he said. "This is making my job harder."

"Maybe you should retire," I suggested.

"Not with the current priest shortage," he said. "I'll probably have to say Mass till I'm eighty."

And as for German, yes, he said Amish children are taught to write the language, but no, he couldn't read it himself.

"Latin challenges me enough."

Our rapport felt so good at that moment that I stepped outside so my parents couldn't hear. I asked Father Mountain about anointing me.

"You mean the sacrament of last rites?" His voice was incredulous.

"Yes, Father, but I thought you didn't call it that anymore."

"We don't, but that's still essentially what it is, and you don't sound very close to death to me. We now call it Anointing of the Sick, and you don't even sound sick."

"I'd like it as insurance. I've had some close calls. I think I would feel like God was on my side more."

"I'm concerned about your motivation for this sacrament, Riley. I don't think I'm comfortable anointing you."

"What do you mean?"

"Exactly what I said. You haven't seemed spiritually healthy lately. I don't want you feeling at ease with death."

Suddenly I understood what he couldn't bring himself to say aloud. "You're worried I'm suicidal."

He didn't answer, and was probably thinking back to when my husband died and my neighbor found me in the garage with the car running.

"That's not what's happening here," I said. "I just wanted another form of forgiveness from the church." Of all people, he knew I was still haunted by my actions in a cemetery in Iowa that left one man dead.

"If you need forgiveness, Riley, come to confession."

"Please, Father Mountain, don't tell my parents about this."

"Then don't give me a reason to."

CHAPTER 58

Husky followed me out to the car, so I let him climb in the backseat to go home with me. My parents waved to us, pleased that they got to spend so much time with me. They saw more of me in the last week than in the last year and had no idea about my tense conversation with Father Mountain.

On the way back to the station, I stopped at the Kueppers' farm to see if Michelle had heard anything more about her husband's DNA test.

While Bowser and Husky ran between the barn and shed, I went inside with Michelle for another look at the Amish table she and her husband had purchased from Sarah. I admired the dark wood and clean lines. A framed military photo of Brian and the American flag were still displayed.

"This is quite patriotic," I said. "Do you mind if I take a picture with my cell phone?"

I wasn't sure whether it might be useful, but I liked to be prepared in case something turned into news. She had no objection.

When the time came to leave, I couldn't find my dog.

"Husky," I called. "Time for home." But he didn't come running. The hounds were probably in the back field, but I stuck my head in an open shed door to check if they were there anyway.

A dog bed in the corner caught my eye. Stunning colors stood out even in the dim light. As I got closer, I realized both dogs were sleeping on a handmade quilt with small, precise stitches and numerous bright fabric patches of green, gold, and maroon.

It looked Amish to me, even heirloom quality.

I'd been craving such a quilt as a souvenir and might have even offered to buy it from the Kueppers family except it smelled awful. That's what happens when dogs sleep on art. I vowed that when Ike made good on his quilt promise to me, Husky would not be allowed anywhere near it.

When I went back into the house, I mentioned to Michelle that Bowser had nicer bedding than me. She didn't seem to know what I was talking about.

I decided to be direct. "How could you give such a beautiful quilt to your dog?"

"What?" Then, hands on her hips, she mumbled something like, So that's where it went. "Show me this dog bed."

I motioned for her to follow me out to the shed. "Tell me what Bowser did to deserve such a prize."

She shook her head. "Bowser must have stolen that quilt from the trash. I had tossed it in a pile of rubbish to be burned."

I pointed in the corner of the dark building. Both dogs, still nestled on the cloth trophy, raised their heads. "How come you didn't want the quilt?"

"It's complicated, Riley."

"Don't forget, reporters love stories."

The one she told was a whopper. "That quilt kept Josh warm in the sinkhole."

Now I was really confused. "Josh brought a quilt on his hunting adventure?"

Michelle shook her head. "The quilt was already in the hole."

She explained that the quilt had been wrapped around Sarah Yoder's body. Josh had used it to keep from freezing, and was still huddled under it when he was rescued. The sheriff ushered mother and son to the back of his squad car. Once Josh started sobbing about the zombie body underground, the interview was cut short and a deputy was ordered to drive them home while the law worked to verify his tale. Michelle didn't learn about the connection regarding the quilt and the body until later when she and Josh talked.

"The cops described the woman as naked," I said. "But you're telling me she was originally shrouded in a quilt? That quilt?"

Now Michelle squirmed. "It smelled horrible. I couldn't have it in the house. Bowser and I had a tug of war. I won. But he must have retrieved it later."

Michelle did not seem to realize that the quilt was a part of the crime scene and an important clue.

"Did you wash it?" I asked.

Her answer was critical. "No, the stench was too icky. And knowing its history, I didn't want it near me or Josh. I threw it out and didn't think about it till now."

Maybe it wasn't too late. I explained that the quilt was evidence. And how the chain of evidence worked.

"Investigators will need to interview you and Josh to establish the connection between the quilt and the body. The crime lab will want to run forensics. They'll be looking for DNA of the victim and the killer and whatever else comes to mind. They'll want samples of your hair, Josh's hair, even Bowser's hair."

"Am I in trouble?" Michelle seemed worried. "Did I tamper with evidence?"

"The cops aren't going to be happy, but you haven't committed a crime. This is more their fault than yours. They should have asked more questions and confiscated the quilt. But it sounds like by the time the experienced homicide team arrived, the quilt was already gone."

I could see how, with all the furor about a dead body, Josh's situation became a lower priority. "It's important that you contact them before more time passes. It might even help prove your husband wasn't involved."

I suspected too much time had passed. But I played optimist rather than realist and sent her inside to call the sheriff. That was a call I was glad not to have to make. While we waited for law enforcement, I brought the quilt out from the shed. I covered my nose with one hand, but could still smell the stench.

I resisted shaking it clean, but spread it on the lawn to take a closer look. Other than dirt, the odor, and a few stains that might or might not have been blood, the quilt was inspiring in both its simplicity and complexity—a geometric pattern with a star.

I recalled Ike's initial sales pitch. "No two Amish quilts are alike. *Each is as unique as a fingerprint.*" If forensics came up a bust, could ownership of the quilt itself identify the killer?

The quilt belonged to either the victim or the killer. If it belonged to the victim: dead end. But if it belonged to the killer, might someone else recognize it?

I pulled my cell phone from my pocket and took a picture of the quilt.

The quilt story was the lead for ten. While Bryce wasn't interested in Amish culture, and was still mad at me about the missing camera, he appreciated the visual nature of the quilt.

((ANCHOR BOX))
TONIGHT WE BRING YOU AN
EXCLUSIVE CLUE IN THE AMISH
MURDER, A CLUE CHANNEL 3
BROUGHT TO THE ATTENTION OF
LAW ENFORCEMENT.

((TWOSHOT))
RILEY SPARTZ JOINS US NOW WITH
THE DETAILS.

((RILEY CU))
WHEN THE BODY OF SARAH
YODER WAS DISCOVERED IN A
SINKHOLE, DETECTIVES WERE
OPERATING ON THE THEORY SHE
HAD BEEN DUMPED THERE NAKED.
TODAY CHANNEL 3 LEARNED
THAT THE BODY WAS WRAPPED
IN A QUILT, THEN DUMPED.
INVESTIGATORS ARE NOW
EXAMINING THE BEDDING FOR
FORENSIC EVIDENCE.

((RILEY QUILT SHOT))
HERE IS A PHOTO OF THAT QUILT.
I HAVE SEEN IT UP CLOSE AND
IT IS HANDMADE AND QUITE
DISTINCTIVE. IF YOU HAVE
EVER SEEN THIS QUILT PLEASE
CONTACT LAW ENFORCEMENT.

Because there wasn't much video to pair with the quilt story, the newscast producer thought it best that the anchor debrief me in a question-and-answer session to get the rest of the facts out.

(RILEY ANCHOR DEBRIEF)
RILEY, HOW DID THIS QUILT COME
OUT OF NOWHERE? AND WHY THE
CONFUSION AS TO WHETHER THE
BODY WAS NAKED OR NOT?

((RILEY CU))
HERE'S WHERE THE STORY
GETS A BIT INCREDIBLE: JOSH

KUEPPERS, THE BOY WHO FELL
IN THE SINKHOLE, USED THE
QUILT TO KEEP WARM THAT
NIGHT. IN THE FLURRY OF THE
RESCUE, THE QUILT WENT HOME
WITH HIM. THIS ALL CAME TO
LIGHT WHILE I WAS VISITING
THEIR FARM. I ADVISED THEM TO
TURN THE QUILT OVER TO LAW
ENFORCEMENT AND THEY DID SO.

I found it ironic that pictures were playing such an important role in this case. First, pictures of a face. Now a quilt.

CHAPTER 59

T he next morning I was taping a photo of the quilt to the war wall in my office when the front desk called to ask if I was expecting a guest. I wasn't.

"Well, you have one. What is your name again? Thao Pheng."

The biggest change at Channel 3 following the spree killing was that off-duty police officers now manned the front and back doors. They flaunted handguns and Tasers and did not seem afraid to use them.

"Thao Pheng?" I repeated. "Never heard of him. What does he want?"

Part of the new security rules said that employees were to alert the front desk of any scheduled visitors. Such precautions made the station's general manager feel he was making the building safer, but that change wouldn't have prevented the newsroom disaster.

The shooter was expected. The shooting wasn't.

"He says it's important that he speak to you," the guard said.

"Can you press him for more details?" I said. "This is sort of a bad time for me to meet."

The security guards also stressed that if an employee did not know the walk-up guest, they should meet in a public place, outside the station. That way, the coffee shop up the street could be shot up instead of Channel 3.

These restrictions made it harder for sources to show up spontaneously, like a few years ago when a snitch talked his way into the TV station and handed me a lead story about the chief.

We became friends, and when he wasn't behind bars, he helped me nail news. Once he confided to me that he didn't mind getting arrested in one of the northern metro counties because a lady jailer there liked having sex with him in his cell. Thinking he was just trying to impress me, I ignored him. A year later, that county attorney charged one of the jailers with having sex with inmates. The story could have been mine if I hadn't been skeptical.

But that caliber of source didn't happen often and I was about to tell the desk I was busy when the guard blurted out that the man wanted to talk to me about the quilt.

"*The* quilt?" I said. "Tell him I'll be right out."

Thao Pheng was a young Asian man, dressed a bit funky. Because I didn't know my new source's backstory, I invited him to chat over a cup of coffee down the block. His English was good, but he definitely had an accent. We were just getting settled when he began insisting that his *pog* had made the quilt in my report just as his *pog* made many quilts. And he was reluctant to call the police, so he had come to me.

I decided he was a whacko. Plenty of them out there wanting to get on TV.

"*Pog?*" I asked.

He looked flustered and then explained that *pog* was Hmong for grandmother. "Will I be rewarded for this information?"

I should have guessed. He wanted money.

His grandmother couldn't possibly have made the quilt. Thao Pheng was clearly Hmong and the quilt was clearly Amish. I was familiar with exquisite Hmong handwork, which traditionally depicted story lines of animals, refugees, and famous Laotian landmarks. The quilt in question was an early American pattern.

I pulled up the picture of it on my cell phone and showed him the screen. "This quilt."

He pointed at it with confidence. "Yes, that one. My *pog* sewed it."

"But isn't your *pog*—grandmother—Hmong?"

With more than 40,000 Hmong citizens, St. Paul is home to the largest urban Hmong population in the United States. They started settling in Minnesota more than thirty years ago after living in refugee camps in Thailand following the Vietnam war.

"Certainly, she is Hmong. Why do you ask?"

I explained that this particular quilt was an Amish design, not a Hmong design.

"Of course," he agreed, countering that his grandmother was a talented seamstress who sewed whatever buyers wanted. "She has a flair for the needle."

My bewilderment grew. "Who does she quilt for?"

He explained that a man bought her quilts and those of other Hmong and sold them in his store.

"Where is his store?"

He shrugged. "Far." He waved his hand. "Not here."

"May I speak to your grandmother?" Clearly, he hadn't been expecting that question. "Before this goes any further, I need her to verify that she created the quilt."

I didn't say it right then, but I was thinking I would require more than simply her word. I'd need to be put in touch with her buyer.

Thao Pheng stepped aside to make a cell phone call. By the time he hung up, a plan was in place. We exchanged phone numbers and he gave me a time and an address to meet his *pog* that night.

CHAPTER 60

I had two reasons for coaxing Lee Xiong—the newsroom's computer genius—into going along with me to the quilt meeting. First, as my guide to Hmong culture, he could keep me from committing a social blunder on a sensitive story. Like what had happened with the Amish early on.

Second, much of my day was spent worrying that this whole "grandmother" story was concocted by the killer to get me alone and find out what I knew.

Thao Pheng had showed up at the station almost immediately after the quilt hit air. And his story was a little vague on why he hadn't simply gone to the police. I hoped this was just my reporter paranoia, because I was doubtful Xiong could provide much physical protection if the situation turned tense.

Normally he took the bus home to St. Paul after work and did the crossword puzzle during rush-hour traffic. But he agreed to ride along with me and give me a crash course on Hmong elders and etiquette.

"Do not look her directly in the eye," he said. "That is rude. Do not assume she is hiding something because she does not look you in the eye. Lack of eye contact shows respect."

He ran through a list of other dos and don'ts. No staring. No handshakes. Sit, don't stand. Smile, don't laugh. If offered food or drink, take a bite or sip. Do not say "no." No is insulting.

"It is polite to ask if it is spiritually well before entering a Hmong home—*nej puas caiv os*—but I will handle that," he said.

That seemed wise. "She may not speak English," I said. "So you might have to translate."

"What is it you wish to learn? Perhaps I should handle the talking."

This was bold of Xiong. Normally he was a timid, geeky sort of guy who wore sweater vests and followed orders. Now he was essentially telling me things might go better if I kept my mouth shut and put him in charge.

Conceding that he could be right, I briefed him on our ultimate goal: tracing ownership of the quilt. "Like following the money. Or a paper trail."

Xiong seemed enthused at the prospect of partnering up on the ground and I realized his job very seldom let him leave the newsroom. As our computer projects producer, he was invaluable to the staff, but invisible to viewers.

My only fear was that he harbored a secret wish to broadcast on the air. I had enough competition from within the newsroom ranks.

Many Hmong settled in St. Paul's old Frogtown neighborhood, west of the state capitol. The area was gritty, but the housing stock was cheap. Crime has since gone down, and the community now boasts some of the best Asian food in the city.

The moment Xiong and I were ushered into the basement of an old two-story home where Thao's grandmother lived, I had no problem believing she'd made the quilt.

A row of tables were covered with colorful fabric scraps and threads. A tray of sewing needles were on one side. There was no sewing machine in sight. Organization was clear. Amazing hand-stitched quilts hung all over on the walls, and no two alike.

I fingered a blue one, with small colored blocks, in awe. The precise detail represented hours of work.

Strangely, they all looked Amish, not Hmong.

Thao seemed unhappy that Xiong had accompanied me, but I presented him as a work colleague, there to help with the story.

I was glad to have him along because, from the introductions, Thao's *pog* did indeed speak little English, and I would have been nervous relying on Thao to translate.

Xiong and I were invited to sit. The gesture encouraged me. She was wearing a traditional Hmong hat of many colors. I was sporting a stylish scarf because I was still self-conscious about my haircut.

"Tell her I love her hat." I pointed to my own as he interpreted.

She seemed pleased by the flattery, but did not look us in the eye.

"Compliment her on her stitching," I said.

Xiong spoke quietly and sincerely. She responded briefly and courteously.

"Ask why she is not sewing in the style of the Hmong," I said. "But make it clear we are simply curious and not upset."

After a few minutes of back and forth, Xiong essentially reiterated the same story her grandson had told earlier in the day. "She says Hmong work is not worth as much as Amish work. So she sews Amish."

Just then Thao excused himself—both in Hmong and English—to take a phone call in another room.

"Does that make her sad, not sewing in her custom?"

I knew how much tradition meant to the Hmong. This was a trait they shared with the Amish. Despite coming from opposite ends of the earth, the two cultures had much in common: cloistered societies that deeply value agriculture and religion.

The main difference between the two cultures was that the Hmong are more integrated with the outside community. Their children attend public schools. They run for public office. And they watch plenty of TV.

Xiong translated her answer: "She enjoys her work and the man who buys her quilts pays well. He also pays other relatives to sew and weave baskets. A good family craft business to support them."

I handed her my cell phone with the picture of the quilt. "See if she recognizes this one."

"She says this quilt was a personal favorite," he said. "She is honored you appreciate her workmanship."

I told Xiong to see what he could find out about the buyer. Within a few minutes, he reported that the man came once a month, always paid cash, and that a pick-up was scheduled for the following evening. That was why she had so much stock available.

"Do you have enough detail on time and place that we could watch for his arrival?" He assured me he did. I didn't suggest a camera interview because that might make our encounter too worrisome for her. If the quilt ended up being a crucial clue, I'd come back later for sound.

I told him to discuss other matters so we appeared to have broad interests.

As we were prepared to leave, Thao's *pog* pulled a stunning log cabin quilt from a corner pile and handed it to me. The texture and detailed stitching tempted me.

"It's beautiful, but I can't afford it," I said.

Xiong explained that the quilt was a present.

"Oh no, I can't accept such a gift."

Xiong reminded me that saying "no" was rude.

"But you know I can't take such an expensive item. Explain that the station has strict rules without me coming off as insulting."

He did his best, but I still detected Pog's disappointment. "Tell her I promise to return someday to purchase one."

I suspected I would have slept well under that quilt, but the station had a firm payola policy designed to keep people from buying news. Thus, while I could buy sources lunch, they could not buy me lunch. And I reminded myself that Ike was off in Ohio, selecting a special quilt for us, anyway.

As we left, Xiong and I continued this animated discussion until we found Thao standing in the alley behind the house where we were parked. He hung up abruptly. And again, brought up the subject of a reward.

"TV stations don't give rewards or pay for news, Thao." But I assured him that if the quilt lead panned out, we'd tell the police about his involvement. "We will give you credit then, but it's best you stay quiet now. Certainly do not tell the buyer that you have spoken to us. That might upset him and he might stop doing business with your grandmother."

"But I need money now." He said it like he meant it, his fingers curled into fists.

"We don't have any cash with us." I held my purse against my body and started walking backward toward my car. Just as I was regretting dragging Xiong into this clash, I heard an odd sound, and turning, saw him posed in some sort of martial arts stance. Suddenly, Xiong threw a stylish kick in the air and ordered me to start the car. I scrambled for my keys, climbed behind the wheel, and revved the engine.

Even though he was short, Xiong looked imposing with his legs spread wide and his arms stiffly raised. He said something to Thao that I didn't understand and performed a threatening, yet graceful, spin, feet extended. Thao turned congenial; Xiong turned back into a geek. And we drove away without any further trouble.

"I'm impressed," I said. "I thought Hmong were peaceful farmers. Where did you learn those maneuvers?"

He explained that Lawj Xeeb—a form of martial arts—was part of the Hmong heritage. "Many have forgotten, but my father taught me and his father taught him and so it has been for my family."

"Maybe you could teach me?" Normally I use words as weapons, but I've been in enough tight scrapes where throwing a good whack could be more powerful.

Xiong looked doubtful. "Lawj Xeeb takes much dedication." Then he indicated I should take the next left turn to drop him off at his house.

My phone showed a * text had come in an hour earlier, but it was too late for me to help Nicole. The good part about spending a lot of time working in the field was that I didn't have to go into Bryce's office.

CHAPTER 61

The following evening, I parked an unmarked station van up the alley and out of sight, but where I still had a clear view of the Hmong family's back door.

Xiong came along again, not just for company, but for protection. He made me promise not to divulge his martial arts powers. He believed secret skills were best kept secret.

In the Channel 3 basement garage, I made him show me a slow-motion version of his kick. I practiced the move a few times, but I could tell by the look on his face, I had some more work to do.

"Riley, you have other talents."

I didn't tell Bryce about the fake Amish quilts or what I was up to, just in case nothing panned out. No one objected when I took a Channel 3 camera home under the guise of wanting to familiarize myself with its many features.

We parked on the street, Xiong slouched down in the middle row of seats, car keys in hand, in case we needed to leave in a hurry, and I crouched way in the back, camera poised.

We waited in the shadows. Enough light shone from a lamp-post for a decent shot most of the time. After a while, it started to snow.

"Are you sure about the time, Xiong?"

"That's what she said."

Twenty minutes later, we heard a large truck backing into the alley. I hit record on the camera. Rear-end lights glowed and a tailgate came down. I watched the back of a dark figure entering the house. The truck was licensed in Minnesota and I shot the number so we could run the plates for ownership records later.

A couple of people started loading boxes into the truck. I zoomed in with the camera lens to catch the colorful pattern of a quilt in an open box. I also caught a glimpse of a Hmong woman, younger than Thao's *pog*.

The clouds had shifted, and moonlight made another face recognizable. I had to be seeing things. Perhaps subconsciously, my thumb hit stop on the camera because I didn't want proof that Ike Hochstetler, my new boyfriend, was the man loading the truck.

"Xiong, say something so I know I'm not dreaming."

"You are not dreaming, Riley. Are you not well?"

How could I tell him my heart was breaking?

So this was the reason for Ike's monthly trip to Ohio. Ike appeared to be buying quilts made by Hmong women and passing them off as Amish. Counterfeit Amish.

This was an insult to both cultures. Everything Amish, indeed. I felt duped, just like Ike's customers would when this news got out. But it was worse for me—I'd been scammed in love as well as merchandise.

Just then, the truck began moving. I knew I needed to get a clearer look. Xiong and I had developed a plan to let the truck depart and leave a few minutes later. I had figured the alley shot would be enough, but now I couldn't risk losing visual contact with the load.

I grabbed the keys. That's when Xiong got cold feet.

"I will walk home," he said. "The Hmong part of the story is finished."

"Xiong, I might need your help." Surveillance generally works best as a two-person activity. "The new Xiong would want to see some action."

He shook his head and climbed out of the van. "I will run the license plate tomorrow at the station. That will give us verification."

There was no time to argue. The truck had just turned the corner, sliding by a garbage Dumpster as the snow continued to fall. I needed pictures to prove Ike was behind the wheel.

Being wider than the rest of the traffic, the vehicle was easy to trail on the narrow St. Paul residential streets. I gave the driver space on University Avenue, expecting him to turn onto one of the streets leading to the freeway.

Instead, the vehicle pulled into a driveway behind an old warehouse. It was too risky to follow on wheels, so I parked a block away, sneaked into the lot and watched as they loaded a table and chairs. Presumably fake Amish furniture. I knew no real Amish had settled anywhere near this urban neighborhood, heavily populated by Hmong.

I rushed back to my van and waited until the headlights from the truck shone in my side mirror. Within minutes, we were headed south toward Minnesota's Amish country.

CHAPTER 62

Trailing the truck on the freeway was easy. It was dark and there was a lot of other traffic. Plus, I had a funny feeling I knew where we were headed.

The closer we got to Harmony, the snowier and icier the road. I beat the truck to Everything Amish, parked around the corner and killed my headlights.

I prayed that the truck would pass by me and the warehouse and drive far outside our Designated Market Area. Iowa. Indiana. Ohio. Any Amish country but Minnesota.

Instead, the vehicle turned into the lot and backed up against the Everything Amish loading ramp. My throat tightened and any chance for clearing Ike Hochstetler vanished.

There would be no happily ever after with him. This was not an Amish romance novel.

An outside light came on, so I did my job and watched through the viewfinder as Ike carried a chunky chair into the warehouse. I wanted answers that mitigated the wrong, but the obvious motivation playing out before my camera was greed.

Snow blew in my eyes and they started to water. The smart thing would have been to climb behind the wheel and drive far away from this story. Maybe even as far as Washington, DC. Into the arms of a man I could trust.

Instead, I walked over to the truck and asked Ike how the weather was in Ohio.

"Riley? How great you're here. What brings you back to Harmony so soon? More news?"

"I guess you could say that."

He handed me a box to carry inside and suggested we head to his house for a hot drink. "And maybe you'd like to handpick a quilt to bring along for later." He gave a playful wink.

"Actually, there is a certain quilt that interests me greatly." I set the box of counterfeit Amish goods down on the ramp, reached for my cell phone, and opened the photo of the sinkhole quilt. "Does this one look familiar?"

He seemed surprised. "Certainly. I just never expected to see it again. Someone shoplifted it from the store."

Convenient, I thought. "Did you file a police report? That's what I did when someone stole my camera."

He shook his head. "I thought Sarah Yoder might have taken it, and I was hoping to resolve things privately."

"You thought Sarah stole the quilt?"

"Yes, it disappeared the same night she did."

"You're right about that."

I explained that the quilt had been found wrapped around her dead body. "That makes it evidence. Remember telling me how a handmade quilt can be as individual as a fingerprint? Think of this quilt as fabric forensics. And it's pointing right at you."

"I didn't kill her, if that's what you're suggesting."

"You can tell that to the police."

"I'm not a murderer."

"Maybe not, but you're definitely a swindler."

I spelled out how I'd discovered the source of his stock. He was a fraud and probably a murderer.

He didn't answer.

"I saw your private sweatshop and I followed you more than a hundred miles from that Frogtown alley tonight." I explained that Channel 3 was going to broadcast a story on consumer fraud with counterfeit Amish merchandise the next day. "If you have a comment to make, I suggest you do so now."

Saying nothing, he just collapsed into a rocking chair sitting on the truck tailgate. Back and forth. Back and forth. He stopped the rocking long enough to give what those of us in the news biz call the mercy plea. "Riley, I'm just a small businessman looking for a break."

"You're a cheat, Ike. I think that's one thing the Amish and English will both agree on."

"But, what about us?"

He rose from the rocker and before I realized what was happening, he was kissing me. His arms felt good, but his lips felt dirty. I pushed him away and slapped him hard across his handsome once-Amish face.

"There is no us," I said. "There never was."

Turning the radio up loud to try to distract myself from my encounter with Ike, I pushed all thoughts of what might have been out of mind. I had been courted by a killer. And if he cheated tourists, no doubt he'd cheat me. And maybe even worse. I tried not thinking about Sarah.

I hated cheats. In love and business. Best that I found out before Ike met my parents. Regardless, I felt like a fool, falling for him. But soon, fidelity would be the least of my problems.

My phone was buzzing on the passenger side of the dashboard as I drove out of town. Ike's number came up onscreen. I didn't answer. Whatever he wanted to say wouldn't change anything. And if I could take back my kisses, I would. His tongue, not mine, was that of the devil.

All this talk of simple life was beginning to feel like a scam. How could such a small town hold so many big secrets?

My car was approaching the turnoff where I needed to decide

whether to continue north to the Twin Cities or head east to the farm. Showing up unexpectedly at my childhood home would lead to questions. While my parents would be pleased to see me, they'd also be suspicious and wonder what was wrong. If I headed back to my own place, I could sulk in private, but I'd have to drive hours through snow.

As I slowed for an internal debate of which would be worse, something rammed the back of my vehicle, throwing me into a skid. I'd been rear-ended. My first thought was that another driver had crashed into me because of the slippery weather.

As I tried to recover, I recognized the other vehicle. It was a truck with no lights. And the rig seemed to be coming at me again.

CHAPTER 63

The truck pulled alongside me in the outside lane. Ike stared right at me as he swerved over, trying to push me off the road and into a ditch.

Just as his truck scraped the side of my van, the road went up an incline, which slowed him down. I reached for my cell phone as I put distance between us. The phone was gone. The hurling action from the impact must have catapulted it to the back of the van.

Seeing Ike's menacing face behind the wheel, I had no doubt now that he'd murdered Sarah. After all, he was trying to kill me.

My game plan was to outdrive him. Once on the highway, other traffic would keep me safe until I could find a gas station with people. There is safety in numbers. But I didn't make it far enough to find witnesses.

Suddenly, my vehicle started losing power. The crash must have caused some internal damage. I needed to find a safe place to stop, but this stretch of road was mostly woods with no houses in sight.

The van was stalling, and my pursuer was less than a minute behind me. I decided I could run faster than this engine, so I pulled over and scrambled to get unbuckled. I headed for the back of the van, feeling along the floor for my phone. Nothing.

Then I realized I was not far from Walden's den. Even at

night, thousands of viewers would be watching Walden via web-cam and infrared light. Some might even have the audio channel open. A strange woman pleading for someone to call the police from inside his den would certainly attract attention. I'd even welcome trespassing charges.

Suddenly, I smelled danger. As the odor became more distinct I recognized it was gasoline.

During my career, I'd faced deadlines by the thousands. But this one was the most critical of my life because I didn't know how much time I had left. All I knew was that I needed to get as far away from the van as possible. Fast.

I fumbled for the door handle and cold air rushed at my face. In my haste to escape, I slipped on the icy ground and twisted my ankle. The smell grew stronger and I realized the truck had hit my gas tank. Gas was now leaking onto the snow.

I stumbled to get upright, and ran limping through the snow. I didn't stop until the blast knocked me off my feet. If I'd been facing the direction of the wreck, my eyebrows would have been gone.

There I lay, about a hundred yards from the explosion, watching the fire and thinking about how if I'd been any slower, I wouldn't be a widow anymore. I'd be with my man in the here-after.

Ike's truck was parked along the road illuminated by fire. Best-case scenario: he'd think me dead and flee the scene.

I said a silent prayer to God even though God and I had been estranged as of late. I felt cheap turning to the Almighty only in emergencies and wished Father Mountain had agreed to anoint me. But instead of making the truck pull away, God showed me a shadowy shape emerging from the cab with a flashlight.

Flames kept the silhouette back, but then I recognized Ike. No doubt he was hoping for evidence of charred remains. Forensi-cally, I wasn't sure how much of a body was left after a car explosion. But I knew we weren't talking ashes and dust. And Ike could see that my driver's seat was empty.

That's when he started swinging his beam of light downward along the ground around the scene. I knew what he was looking for. Tracks. He was seconds from finding my trail in the snow, and less than a minute from finding me.

My head start wasn't enough to keep me out of jeopardy. My footprints would be obvious in the moonlight. If I hid, Ike would find me. If I kept moving, he would overtake me.

I had no time to orientate myself. Turning what I hoped was east seemed the right direction toward the bear cave. It was another half mile by my guess. Pantyhose were poor insulation in frigid temperatures, and my feet were getting numb.

There was no hope of disarming my opponent with Xiong's surprise kick. Keep moving, I told myself, wrapping my arms around my chest. Reaching Walden would be its own reward. A bear would certainly throw off some body heat even if its temperature dropped during hibernation. Hopefully my visit wouldn't wake him.

That's when I started fantasizing about fur.

CHAPTER 64

Hypothermia can lead to mental confusion. So when the surroundings started to look familiar, I wasn't sure if it was because I was close or simply delusional.

But when I reached the landmark maple tree, I knew Walden was near. On my knees, trying to block my face from the wind, I found the opening to the bear den.

Crawling inside the tunnel felt like crawling toward salvation. In the far chamber, Walden lay curled and silent under the webcam. His radio collar and ribbons were quite noticeable. I snuggled against him, my ear against his chest, waving my hands in front of the camera to signal my presence.

"Help." I hoped my whispers were loud enough for Internet viewers to hear, but not so loud as to wake a sleeping bear in its winter den. "Please call the sheriff."

I realized my plan for rescue was ridiculous and dangerous. But the bear cam seemed like my only chance to reach 911.

Whether any of the viewers would even have their audio open to hear my panicked plea, I didn't know. I wished I had a sign to hold up to the camera, but my purse was toast back in the van. Then I felt my pants pocket and found a pen. After all, my job as a reporter was to never be without a pen. I wrote HELP on my palm and held my arm straight toward the lens. CALL POLICE.

I was on the verge of the most important standup of my life.

Success wouldn't land me a job, an award, or ratings. But it just might keep me alive.

"I'm being chased by a man—"

Suddenly I heard a beating heart echo within the den, and knew Walden was on the verge of stirring. I recalled Teresa telling me that black bears are most dangerous when they feel threatened. Within a couple minutes, his blood flow would reach his extremities, then Walden might be alert enough to protect himself from peril. And he would view me not as an observer, but as an interloper.

"I need help." I hoped one of the bear's cyberfans would report me as an intruder. Walden lifted his head. I knew he was waking, and that I needed to move.

I shuffled backward through the tunnel until outside the cave, then scrambled to my feet. My instincts told me to put some distance between us, but I had no idea where to head and I worried that if I left the scene, help wouldn't find me. But if I stayed too close, Walden might find me. And I also worried that if I ventured too far from the den entrance, Ike would track me.

So I decided to take a gamble by climbing onto a low-hanging branch on the large tree near the cave. Once up, I moved higher so I could watch the area in case rescuers arrived. I couldn't see far in the moonlight.

Then a roar, more like a lion than a bear, came from the burrow. But Walden stayed inside. I prayed for him to turn around several times, get comfortable, then slip back into his long seasonal siesta. I only hoped I wouldn't freeze to death first.

Just then, a dark figure approached.

CHAPTER 65

The wind was harsher up in that tree than it was below. I pressed my body flat against the trunk, trying to blend into the wood in case Ike looked in my direction. Don't look up, I mumbled to myself, over and over. I had no desire to stare into the eyes of my assassin.

Luckily, his face stayed glued to the trail on the ground. He paused at the entrance of the den. Even in the dark my path was visible. But while my tracks unmistakably led inside, it was not so clear I had exited.

Looking back, perhaps I could have or should have yelled a warning. But the cold had dulled my senses and I wasn't thinking fast. I just remember being relieved Ike never looked up.

He probably thought he had me trapped and the showdown would be over in a manner of minutes. He was right about half of his hypothesis. Entering the bear den was the last blunder he would ever make.

From my perch, I could hear the confrontation. My stomach grew tight when Ike's screams ended.

A few minutes later, Walden exited. He shook angrily from side to side and clawed the air. I stopped breathing, closed my eyes, and prayed some more. I'd heard of bears being treed, so I knew Walden could climb, but luckily for me, he didn't.

When I opened my eyes, the black bear was gone. He might

have disappeared into the darkness. Or retreated back into his cave. I wasn't sure so I stayed quiet and waited.

Teresa from the bear center had been typing a research report in town while watching the webcam of Walden hibernating when my cyberface popped up on her computer screen. She assumed my appearance to be an obnoxious television stunt and left immediately to chew me out for breaking my promise not to interfere with nature. Then she planned to have me arrested as a caution to other media.

She missed the ensuing online action.

Around the world, just under two thousand people watched the live webcam melee between Walden and Ike. Then someone posted the attack on YouTube and the confrontation went viral before the video could be taken down.

The bear clicked his teeth when Ike entered his lair. But the man didn't heed the warning. With the bear clawing at his face and biting at his arms, the two rolled on the ground together. Faces were only seen twice and then only briefly. Blood spattered everywhere until the pinhole on the camera lens was covered and the scene went black.

Fortunately, the episode was in black and white, not color. Or it would have surpassed the gore of any B-list horror film.

Visually, the whole ordeal lasted only thirty-four seconds. But the audio dragged on for nearly five minutes. Roars mixed with screams. Low human moans were the final sound.

The medical examiner's report listed the immediate cause of death for Isaac Hochstetler in clinical terms: *multiple injuries, shock, hemorrhage, due as a consequence of mauling by bear.*

But thousands of witnesses, including me, knew he had been torn to pieces. Like the headless Amish doll.

CHAPTER 66

Walden's fate was debated late that night by state wildlife officials who conceded that while the creature had been unfairly provoked, once he'd gotten a taste for human blood, he presented a "very real danger to people."

They determined the big bear needed to be destroyed.

The bear center folks, especially Teresa, pleaded for compassion. As did other bear researchers worldwide, but no one for miles around wanted to risk living near Walden. So no local public support was forthcoming. The hastily assembled online outcry to Save Walden came from nature lovers who lived a safe distance away from the rogue bear.

Using his radio collar, the animal was tracked and killed later that day.

No media were allowed to record the execution. But shots of bloody snow led all the newscasts that evening.

CHAPTER 67

I speculated that Sarah must have discovered the Amish coun-
terfeiting scheme while working at the store and threatened
to talk. Maybe she tried to blackmail Ike. Or maybe she was simply offended by the deception.

With both players dead, we'd never know the truth.

The chain of evidence linking the quilt from Ike's store to Sarah's sinkhole convinced Sheriff Eide that he'd solved his first and
only murder and could close the case with pride—two weeks before the election.

The Channel 3 van still sat torched by the side of the road. That Ike
and Walden had both perished, and the fact that I had almost died,
all weighed heavier on my mind. However, those casualties didn't
cost the station any actual money, so Bryce was more concerned
that the price of my Amish murder investigation—one company
vehicle, two broadcast cameras, and assorted other news gear, including my cell phone—was nearing sixty grand. For a television
news director whose dream was to make more money being number two than number one, that's a steep tab for any story.

I felt isolated without calls, texts, or emails. Although the
good news was I didn't have to worry about Bryce being on the
other end of any communication.

I had unfinished business around Harmony, so my dad let me borrow their car, keeping the pickup for themselves. And because my purse had also gone up in flames, Mom gave me eighty-two dollars—the cash stash she kept tucked under the good china. I'd also used their phone to call the neighbor boy to take over Husky duties until I got back to the cities to hug my dog.

Knowing I'd be unwelcome, I stopped at the Yoder farm anyway just to clear things up between us before I left town. Even though snow was on the ground, Miriam was hanging dresses and pants on the line. A large basket of wet clothing sat by her feet.

She had already heard the news that Sarah's killer had been found.

"It matters not," she said. "Judge not, that ye be not judged." Not wanting to be drawn into the whole forgiveness debate, I got right to the point. "Here's what her murderer's death means in terms of the media and you. Because the case is closed, there won't be a trial. Which means Sarah won't be in the news much longer."

"No more stories?" she asked.

"Not from me."

I was too personally involved in the case to cover it anymore. Bryce had sent Nicole down to report on Ike's death. The law had put crime-scene tape around the bear den. I'd stood there, for my interview, pointing at the tree where I hid in fear, unsure if I'd die by man or beast.

"No more putting her picture on TV?" Miriam asked.

"I think that's over, Miriam. The whole point of my questions and quest to tell her story was to bring her justice by identifying her killer. I know that's hard for you to understand, but from my perspective, now Sarah can rest."

Miriam was so relieved, she stumbled, dropping wooden clothespins on the ground.

"I'm sorry for the loss of your daughter, Miriam. And I'm especially sorry for all the ensuing intrusions into your world."

My recent encounters with the Amish had taught me that the adults were generally an unemotional lot in public. So I was taken aback when Miriam began weeping. She probably felt some guilt over Sarah's homicide. If they hadn't shunned Sarah, she wouldn't have left, and wouldn't be dead.

"It's never too late for a good cry," I told her.

Then I wrapped my arms around Miriam, and she sobbed against my shoulder like she was a child instead of a mom. I didn't often get a chance to physically comfort someone troubled. Usually a camera was rolling and I had to stay professional during an emotional interview. As she quieted, I was glad I had come to visit.

"Hey, Miriam, I don't get down this way very often, but if there was any way we could be friends, I'd like that."

Sometimes families want to stay in touch even after their news cycle ends. Other times they want no reminders of the torment. But she shook her head, and I understood this was goodbye for us.

Then her son, Gideon, pulled into the yard with the buggy. I didn't hear the clip-clop warning because of the snow-packed road. He jumped out before the horse even stopped and raced over to us, shouting for me to go away.

Then for the first time since I met her, Miriam raised her voice. "Be still," she told him.

And for the first time, I saw her flex her maternal muscles and take charge of her son. While I understood she and I could never be true friends, she had apparently decided not to let him be rude to my face. "The stories are finished, Gideon. She has promised to stop showing Sarah's picture. It is finally over."

That calmed him down. And while I should have just walked to my car without another word, and driven off without a look backward, I wasn't as fond of him as of his mother.

Of course, she hadn't held me down in the dark and cut off

my hair. I pulled off my hat and threw it at Gideon. It bounced against the brim of his own.

"I know you can't give me back my hair, but at least give me back my camera."

He didn't answer.

"You told the sheriff the truth about painting over Sarah's billboard, why don't you tell me the truth now? What did you do with my camera?"

He started toward me, angrily, but Miriam held him back. I noted that he kept rather quiet so I took his silence as an admission of guilt.

Because I was a one-man band, I didn't have anyone to hold me back and keep me calm. "You think this haircut sent me a message, Gideon? Just be glad I don't send you a message of my own."

"What is all this talk about cameras and hair?" Miriam seemed to be asking both of us.

"Ask your son," I told her.

Then I left the world of the Amish behind. No regrets. I had expected a taste of mystery and had gotten an overdose of misery.

Just then, the modern world didn't seem so tainted. And if there was a devil, I was more convinced than ever that his weapon of choice was not TV.

I was an hour on the road before I remembered Sarah's journal, hidden in my top drawer at the station. Between Walden and the quilt, I'd had no time to find someone to translate the German writing.

Now that her killer was found, the urgency was gone. Sarah's final thoughts no longer mattered. As a journalist, I respected that diaries are supposed to be confidential. So I was torn between honoring Sarah's privacy and giving the journal to her mother.

CHAPTER 68

I was too sleep deprived to head to the station. I'd been working on adrenaline and caffeine the last thirty-six hours and was completely spent. I drove home torn between wanting to crawl between clean sheets and wanting to climb into a hot bath. Since it was just me, I decided the bath could wait.

Except I wasn't alone. A rental vehicle was parked in front of my house. And behind the wheel, reading a newspaper, was my former fiancé.

He didn't recognize me at first, probably because of my car and hair. I pounded on the driver's-side window to get his attention. Within seconds, his arms were wrapped around me, and then our lips took over. Familiar kisses felt reassuring.

"I heard what happened with the bear, Riley." My lover had a Google Alert on my name. That's how he always knew about my latest story or mishap. "I couldn't reach you, and I decided enough with waiting for you to want me. I want you enough for both of us."

Soon we were inside, and rather than mention that I smelled like a combination of smoke, gasoline, bear, and blood, he merely turned on the shower and helped me undress.

"Oh Nick, I'm too tired for a shower."

"I'll do all the work, Riley. You just stand there. I'll scrub your back, shampoo your hair, and give you a nice towel dry."

The steam and heat felt soothing. I closed my eyes and pretended Ike Hochstetler had never happened. Minutes later, Garnett and I climbed between the bedcovers.

"Are you going to do all the work between the covers, too?" I figured Garnett didn't fly all the way from Washington, DC, for a hot shower. Before he could even answer, I fell asleep curled against him and didn't wake for fourteen hours.

When I saw the clock, I panicked. I should have been at work hours ago. Without a phone, the desk couldn't reach me. Bryce would be furious. He'd probably write me up as AWOL.

"Relax." Garnet was typing away on his laptop computer. "I called the station and told them you were sick."

"Sick? I'm not allowed to be sick. I work in TV news."

"Sometimes you need an objective observer to decide what's best for you, and I decided you were sick."

He was probably right. "The whole episode feels unreal. I almost wonder if I went a little mad out there in the woods. Maybe I still am."

"We all go a little mad sometimes." Garnett leaned back as he said the line with meaning.

I responded immediately. "*Psycho*. Anthony Perkins, 1960."

"See, that was a test, Riley, and you passed. Now I know you're cured of any madness."

"Maybe I'm just mad about you, Nick." And I took his hand and led him back to bed and proved it.

CHAPTER 69

The next day I insisted I was well enough to return to work. Garnett had to fly back to Washington anyway after finishing a security meeting out at Minneapolis–St. Paul International Airport.

Usually he would try to talk me into going back east with him, and I would claim to be too busy at the station. But actually, I really didn't like flying.

Neither of us brought up any future plans this time, probably because we didn't want to jinx our present status. The past also seemed better left off-limits. So that restricted our conversation topics.

Both of our lives had changed forever that afternoon at Channel 3 when Garnett killed the gunman who was shooting up the newsroom. Even though he'd been a cop his entire life, he'd never actually taken a life. And I was struggling with my own disturbing problems after facing a psycho in an Iowa cemetery. I guess I thought if we didn't talk about the bad, it wouldn't be real and might just go away. But I'd since learned that theory was worthless. Maybe Garnett had, too. Maybe that was why he was back in my bed. I was afraid to ask him.

"Want to walk the dog with me?" I said instead.

"You have a dog?" He looked around the kitchen. "Where do you keep him?"

"Husky. He's with a neighbor. Remember him? First he belonged to Toby, then Noreen, now me. He rotates between living here and down at the farm."

Soon we were heading toward Lake Nokomis, just the three of us. We almost resembled a family. I wondered if Garnett still had the engagement ring that he had given me and I had given back. It held a deep red stone—a garnet. But instead of asking me to marry him again, he asked how things were at the station.

"How's the new boss working out?"

"I hate him."

"Still making you shoot your own video?"

"That's the least of it." If I told Garnett about Bryce's technique for supervising women, he'd pound him. So I kept quiet because I didn't want my once-again boyfriend behind bars. "Although if I'd had a photographer assigned to me, I wouldn't have been running for my life alone the other night."

"There'd probably just be one more dead bear victim," he said.

"Walden got a bum rap. He deserved to see spring. I wish things could have ended differently for him."

"Well, the way I read the situation, if the bear hadn't killed this guy, the guy would have killed you. I'd rather hear about a dead bear than a dead Riley."

"That might be the most romantic thing you've ever said." Garnett was better at quoting movie lines than coming up with his own dialogue.

"I do my best."

My ankle was still bothering me, so I suggested we turn back so I could elevate my foot.

"Fine with me," Garnett said. "All the walking is making me hungry. Do you have anything in your refrigerator?"

I weighed the last time I'd been shopping with the last time I'd taken out the garbage. "Probably nothing edible."

We stopped by a local deli and I ran to use the ladies' room and grab something to eat. This bathroom water was a little on the hot side, but what really got my attention was that one of the workers making sandwiches wasn't wearing gloves. I knew that was a health violation, so I just stuck with two coffees and muffins in plastic wrap. When I came outside, Husky was rubbing against Garnett's legs while he got his ears scratched. I made a mental note to swing by the grocery store on my way home from the station and pick up some basics like milk, eggs, and dog biscuits.

Then I remembered owing Bryce another food story that was cheap, fast, and foolproof. That would probably be the first thing he asked me about when I returned to work. Not, how was I doing? But, what have I got for sweeps?

I forced myself to think food. And suddenly, restaurant inspections came to mind. Instead of Channel 3 putting eateries to the test, we'd simply report what city health inspectors found. Cheap. Fast. Foolproof. Now I wasn't dreading returning to work so much.

Husky was eager for the walk to end. He didn't like cold paws. When we got back to the house, he rushed to the door to embrace his indoor-dog status. Garnett and I clung together for a brief kiss and went back to our professional—but at times, unprofessional—worlds.

CHAPTER 70

As I drove to Channel 3, I was reveling in the benefits of not having a cell phone and not being constantly on call. I'd traded convenience for freedom. I'd decided to wait until the station ordered me to buy a new phone.

But I didn't go straight to the office. I stopped first at the Minneapolis Health Department to talk about health code violations, which are public record. Within minutes I was sitting at a small table with a large stack of files. The last three months of city restaurant inspections. I made a food index, noting which places had high grades and which had tanked. My story would be a report card to Minneapolis's dining establishments. I wished all my research could be so easy. I set to work making photocopies.

The best part about my Channel 3 office was the location. Tucked in the rear of the building, I could enter through the station's back alley entrance when I wanted to keep a low profile. I didn't have to walk by the news director's office or the assignment desk.

By the time I arrived at work, the news huddle was long over. Most of the staff had scattered. I logged onto my computer, and made a spreadsheet of the restaurants and their scores. Just as I was heading to tell Bryce the good news, I ran into Nicole who was leaving his office.

"Why didn't you interrupt us?" She held up her cell phone. "I texted you."

"I'm phoneless, Nicole. What happened?"

She looked around to see if anyone was watching us. I motioned for her to follow me to the ladies' room. The restroom hadn't been updated since the station was built, and had gotten shabby over the years. The faucet water was on the cool side. The women of Channel 3 had been campaigning long for a remodel, but had always been turned down due to budget constraints.

However, the stalls were empty, and it was just the place for a private chat.

"What happened?"

"He complimented me on my job covering the bear attack. Then he asked if I'd received his message. I told him I have conservative Christian values and didn't appreciate that kind of picture. That I had deleted the photo and didn't want any more."

"That's actually good. You put him on notice."

She looked relieved. "Really? Do you think he'll stop then?"

"No, Nicole. If anything, he'll want to prove he's in charge."

CHAPTER 71

I walked into Bryce's office waving a printout of my spreadsheet. "Here's your food story, boss, and it's terrific."

My enthusiasm surprised him and he instructed me to close
the door for our discussion so he could better concentrate. I
thought about refusing, but figured that would just piss him
off.

I gave him the bottom line: Channel 3 would broadcast restaurant inspection scores. "We have some popular places with
violations that will surprise viewers."

"So we're good to air?" He sounded surprised.

"Sure are, boss."

"This seems too easy." He sounded suspicious.

"Call Miles," I said. "I'm not worried. Because a couple of
these places with failing marks are large restaurant chains with
their own staff attorneys, now might be a good time to bring
him in to flag any legal issues."

While we waited for Miles, I explained the difference between
critical and noncritical food violations. "Critical ones could
cause food-borne illnesses. They might involve sanitation or un-
dercooked meat."

Within a couple minutes, Miles had arrived. He shut the door
for our attorney-client talk, but that was fine with me because I
wasn't alone with Bryce anymore.

Miles had no objection to broadcasting the inspection scores as long as we gave the restaurants an opportunity to respond. Whether they decided to comment or not would be up to them.

"Absolutely, we will," I said. "But that affects timing. If we want to hold the story for the November sweeps, I don't think we want to contact them much more than a week in advance. Otherwise they'll have their advertising team call our sales gang to lean on us to kill the story."

"Wait," Bryce said. "This could cost us advertising revenue?"

"Theoretically, yes," I said. "These major restaurant chains might threaten to pull their advertising. But usually that's just a ploy to see if we'll fold. And it wouldn't be fair to just report mom-and-pop places that can't afford to advertise."

"But conceivably, we could lose money?"

"Well, yes. But companies that make a stink about pulling advertising usually end up looking even worse. And that draws more attention to their transgression. In the meantime, we likely gain viewers who tune in to watch all the fuss."

Bryce got quiet fast. And I feared he might be mulling over killing this story, too. "But aren't these health code inspections just a snapshot in time? The restaurants might have improved."

"That's certainly true," I said. "And that's what they'll probably argue, if they choose to do an interview. But the restaurants might also have gotten worse."

"I'm not comfortable airing it without comment from the restaurants," Bryce said.

"That would be their choice," I said. "Are we never going to air a crime story if a suspect refuses to talk to us? Are we going to steer away from political controversies if a candidate declines an interview?"

"What if the restaurants sue us?" Bryce asked.

"I don't see it as a legal problem," Miles said. "We're merely reporting what the city found. Very low libel risk."

"We'll add some context with an interview from the health

department," I said. "And we'll also salute restaurants which scored high, to prove it's possible."

I thought that settled things. But not so. Ten seconds later, my restaurant inspection story was dead.

Miles left, but I wanted answers. "How can this be, Bryce? The calorie-fat testing story also involved some advertisers." Then I realized that was why he killed it, not because the food tests were too expensive or risky. My new boss didn't want to offend advertisers.

Before I said something that would land me in trouble, I stood up to leave.

"Just a minute," he said.

Uh-oh, I thought. He wants a high five. But he just wanted to admonish me about being out of touch with the assignment desk.

"They couldn't reach you for the last couple days. In this world of breaking news, our staff needs to be available 24-7."

I reminded him that my cell phone blew up with the station van. "My phone died in the line of duty, Bryce. I think the station should replace it."

He disagreed. "You're lucky I don't make you pay for the van, too, and not just the phone."

As I walked out Bryce made some comment about writing me up for negligence with company property and scoring me poorly on availability in my upcoming job review.

"And don't forget, Riley, I still expect you to come up with a food story."

A letter came in that day's mail from Michelle Kueppers. She thanked me for spotting the Amish quilt in their shed and helping find Sarah Yoder's killer. She enclosed a picture of her and Josh holding Brian's military photo. The picture looked good enough for a Christmas card and I wouldn't be surprised if it ended up on one.

It is such a relief to Josh and myself not to worry about this murder anymore. And even though I believed my husband when he told me he was not involved with this woman, to be honest, I was anxious about what his DNA might show. Josh had been blaming himself for finding her body. I told him what he did was good and brave and God will reward him. "But not if it hurts our family," he said.

Thank you for being smart and brave too, and doing your job.

My bottom desk drawer has a file of my favorite letters from viewers. This one belonged with that bunch.

Also in the drawer was a file from viewers who considered me liberal media scum. I kept those close to remind myself that journalists can't please everyone. If hell had mail delivery and Ike could send a letter, it would likely go in that file.

I thought about burning some of the really hateful letters in the alley behind the station. But I had vowed to save them all. Someday, to celebrate my retirement from television news, I would donate my top ten to a charity's silent auction where autograph hounds might bid for them.

Not that any collector would care about me, the recipient. The senders of the letters—politicians, athletes, even murderers—would attract the money.

CHAPTER 72

Malik greeted me the next morning with a gleam in his eye that I hadn't seen since the day he froze during his live shot.

"No, we don't get any more meals to test," I said. "If what you're hoping for is a free lunch."

But it was something else. "Remember how I've been missing that certain camera you lost? I knew every centimeter on that camera's body from viewfinder to lens. I could operate that camera blind."

"Which one? The torched one or the stolen one?"

"The stolen one. That camera was perfection."

"Well, if you lobby Bryce, maybe he'll buy you another. But I'm not bringing it up because he'll probably make me pay for it."

"They don't make 'em like that one anymore."

"I have to write the food script, Malik. Stop trying to make me feel guilty and let me get back to work."

Instead, he pushed my growing stack of food files aside and pulled a chair up next to my computer.

"Move over, Riley. Let me at that mouse."

I stored my script and abandoned my workstation, seeking coffee and a chance to stretch my legs. When I returned,

Malik motioned me over to the monitor and I saw he'd called up Craigslist, a website for selling used merchandise.

He clicked to an ad where a picture of a video camera, priced at a thousand dollars, came up on the screen.

"That's our camera," he said, pointing.

"Are you sure?" My memory of the camera was muddled. I hadn't been a one-man band long enough to be an expert. "Seems like an awfully good price."

"Most stolen goods are priced to move."

"But the Amish don't have computers or Internet access, how would they be advertising online?"

"Maybe an English friend is helping them out. See, the seller location says Preston, Minnesota. That's very near Harmony."

He was right about that. And I had a hard time believing there'd be two such cameras in one rural county. "So what do we do?"

"There's only one way to be sure, Riley. The serial number."

"And if it matches ours," I said, "we can contact authorities and probably report the theft as news."

If we retrieved the camera, our status with Bryce would definitely improve, because the station had self-insured camera equipment and the loss was coming out of the news budget. I had to return my parents' car soon anyway, and I could also bring Husky along and drop him off at the farm so I could get a dog break.

"Want to take a road trip, Malik?" The only problem was I might be recognized by the person selling the camera. "You'll have to call, get the address, and set up an appointment. Also get approval from Bryce, because my last meeting with him went bad."

He gave me a thumbs-up. But then, because Malik had been on air recently, I started worrying he might look familiar, too. We could both wear disguises, but ordinary folks from around the area might be less suspicious customers than out-of-town strangers.

"Let's send my mom and dad to check the serial number."

So I called them on my newly purchased cell phone.

Malik brought the same model of video camera along as a prop, to show my parents where the serial number was located—on the bottom, near the battery compartment.

"I can't read the numbers very well," Mom said. "They're too tiny."

"My eyes are okay," Dad said. "It's my knees that are bad."

I wrote the digits of the serial number on his palm.

"If the numbers correspond, offer to write our dealer a check. I'm guessing he'll insist on cash, and you'll have to meet him another time." I handed Dad a twenty-dollar bill. "See if he'll take this as a deposit."

The Craigslist seller didn't give out any home address, just arranged for a get-together in a parking lot by the town swimming pool. Off season, the area was deserted.

Malik and I parked the van across the street and waited with the camera ready to shoot. My parents sat in the pickup with a wireless microphone hidden under Dad's jacket. I had them face the dashboard toward the road so they had good visibility and so did we.

An Amish buggy drove by with a beardless man inside, but didn't stop. I wondered if he'd circle back. I checked the video. Malik had recorded a close-up and the driver was definitely not Gideon.

Just then a dark-green sport utility vehicle pulled into the lot alongside the pickup and rolled down the window.

"Quick," I said. "Get the license plate."

He read the numbers and letters out loud. I called the newsroom for Xiong and asked him to track the owner from our computer vehicle database.

The driver handed the camera over to my mother on the passenger side. She tried to practice pointing and shooting. Then she passed it over to my dad. "Here, honey, you try."

While he fumbled, I heard her asking the guy how old the camera was and how good a picture did it take. I had told her to try and distract him while Dad was looking for the serial number.

His voice wasn't clear because he was so far from the hidden microphone, but sounded like he was saying, "First rate, lady."

"We'll take it," Dad said.

That was our cue that the numbers matched. The camera belonged to Channel 3 and had been stolen from me.

Then Xiong texted me that the SUV belonged to Roger Alton. That name sounded familiar. Xiong included an address in Preston, Minnesota. He also sent the man's height and weight information from the separate driver's license database.

My parents had already agreed to pay the thousand dollars, even though my mom, a garage-sale buff, had wanted to see how low she could negotiate.

"I'll write you a check," Mom said. "Who should I make it out to?"

Thieves don't want checks in case they bounce; they also don't like giving out their names to buyers or having to endorse the check later.

"Didn't you bring any real money?" The guy's voice was louder now, full of incredulity.

"No one carries that much cash," Mom answered. "What if we were robbed?"

Dad offered him the twenty from his wallet as a deposit. "How 'bout we come back to meet you later? We just need to make a quick trip to the Farmers State Bank of Adams."

The guy agreed to come back that evening at six unless he got another offer. They handed the camera back through the truck window and he took off.

Thirty seconds later, Malik and I waved them over.

"Good job," I said. "So the numbers matched?"

My dad affirmed the match with a proud nod.

We knew a crime had been committed. And we had a suspect.

Just then a Fillmore County Sheriff's vehicle raced by and I remembered where I'd heard the name before.

Roger Alton was Sheriff Eide's election pal. And besides carrying money, he also carried a gun. So he might not be the type of adversary I wanted my parents to face alone.

"He smelled like booze," my mom said.

I had to admit that I might have been wrong to blame Gideon for cutting my hair and filching my camera. The scene at the Lamplight Inn replayed in my mind. One man clean shaven, the other bearded. Both in wide-brimmed hats. A dark room. Then it hit me.

The Amish weren't the only ones around these parts opposed to cameras. Early that same day, Sheriff Eide had tried to steal the video from me in the back of his squad.

The sheriff had a smooth face. The man in the truck definitely sported whiskers. And plain Amish hats were easy to find in tourist country.

I realized the whole attack was a ruse to take my camera. The pair had concocted the ambush based on the latest news about the renegade Amish group. His buddy probably agreed to help to avoid any controversy with his name. So Sheriff Eide got the video, and Roger got the camera.

I got a bad haircut. And now I was getting a worse headache.

CHAPTER 73

Reporting the stolen merchandise posed a problem. I could hardly call the Fillmore County Sheriff for help. And Bryce had told Malik and me to get the camera back free, and absolutely not pay a grand. After all, the equipment belonged to us.

"I didn't bring any cash along," Malik said. "Did you?"

I shook my head. "No big bucks. And none of the ATM machines will let me withdraw a thousand dollars."

My parents offered to run to their bank and get the money. I decided we might need a stack of greenbacks for a prop, so I thanked them and sent them off. Dad drove the pickup and Mom took the car they'd loaned to me. Husky curled up in the backseat for a reunion with the farm dogs.

Then I remembered Deputy Laura Schaefer, the sheriff's election challenger. Her night shift hadn't started yet, but maybe I could catch her at home.

"Darn, not listed," I told Malik.

Cops often put their work addresses on vehicle registrations or driver's licenses because they don't want bad guys knowing where they live. I explained the new problem to Xiong, and within a few minutes he'd found a home address for her in our hunting-license database. Police don't want to risk that piece of mail getting lost. And apparently Laura liked to hunt.

• • •

A Schaefer campaign sign stood next to the mailbox, so I figured I was at the right place. When I knocked, I couldn't tell from her face if she was dissing me or genuinely didn't recognize me again.

"Sorry to bother you at home, Deputy Schaefer."

"Regardless, Ms. Spartz, I don't start patrol until seven."

"I can tell you're off duty." She was dressed like a normal person, not like a cop. Out of uniform, not armed with gun or hammer, she looked good enough for my job. Maybe even better, with her flowing hair.

"And I can save you time," she continued. "We haven't found your camera. And Gideon Yoder didn't know what I was talking about when I grilled him about your attack."

Without leads, I could see how the investigation might have stalled. "Well, Deputy, we can actually save *you* time." I turned to let Malik reveal our big news.

"We found the video camera!" he proclaimed.

She looked plenty confused now. "Then why are you bothering me?"

"It's been stolen," Malik said. "And we need help recovering it."

"And the theft is your case." I explained about Roger Alton, Craigslist, and my parents. "He's coming back tonight for the money."

That scenario made her pause. "The cost of that camera would definitely push the crime into a felony zone," she said. "And felons can't be granted gun permits."

"That will be the least of his problems," I said. "Because Roger didn't do it alone. *Two* men attacked me. That's why I'm coming to you."

Her eyes narrowed and she followed my implication.

"Earlier that same day," I continued, "a man wanted the video in my camera. And tried to take it from me himself. Looks like he might have gotten it after all."

"The sheriff?" she said. "I heard something about the two of you and a skirmish."

"I had mentioned to him where I'd be staying that night. Guess I might be a witness on a couple levels."

Malik turned on his camera, gave her some earbuds, and played the fresh video of my parents and Roger trying to lock in the camera sale.

"I'll also need to talk to your parents," Deputy Schaefer said. "Now. It'll be getting dark in a few hours. We don't have much time."

CHAPTER 74

My parents waiting in a dark truck for a man with a camera didn't bother me. I did that all the time. A man with a gun was something else.

But my dad insisted. I think he wanted something to brag about to his pals down at the American Legion. "And besides, I already have the cash." He'd flashed ten crisp one-hundred-dollar bills at us.

He wanted to bring his own gun along, but Deputy Schaefer refused. "I'll be in the back of the pickup for insurance. Make the handoff. We'll take it from there. The fewer guns on-site, the better."

She had assembled a team from the state Bureau of Criminal Apprehension. Because of the connection between the sheriff and the suspect, they had arrived to take charge of the stolen-goods sting.

Malik and I parked the van across the street even though the light was bad. My mom was with us, fussing about being left out of the real action.

"But if I'm not there," Mom said, "our guy might get suspicious."

"He'll probably just be relieved." I suspected the real reason she wanted in was to boast to her Red Hat ladies. "You have a good seat here, Mom. They don't want a crowd."

Normally Channel 3 wouldn't get to be on the front lines of a law-enforcement undercover operation, but our camera was at stake, as was my father. We had been warned not to cross the road no matter what happened, and to keep our vehicle lights off.

Bryce had wanted to dispatch a second TV crew, but I thought that would spook the cops and get us evicted from the case.

"If it all goes down well," I said, "you can send someone else to cover the news."

Being the victim of the camera theft made it unwise for me to actually report the story. All sorts of conflicts of interest abounded. But without me, the station would never have the access.

The clock read forty-five minutes before showtime. Malik and I had waited in undercover vans plenty of times during our news careers. We were used to the tedium. Surveillance was also easier for him because he could pee in a bottle. Not that he would do that with my mother along. But having to hold my bladder was not nearly as bad as having to listen to her chatter.

"What time is it now?" she kept asking.

"Shhh, Mom. Not yet."

She worried our guy might not show. She worried Dad might doze off. But I knew all that worry was because there was the potential for shots to be fired.

CHAPTER 75

The SUV was five minutes early. Malik spotted him first.

"Is that him? Is that him?" Mom asked.

"Shhh. No talking," I warned. And to my surprise, she grew quiet.

While we had a dim view, we couldn't hear anything. The state cops didn't want Dad to be wired by us. They made it clear, the operation belonged to them, not us. After all, they were the ones armed with loaded guns. Them and Roger. All we had to shoot was a camera. I was beginning to swear this was a misguided idea, casting my dad as bait. Across the road from the action, I feared the worst. I think all three of us did.

Then, within minutes, the sting was over.

My dad had the camera. Roger had the money. The cops had Roger.

They pressed him against the side of the vehicle, searched and cuffed him. If they found a gun, we couldn't tell. Not even with Malik's special low-light lens.

I would have liked to stand next to Roger to get a sense whether he was the man with the scissors at the Lamplight the other night. I remembered that assailant also had facial hair. But I honestly couldn't gauge either of my attackers' heights, since I was being held down during the entire ordeal.

Staying on our side of the road, Malik and I ran up to the

squad car driven by one of the investigators to try to land an interview. But when I got to the side window, instead of pulling out the handheld microphone from my purse, I mistakenly grabbed the rubber spatula I'd been using for the doomed food-testing story. That got me no respect or sound. Just the tail end of the vehicle disappearing into the night.

Roger wasn't being transported to the nearby Fillmore County Jail. They were taking him up to the Olmsted County Jail in Rochester for questioning. The cops had verified that the serial number on the camera did in fact match the one on my police report. So Roger had some explaining to do.

Except he was kind of drunk.

And instead of demanding an attorney after they read him his rights, Roger apparently started bragging about how, yeah, he and the sheriff had cut that damn TV reporter's hair and stolen her camera.

"Sweet," he said. "Everybody thought Amish did it."

I didn't find all that out until later. And much later, when I watched the interrogation room videotape of the investigator questioning him, their back-and-forth was mildly disturbing.

Roger swayed at the table during his interview.

"Me and Ed flipped a coin to see who got to use the scissors," he said. "I won."

"So stealing the camera was your main plan?" the detective asked.

"Yep. Ed wanted the video. He said I could have the camera. Where is my camera anyway? Oh wait, I sold it. Where is my money?"

((ANCHOR BOX))
CHANNEL 3'S OWN RILEY SPARTZ
IS AT THE CENTER OF A STOLEN
CAMERA CASE THAT MIGHT BE

CONNECTED TO A COUNTY SHERIFF
IN SOUTHERN MINNESOTA.

At the time, all I knew was the camera was ours again and Channel 3 had an explosive story.

When we tried to get a reaction from the sheriff, we learned he was also being questioned. Technically, he wasn't under arrest. And his mug shot wasn't on file yet. All that would come later. As would the other troubling development in the Sarah Yoder homicide that Sheriff Eide was keeping quiet from his constituents.

While the DNA tests had come back negative for Brian Kueppers, the results had also come back negative for Ike Hochstetler.

The sheriff had been so set on solving a murder before the election that when the science didn't match, he figured it best to wait until voters had gone to the polls and reelected him before breaking the news that a killer still roamed free.

CHAPTER 76

The counterfeit Amish scandal had angered the residents of Harmony, but infamy can be good for business. This was normally a slow time for tourists, but the town was booming. Visitors were also delighted by the weather. Mild temperatures had melted much of the early snowfall and dry leaves and grass now loomed over the southeastern corner of Minnesota.

Malik and I had both spent the night at the Lamplight. My parents had wanted us to stay out at the farm, but I had an errand to finish in Harmony. The way I had left things with Gideon Yoder was ugly. I wanted to return cool and apologetic for my remarks regarding him and my hair.

We drove in the yard and I headed toward the barn. He was standing by the dairy cows, using a gas engine to operate some milking machinery. I didn't want to start an argument, so I motioned him outside, away from the noise.

He followed but did not look pleased to see me. I expected him to order me gone immediately, so I spoke fast. "I'm sorry, Gideon."

He seemed surprised at my comment, and I kept talking so my message would be clear.

"I'm not here to pick another fight," I said. "I accused you of some things that weren't true. All that stuff I said about my hair and camera, I jumped to conclusions about you and that wasn't fair."

He stared at me like he suspected that this might be a trick. Because he remained quiet, I had to continue talking. "I just wanted to apologize, Gideon. And end things on a better note between us."

Then he held out his hand, and we shook. "I forgive you," he said.

Being forgiven by Gideon made me uncomfortable. And thanking him seemed too weird. So I just nodded. He walked toward the house and I walked back to the van. Each to our very separate lives. Neither wanting to meet up again.

Malik rolled down the window when I got close. "How'd it go? I saw the handshake."

"Yeah, okay." The forgiving part really bothered me. Made me feel like a loser. But I sort of was. I wanted to be a good sport and not look back, but I heard rushed footsteps on the porch and curiosity kicked in. Miriam was standing next to Gideon, not realizing her voice carried across the yard.

"What did the English want?" she asked.

We couldn't understand his answer.

"Apologize?" Her voice sounded disbelieving. "She apologized?"

Gideon nodded and we heard him say something about cameras and cutting hair.

"Did she ask about Sarah?"

He shook his head. "Maybe at last, Mamm, it is finished." They both went inside and shut the door.

Even worse was when we drove down the road and met Hannah walking to school. She was in a hurry and couldn't dawdle, because the bell was already ringing. But when she saw me wave, she raced over to the van, calling, "Hallo."

"Did you bring me a picture of my sister?" she asked.

I had completely forgotten. But clearly my promise had stuck in her mind.

"I'm sorry, Hannah. I didn't realize I would be coming out this way so I don't have one along. But I will bring it next time."

I stopped short of saying, "I promise," because I'd already promised once and she'd seen a test of my reliability.

"How are you doing without her?" I knew Amish often didn't discuss the dead after burial, and sensed this might be proving difficult for her. In fact, I was certain she wanted to talk about Sarah.

"Hannah?" I wished the two of us were alone, without Malik. Maybe then we'd make better headway.

But the school bell rang again and she looked past us like we were annoying English tourists, and ran away swinging her lunch pail.

CHAPTER 77

My paper towel had just landed in the trash when Nicole entered the ladies' room at the station in a rush. Seconds later she was retching, her head over a toilet.

"Are you okay?" I asked.

Normally the desk dislikes us going home sick. But reporters throwing up on air are even more unpopular, so I suggested that maybe she should head home.

"No, Riley, I'll be fine." She glanced under the stalls. "Are we alone?"

"Totally." I handed her a wet towel for her face. "Maybe we should go next door to the greenroom and spiff you up. The lighting is much better there."

"It happened again, Riley. Just like you said."

I didn't follow her immediately. But then I understood. "Did he?"

"Yes, he sexted me again. Do you want to see . . . him?" She reached in her purse for her phone.

"No, Nicole, absolutely not. Put it away." With a row of toilets handy, a picture of Bryce would be enough to make me barf, too.

We discussed her next move. "Right now, Nicole, he could claim a single incident. A misunderstanding. That he hit the wrong Send button. That someone hacked his account. I think he'll continue messing with you, and you'll build a stronger harassment case against him if you wait."

"I'm not sure what I want to do," she said. "There's so much that could go wrong."

We discussed her biggest fear. If she reported him, any investigation might get messy. She could be labeled within the television industry as a troublemaker.

"I don't have a heavy-hitter news reputation to fall back on like you, Riley. I'm just a rookie. I could lose my career over this."

"But it's also possible women at other stations might come forward with the same story," I said. "Believe me, he sexts me, and he's finished."

"Maybe that's why he's bothering me instead of you," she said. "Maybe he senses I'm a coward."

"You may be cautious, but you're no coward. And he doesn't realize we're a team."

Nicole decided to keep quiet for now. And since all the evidence was hers, that was her call. I decided not to pressure her, but simply advised her to hold on to the texts.

I also threw in a little undercover training. "The next time you go into his office, videotape the encounter with your cell phone." I showed her how to tuck her phone in her purse pocket with the lens sticking up. "Set your bag on the table across from his desk. Let Bryce do the talking, and get him to confirm that's him in the photo."

Just then the GM's assistant came in. We shut up and turned on the faucets and washed our hands. Because the water was cool, and our topic of conversation had been on the slimy side, I used plenty of soap.

While scrubbing, I remembered seeing references in the restaurant inspection reports to water temperature. I realized public bathrooms must have codes of how hot is too hot and how cold is too cold when it came to water. I wondered how many famous buildings around town met the standards. It wasn't food, but it might be easier to win Bryce's approval.

• • •

As I walked through the Minneapolis skyway to the city health department I daydreamed about how best to handle Bryce. I was torn between two films in which women teach men a lesson. *Nine to Five* versus *The Girl with the Dragon Tattoo*. I fantasized about imprisoning Bryce at home and running the newsroom my way in his absence. But there was a certain appeal in obtaining revenge by tattooing something mean on his torso.

The Minneapolis health inspector who had helped me with the restaurant files sympathized when he heard my story wasn't working out. I didn't tell him about the advertiser angle. I was ashamed to let anyone outside the station know.

But when he heard I was interested in water temperatures in public bathrooms, he loaned me a professional digital thermometer and told me the water needed to be between 110 and 130 degrees. Not too hot and not too cold.

"To kill germs, right?" I asked.

He shook his head. "Water doesn't kill germs." He explained that comfortable water temperatures make people more likely to wash hands, preventing the spread of illness. "It's the soap and scrubbing that removes germs."

So on my way back to Channel 3, I checked water temperatures at the bathrooms in city hall, the library, and the courthouse. As soon as I got back to the station I went straight to the ladies' room.

Aha, I thought to myself. Too cold. Just as I suspected.

A few minutes later I was telling Bryce my plan for checking bathroom water temperature at the state capitol, the Minnesota Zoo, even the airport. "This should be easy, we simply report the numbers. And the good part is government agencies can't sue the media."

Then I told him the punch line.

((RILEY SOT))
AND AMONG THE BUILDINGS WE
TESTED WAS CHANNEL 3. AND
GUESS WHAT WE FOUND IN OUR
LADIES' ROOM? THE WATER WAS
TOO COLD BY TEN DEGREES.

"We're not running that," Bryce said.

"Viewers love it when we admit our own flaws," I said. "And besides, maybe we'll get the problem fixed around here."

But my boss had his own idea. "If the whole point of the story is to encourage viewers to wash hands, let's set up hidden cameras in public bathrooms and do a 'gotcha' when they don't."

This was such a bad plan, I didn't know where to begin. So I stuck to the basics. "The legality of hidden camera use hinges on whether the person being recorded has a reasonable expectation of privacy. Nowhere would the expectation of privacy be higher than in a bathroom. If we aired someone not washing their hands, and us confronting them about it, they could sue us for invasion of privacy and would probably end up owning the television station."

I could tell Bryce wasn't sure whether to believe me or not. He picked up his phone and dialed an extension. "Miles, don't come down. Just answer one question. Can we put hidden cameras in public restrooms to see if people wash hands?" I couldn't hear Miles's answer, but Bryce hung up almost immediately.

"I'll have to get back to you about the water temperature story, Riley."

For the first time in any of our closed-door office meetings, Bryce kept to his side of the desk. Probably smart, because if he'd come within an arm's reach of me, instead of slapping a high five, he'd have landed a black eye.

CHAPTER 78

Fumbling for a calculator to double-check my mileage expenses, I found Sarah's journal in my desk drawer. Even though the language was foreign, turning the pages took me back to Harmony and her murder.

That reminded me of her forensic drawing. I made a couple photocopies of it and tucked them in my bag in case I ever crossed paths with her little sister again.

Homicides—even when solved—always leave unanswered questions.

I considered mailing Sarah's notebook to her mother anonymously. Let her think angels sent her daughter's final words from heaven.

I called Garnett. As a security official in our nation's capital, he might have a colleague who spoke German, although Arabic and Chinese were more highly valued in government these days.

"Hi, honey," I said.

"What's wrong?" he asked.

"Nothing, why do you assume something is wrong just because I call? Maybe I'm just missing you."

"Are you?" he asked.

"Yeah, Nick. I am."

I realized that was the truth. And at that moment, if he had suggested we spend the rest of our lives together, I would have said yes. But our conversation didn't venture in that direction.

"You usually don't call during the day unless there's a problem, Riley."

He sounded busy and that broke any romantic mood, so I stuck to business.

"Well, I need some advice. You don't know anybody who can translate German, do you?"

"I do, but so do you. What do you need?"

I told him about Sarah's notebook, and he told me cops like diaries in violent crimes to help establish victimology.

"If your homicide had been unsolved, I'd have said you hit the jackpot because fewer people keep such records anymore. Facebook is the diary of today."

"Except, Nick, I can't read any of what Sarah wrote. It really is a secret diary."

Then he told me about a free online website that translates different languages. English to German. German to English. Italian, Russian, Spanish.

"The wording might not always be perfect," he said. "But it's probably good enough for your purpose."

We said our goodbyes and I searched the Internet. The website was slick. *"Ja, Deutsch,"* I said, selecting the German-to-English program. Typing Sarah's last entry was awkward because the letters did not come naturally to my fingers. Luckily she had beautiful penmanship that was easy to read.

2. Oktober

Ich habe beschlossen, dass ich morgen zur Polizei gehe. Ich habe keine Angst, die Wahrheit zu offenbaren. Soll er sich doch verteidigen.

I hit the translate key and immediately Sarah's story unfolded.

"I have decided tomorrow I will go to the English law. I am not afraid to reveal the truth. Let him be judged."

Her last account verified what we had suspected. Sarah had

discovered the fraud under way at Everything Amish. I imagined she felt conflicted. If she lost her job, she might be forced to return home. How Ike found out she was preparing to turn him in was irrelevant.

But since I was snooping and this online translation was so simple, I decided to keep typing because the whole process made me feel like a foreign agent.

1. Oktober

Die Arbeit im Geschäft ist nicht, was ich erwartet habe. Aber nächste Woche habe ich genug Geld, um mein neues Leben anzufangen.

"The store work is not what I expected. But next week I will have money to start my new life."

Translating was addictive. Instant gratification.

September 30—Sarah wrote about a man preparing to leave for war—presumably Brian Kueppers—and shopping for a gift for his wife. He promised to come back with her to pick out a table.

Er fragte, ob ich wirklich amisch sei. Ich wusste nicht, was ich sagen sollte. Bin ich amisch?

"He asked if I was real Amish. I didn't know how to answer. Am I?"

Instead of continuing backward. I turned to the front of the diary to begin fresh with Sarah's life in chronological order. Then I might better understand the context of her remarks.

24. September

Ach Gott, Ich muss hier weg. Ich habe versucht zu verzeihen, aber ich kann nicht . . .

"Oh God, I must leave. I have tried to forgive, but cannot. And living among them, yet isolated from their company, is hardship. They have put the bann on me. So I will make my plans to flee. Apology is not enough. I worry for Hannah and will work to come back for her."

The next entry seemed to show an attempt at humor.

25. September

Es macht mir nichts aus, dass mein Bruder . . .

"I don't mind my brother not speaking to me, or sharing food at my plate. The good thing of the bann means he must avoid me."

Sarah wrote of struggling with her decision to join the Amish church by baptism. I regretted never getting to know her personally. Of all the murder victims I covered, she still remained the most mysterious.

But diaries were traditionally a place to hide secrets. Maybe Sarah wanted to share one with me.

Ich liess mich taufen, damit ich unterrichten kann . . .

"I chose baptism so I could teach. Now with the bann I am disallowed. Shunning by the church is more pain than my family. And I fear for Hannah. At school I could protect her."

The next entry was more emotional—even creepier—than the previous ones.

Ich dachte, der Bann war vorbei, als Mamm in mein Zimmer kam . . .

"I thought Mamm was ending the bann when she came into my room. But no. She opened the Bible and made me read aloud the Matthew verse: Then Peter came to Jesus and asked, 'Lord, how many times shall I forgive my brother when he sins against me? Up to seven times?' Jesus answered, 'I tell you, not seven times, but seventy-seven times.'

"Then she shut the book and left me. In the morning darkness, it was the same. No one greeted me. Or made room at the table. I peeled potatoes but they would not eat them."

Sarah's writing was making me squirm. Was Miriam focused on the issue of forgiveness in the broadest sense? Or did she mean "brother" literally? I felt shivers as I continued to type the German.

27. September

Gestern Abend, als der Mond schien und alle schliefen, bin ich weg . . .

"Last night when the moon shone and my family slept I fled.

First I had practiced silence on the steps and doors. I walked miles to an old house in town. I had heard talk she would house Amish who leave the church. I did not want to wake anyone. So I waited hours on the steps outside until I saw a light. When I knocked she gave me a room."

28. September

Die Frau hat mich nichts gefragt . . .

"The lady at the house didn't ask questions. She helped me find work at a large Amish store outside town. The owner didn't mind I dressed Amish. He said it was good for business. When I earn money I will buy new English clothes."

The next entry wrote of being torn about keeping quiet or going to the law. And it wasn't reporting counterfeit Amish goods that had her divided.

Verzeihen oder beschuldigen? Was ist härter?

"Forgive or accuse? Which is harder?"

And as I continued to type Sarah's words, the translation horrified me.

Gideon had been raping Sarah. For years.

In der Scheune hat er mich überwältigt.

"In the barn, he held me down."

And Miriam knew.

Kämpfe mehr. Bete mehr . . .

"'Fight harder. Pray harder.' That's how Mamm told me to stop him."

She related how Bishop Stoltzfus made Gideon apologize for his acts. Just like the other Amish church leaders in Ohio and Iowa. And Sarah was ordered to forgive him. Just like all the other times.

Aber dieses Mal habe ich mich geweigert . . .

"But this time I refused."

And that's why they were shunning Sarah.

CHAPTER 79

Sarah's tale of abuse and cover-up made me wonder how people who profess to be so God-fearing can be so god-awful. Did Gideon kill his sister to keep her quiet?

Hovering over the English translation, I printed each page of the diary, and reread each line. Garnett was right about victim-ology coming alive in words by the deceased.

Gideon soll meine Schreie in seinen Albträumen hören . . .

"May Gideon hear my screams in his nightmares."

I had no firsthand knowledge of the abuse and this evidence alone could not convict, but I owed it to Sarah to investigate further.

Yes, her written words might be admitted at trial, but Sarah could not be cross-examined. Gideon could not be forced to incriminate himself. Same story with Miriam, unless the state offered her a deal. I'd hate to see that, but there might be no choice. Without corroborating evidence, the sexual assault case against Gideon would be weak.

Unless another witness could be found.

And I was convinced I knew one. Hannah.

The child seemed fearful. And in her writing, Sarah seemed to allude to a reason for her apprehension. Did Hannah miss her sister, distrust her mother, or dread her brother?

Each time I'd seen the little girl, I'd concentrated on the obvious, first question. Next time we met, I'd push her deeper for answers to the more intrusive queries.

As for her other two family members and their objections to the drawing of Sarah, did they really not like seeing her face because of their Amish aversion to pride, or did staring at her make them feel guilty?

Just then Garnett rang to see how the diary translation was going. "As a former homicide cop, I'm still curious about our victim."

"It's real bad." I told him our murder victim appeared to also be a victim of incest. I read him the last entry of the diary: 'I have decided tomorrow I will go to the English law.' Who was she prepared to turn in? Her boss for fraud or her brother for rape?"

"What does your gut tell you?"

"I've never liked the brother. He creeped me out from the start."

That's when I revealed to Garnett that I had been fond enough of Ike Hochstetler to kiss him. "So I was quite surprised when he turned out to be her killer, and almost mine."

Kissing and telling proved to be a bad idea. Garnett was angry, I could tell, even from a thousand miles away.

"So you kissed the first guy who leered at you? Did his Amish past seem exotic?"

"You and I were broken up, Nick."

"Not totally," he responded. "We'd started talking again. And I'd offered to fly back and make up. Was he why you turned me down?"

"Maybe I kissed Ike as a test. Just to see if anyone else had the same spark we do."

"And did he? Riley?"

Garnett thought my pause meant yes, but I was actually trying to recall Ike's lips. I did remember enjoying him enough that we almost went all the way in his sports car. But I also recalled being repulsed by his final touch. I thought best not to share either nuance with Garnett.

"Did you sleep with him?" he said.

"No." That answer came without pause. But even immediately was too late. Garnett was furious he'd had to ask.

"Well, just for your information, Ms. Spartz, I've got someone in Washington who I kiss."

"Who?" I wasn't sure if he was telling the truth, or trying to hurt me because I'd hurt him.

"None of your business," he said.

"Of course it's my business, Nick. We slept together just the other night. If you've kissed someone since then, you'll never kiss me again."

That night I slept poorly. Nick probably did, too. At least, that's what I told myself as I stared alone at the stars. Our affair could not end this unhappily-ever-after. Or could it?

This was another one of those times a loyal dog curled next to me would have made the hours go by faster. Instead, a parade of star-crossed literary lovers kept me awake. Romeo and Juliet. Catherine and Heathcliff. Adam and Eve. By the time I got to Jack and Ennis from *Brokeback Mountain* I was convinced Nick Garnett and I were history.

I hoped Husky was happy down at the farm.

CHAPTER 80

My cell phone buzzed the next morning at work, but it wasn't Garnett. He hadn't called me and I hadn't called him. I was working up how best to tell Bryce about Sarah's diary when Nicole texted. Her message read :) instead of *.

Curious, I texted back: Meet in basement. I didn't want too many people to look back and recall us hanging around together in case the Bryce situation got ugly.

The Channel 3 lower level featured dark and lonely hallways with storage rooms tucked in undesirable corners. The photo lounge, just off the elevator, was the only habitable spot. I put my finger against my lip to signal Nicole to follow me silently to a large space with cement floors and high ceilings. Boxes with dates and story slugs scrawled on the sides were stacked everywhere, covered with dust.

"What is this place?" she asked.

"It's the old news graveyard."

Channel 3 preserved investigative files and tapes five years against possible litigation. Some stations were moving toward purging all video immediately so they wouldn't have to deal with subpoenas. But I always felt that if I ever got sued, my work was my best defense.

We each sat on a box behind a wall of other boxes in dim light.

"So what happened?" I asked.

"Riley, it worked just like you predicted. Watch."

Nicole held out her cell-phone screen toward me. A bouncy shot through the newsroom made up the opening scene. Then Bryce greeted her and instructed her to close the door. The bag camera was off center, but adequate. When he sat, his face was visible.

"I've been thinking, Nicole." He reached across his desk and tapped his finger against her nose like she was a small child.

"Yes, Bryce?" It must have taken a lot of willpower for her not to try rubbing the germs off. But she stayed still and let him talk.

"Even though you're still technically on probation, maybe I should rotate you behind the anchor desk for a day. I'd love to see how you do as a lead anchor."

"Really? Me?" Dangling the anchor job in front of her wasn't what she was expecting Bryce to do. Her voice sounded more thrilled than I liked, but she was at that stage of her career where lead anchor sounded seductive.

"I don't see why not?" he answered. "I sense you might have that special camera magic that lights up a TV screen."

But then she remembered her mission. "Speaking of cameras, Bryce, is that really you in those pictures you keep sending me?"

"Do you like?" he asked.

"To be honest, not really. Women aren't into photos of male nudity."

"You prefer the real thing?" He stood behind his desk and while his face was no longer in view, his fingers undid the top button on his pants.

"No, no," she said. "Please, don't."

"Oh, not here. I understand. You don't like mixing business with pleasure." He started moving in her direction and she grabbed her handbag.

"I just remembered, Bryce, I have an interview at city hall. I need to run."

Her voice lost that marvelous broadcast quality and turned shrill. Her last words blurred together in a panic, and the video kept rolling chaotically as she dashed out of his office and into the elevator.

I wasn't sure what to say to Nicole. All I could think was that we were definitely working for a pig.

"On a whole lot of levels, you handled that well, Nicole. And for hidden camera work, the quality was amazing. You'd make a fabulous one-man band."

She smiled coyly, like she was weighing my compliment, but she was really fishing for something else. "Do you think I'd make a fabulous anchor?"

"You're not thinking—"

"Well, somebody's going to get the job, Riley. Why not me? He might not have a choice." She waved her cell phone, craftily.

"Blackmail is wrong. Instead of punishing him, you'd be part of the problem."

"So what should I do?" she asked.

I suggested she march up to the GM's office and show him the video and the sexts and get Bryce his pink slip. She told me she'd think about it. If the video were mine, I might be tempted to switch it with a newscast tape so it would roll on the air for all to see—a little personal revenge mixed with public ridicule.

Back in the elevator, I got a text from Bryce. I didn't want to look at it, so Nicole peeked and read that he wanted me to come to his office.

"You're not going to mention me to him, are you?" she asked.

"Absolutely not," I assured her.

Minutes later, I was sitting across from Bryce, skimming a handful of papers he referred to as my "job review."

"Have you actually supervised me long enough to evaluate me?" I asked.

"I think I have, and I believe in giving timely employee feed-back."

He had ranked me as Meets Expectations in three areas and Needs to Improve in four others including teamwork, news judgment, technical skill, and on-air appearance.

This was the first employment review I'd had in years. Noreen had thought all that paperwork was a waste of time. I figured Bryce was laying a paper trail so that my contract wouldn't be renewed.

"Didn't I exceed your expectation anywhere?" I asked.

"No," he said. "But this will give you something to work toward."

The only thing I wanted to work toward was finding a new job and a new boss. Unless Nicole could get rid of this one ASAP.

Luckily the weekend was only a few hours away. I had already decided to drive down to the farm and surprise my parents. At that moment, I had no idea of the surprise that awaited me.

CHAPTER 81

The Amish schoolhouse looked empty from the road and even emptier through the window. The room's accessories reminded me of my own early education years. Blackboard, American flag, and wall rack with hooks for hats and coats. The wooden lift-top desks looked exactly like the ones in my country school.

I'd hoped to catch up with Hannah near school, rather than at home. I wasn't ready to confront Gideon concerning his dead sister's last written words.

Eyeing the path Hannah was most likely to walk, I spotted a little white head bouncing through a harvested farm field so I parked where she'd likely exit.

"Hannah," I called her name from my car when she became closer.

She looked at me dubiously, keeping her distance. Probably because she didn't recognize my vehicle: I'd always driven a van before. But when I waved a laminated sketch of Sarah, she approached, reaching for the picture. She fingered the plastic coating uncertainly, checking the front and back.

"This way it will stay nice for you, Hannah. Even if you have to keep your sister's picture hidden outside."

"*Danke.*" She kissed her sister on her penciled lips.

"Do you have a minute to chat about Sarah?"

I opened the car door and patted the seat beside me, realizing she'd probably been instructed not to talk to English or get into cars with strangers. She glanced around up and down the road. No other vehicles, buggy or motorized, were in sight. So she climbed inside.

"My name's Riley." I wasn't sure how to proceed. "I've been telling your sister's story for the news." Under some circumstances, I could be accused of child abduction. Best to just start talking and see if the child joined in. "Did Sarah and Gideon ever have problems?"

Hannah didn't answer. She merely ran her finger over the outline of her sister's sketch, as if committing the pieces of her face to memory.

"You and Sarah sure look like sisters," I said. "And it sounds like you had fun with her. Tell me about Gideon."

I didn't want to be specific, because I didn't want to plant ideas. The girl was nervous, that much was clear. But whether Hannah was uncomfortable about being in my car or talking about her brother, who could tell?

"Gideon is mean."

If she mentioned the word "touch" along with her brother's name, I was prepared to drive her and Sarah's diary to the county child protection services.

"How is he mean?" I asked.

But Hannah merely fidgeted, without offering specifics.

"Have you told this to your mother?"

Soon, her mother might worry about her. And question her about why she was late. Hannah must have had the same fears. She rolled the picture inside her lunch pail, then opened the car door to leave.

"If there is anything I can do to help you, Hannah, I will." I realized building up the kind of trust needed for this conversation might take time. "I'd like to talk more about this when you're not in such a hurry. Is there any place we might see each other again?"

She stared straight at me, like she was judging me. Then she apparently made a decision. "Tonight, I'm going to the corn maze." For the first time since we met, she sounded enthusiastic.

"The corn maze is a great time." I saw potential for us to meet among the twists and turns. "Will all three of you be there?"

She nodded. "We went last year." Then she paused. "Sarah, too."

The corn maze was low-tech family entertainment for autumn. No devil's tail or other technology afoot there. Just good old-fashioned family fun.

"As it turns out," I said, "I'm also going to be at the corn maze tonight. Should our paths cross, maybe we can duck away to chat in the rows of corn. But if your mother or brother are around, act like you don't know me."

She nodded to show she understood. I was the kind of friend her family wouldn't approve of.

CHAPTER 82

I could feel it in the air: a storm was coming. Distant shimmers of lightning flashed across the sky, out of season. But the climate had been unusual this autumn. As a child, during quiet weather, I remembered my grandpa teasing me about listening carefully to hear the corn grow.

But tonight, shrieks of delight came from the fields. Young and old visitors arrived to tour Maze of Mystery. Horses and buggies were hitched across from motor vehicles.

But no sign of the Yoder family.

The Amish were hard to distinguish from each other with their uniform garb, so I kept close watch for the trio. Finally, I saw them clutching their tickets, and followed them inside the corn maze.

I kept quiet and distant, surprised to see Miriam carrying a kerosene lantern from the buggy. A sign by the entrance the other day had cautioned No Open Flames, but technically her fire was enclosed by glass and steel.

As for me, I had a flashlight tucked in my purse.

Staying behind the Yoders proved easy for the next half hour. Then the three split up, apparently racing each other among the corn stalks for the exit.

Hannah disappeared with a pack of other children, so even though she was the one I most wanted to talk to, I decided to stick with Miriam. I would confront her about what I found in Sarah's diary. She moved slowly, like she was giving the rest of her family a head start. Using her lantern, she also paused to admire scarecrows holding scythes and pumpkin decorations displayed along the paths.

I didn't want to stall too long before approaching her directly, in case she caught up with the other two. So I hid off the path, lurking in the corn, waiting for her to come my way.

"Hello, Miriam," I called out a minute later.

She didn't recognize me in the dark, so I shined the flashlight on my face. Then on hers. Seeing me, she looked upset.

"It's me, Riley Spartz."

"You?" Miriam swung the lantern back and forth, as if checking to see if anyone else might interrupt us and rescue her.

"Back with your devil's tongue?" she whispered. "You said Sarah could rest. Your English questions would end. Yet here you are."

That was the most I'd ever heard Miriam say in one stretch.

"Except I found this. So I had to return." I showed her Sarah's journal and flipped through the pages so she could place her handwriting. "I know now why you were shunning your daughter. She wrote down the evil things her brother did to her. Apparently you found it easier to forgive him than her."

Miriam didn't ask what I was talking about. She already knew.

She reached for the notebook. "Her words belong to me. I am her mother."

"No." I clutched the diary tight to my chest. "This is evidence. Sarah wrote what happened between her and Gideon. And you. How could you protect your son, and leave your daughter in such danger?"

I knew the answer even though she remained quiet. In the Amish culture, men were dominant and women submissive. This was proof.

"Even worse than his abuse, have you considered that he probably killed Sarah?"

"No." She shook her head, and the lantern waved erratically. I moved to the center of the path, putting space between me, fire, and dry corn tassels.

"Have you ever asked him?" I said. "Or were you afraid of the answer?"

"She had no need," said a voice from behind me. Gideon stood watching us. "She knows I didn't commit murder."

Gideon was armed with a weapon, a scythe, apparently stolen from one of the scarecrows.

With wooden shaft and curved metal blade, scythes were the preferred tool for mowing grass or reaping crops centuries ago. I had dismissed these as mere props, but just then Gideon swung the edge at a row of corn and with a whoosh sound, cut the stalks clean.

Suddenly, Gideon looked less like an Amish man and more like the Grim Reaper.

Medieval folklore always depicted Death holding a scythe as a harvester of souls. At that moment, I had no doubt Gideon had slain Sarah. Now Death was stalking me.

"I know you killed your sister, Gideon."

"That I did not."

By now, the maze seemed empty of other visitors. And we were farthest from the exit. The odds of an outsider intervening were slim. But I spoke loudly, just in case.

"I have read her journal, Gideon. I know what you did. And you wanted her to forgive your abuse. I would not have pardoned you either."

"I did not kill her."

He swung, and like a razor, the scythe came close to my arm.

"Yet you almost killed me now."

He didn't disagree.

"She was going to turn you in to the English law," I said.

"That's why you turned from molester to murderer. Did you confess that sin to your church?"

He screamed at me to stop, then took another plunge with the blade. I held my purse out for protection and he slit it, contents spilling onto the ground, including my cell phone.

I was afraid to turn and run, because the time I needed to pivot would be all the time he needed to kill. To survive, I needed to keep my eye on the scythe.

All I could do was back up. Slowly and carefully. But defense seldom saves lives. I needed to act. But how? I had no weapon. Fumbling in a side pocket of my purse, all I could find was the cursed rubber spatula. I flung it at him.

As he laughed, I noticed Gideon's pacing becoming predictable. Swing. Pause. Swing.

Then I remembered Xiong's glorious martial-arts kick in the alley behind the Hmong quilt house. If I kicked Gideon where it hurt men most, just as the blade finished its arc, I might escape the maze alive.

CHAPTER 83

Stop blaming my son." This time, Miriam's voice came from behind me. I felt like the Yoders had me surrounded.

Miriam chose that moment to distract me from my counter-attack on Gideon by claiming that she had killed Sarah. I had a hard time seeing this as a case of maternal filicide—child murder—but then I remembered Miriam tearing the head off my Amish doll. So I kept quiet to hear her story.

Gideon also appeared intent on listening to what his mother had to say because his scythe swing slowed. For safety, I kept my eye on him. For reparation, I kept my ears on her.

"I went to save her soul." Miriam recounted an ill-fated visit to Everything Amish and how hopeful she felt seeing Sarah still garbed in apron and bonnet.

"The buggy is waiting outside, I told her. But she refused to follow. 'No, Mamm,' she told me, 'I am staying here.'"

"I assured her she would be welcomed back to the church when she knelt and confessed her error. All would be forgiven, and she would be able to teach school." Miriam wiped her eyes. "Hannah missed her sister so much."

But Sarah had apparently held fast to her decision to remain with the English. An argument ensued between them, Miriam calling her daughter "insolent."

"No, Mamm. I am not the one damaging our family."

Miriam explained that during the shunning, Sarah had seemed her most docile. She puzzled, how could her daughter have changed so much in so few days? And she panicked when she heard Sarah's plan.

"I'm going to tell the English about Gideon," Sarah had told her. "I have made up my mind. This will protect Hannah. They will remove him or they will remove her. Our family secret will be finished."

"I told her she must keep quiet." Reliving the scene was upsetting to Miriam, and she moved closer toward her son. "But Sarah would not listen. I told her she was also to blame."

"Me? Blame?" Sarah had apparently reacted with shock in that appraisal from her mother. I also was stunned by Miriam's attributing the guilt to her daughter.

"Bishop Stoltzfus and I have discussed this," Miriam had said. "The trouble with you and Gideon has happened so many times for so many years, you must also be at fault."

Gideon had stopped swinging the scythe. I wasn't sure whether it was because he agreed or disagreed with his mother about the blame. Since he seemed momentarily catatonic, I stole a glance at Miriam. She was crying as she reiterated their final encounter, and how Sarah had suddenly accused her.

"Me? How about you, Mamm? Scolding me for the sins of my brother. You are to blame for him. You should have stopped this long ago."

Miriam put her head in her hands, the kerosene lantern wobbling. I imagined her headache was also a heartache. Every night as she tried to sleep she probably heard Sarah's words repeated. *You are to blame for him.*

That's when Miriam stopped talking. However the tale ended, it seemed too painful for her to continue. But news stories need closure and reporters need answers.

"What happened next?" I asked her.

Miriam didn't answer.

"How did Sarah die?" I continued.

She looked at Gideon, even though I was the one with the persistent questions. He volunteered nothing to defend or accuse his mother. He seemed almost mesmerized by her narrative, like he was hearing some of the details for the first time.

"Miriam, you said you killed Sarah. So how did she die?" I repeated.

That appeared one question too many. Gideon jumped in to end the conversation. "When Sarah left the Amish, she was already dead to us. It makes no difference how she died."

"I imagine it mattered to Sarah," I said. "And I'd like to hear the truth, Miriam, if you're ready to tell it."

"Stop asking your English questions," Gideon said. "My mother has been forgiven by the bishop, she does not have to talk to you."

His talk of forgiveness was interesting. "What did your church forgive you for?" I asked her.

"Don't answer," Gideon said.

"No, I want to speak," Miriam replied. "She fell. We quarreled and Sarah fell."

It seemed a stretch for a young woman to die in a fall, then end up naked in a sinkhole. But Miriam insisted it was an accident, and described how she had grabbed her daughter's arm, to take her home.

"She told me, 'I am staying, Mamm. You're the one who should leave,'" Miriam said. "I tried to drag her toward the door, but Sarah pulled away from me."

Everything Amish was crowded with furniture displays. Miriam described how Sarah fell, hitting her head against the corner of a sturdy table. She slid downward, her body collapsing to the floor. There was no blood. Sarah was unconscious, but still breathing. The girl looked like she was merely sleeping.

CHAPTER 84

I tried waking her," Miriam continued. "But Sarah didn't move."

"Did you consider calling for help?" I asked. "The store has a telephone."

I knew it wasn't that simple. The Amish were not conditioned to seek medical help during emergencies. They tended to wait it out, and see if the condition improved on its own.

"I thought this was God's way of returning my daughter to me," she said. "I would take her home, and when Sarah woke, she would be glad to be back with her family."

Everything Amish was closing soon. So Miriam alternated between dragging and carrying the girl to the backseat of the buggy. She had yanked a quilt down from the middle of a hanging row on sale and used it to cover Sarah.

"I had wanted to keep her warm," she said.

I didn't ask her whether she also wanted to ensure no one else would see her passenger. Knowing it was unusual for Miriam to be out alone after dark, I pictured her angst as she drove the whole way back to the farm.

She ignored me to glance over at her son as she recounted the happenings of that night, recalling that Gideon had been waiting to take the reins when she arrived home. "He started to ask where I'd been, but I cut him off and ordered him to help me bring his sister inside."

But it was too late. When they pulled back the quilt to check on Sarah, she stared at them accusingly from the back of the buggy. Her eyes were glassy, her body limp. I recalled the medical examiner's conclusion about blunt-force trauma and bleeding on the brain and knew from past cases how unpredictable such injuries could be. At least, Sarah had died quickly.

"I didn't want Hannah to see her, so we pulled the buggy into the barn," Miriam explained, "while we thought about what to do."

No doubt, Sarah's death would mean unwelcome questions from outsiders. I imagined Miriam felt conflicting emotions: guilt and relief. Essentially, she had to decide between her daughter and her son. Except she had already chosen long ago.

"So which one of you had the idea to hide her body?" I asked.

Gideon spoke: "We both agreed it best."

"I asked him to leave Sarah and I alone for a few minutes," she said.

Sarah had wanted to be English, so she would be. Miriam erased her Amish identity by unbinding her hair and removing her garments. Unclothed and decomposed, it would be harder to identify Sarah.

"When I took off her bonnet, I felt a bump on the back of her head." Miriam gave a small sob. She was ashamed of her daughter's nakedness. "So I rolled her in the quilt, and told Gideon to hide her someplace where she would be thought English if found."

And that was how Sarah ended up in the sinkhole.

In the minds of the Amish, English frequently died from violent crimes. The Yoders' hope was for Sarah to rot and never be recognized as Amish again. To anyone who inquired about her whereabouts, they would shrug and simply reply that she was in the bann and had left their world. Eventually the questions would stop. People would forget about Sarah.

But they did not. Her anonymity was short-lived.

By the end of the story, Gideon had remembered he held a scythe. And his next swing demonstrated he had a much worse scheme in mind than cutting off my hair. Visions of the headless Amish doll came to my mind.

"Is your mother telling the truth, Gideon? If you're not a killer, then prove it by not killing me. Amish reject violence. Don't let her destroy your faith."

He seemed momentarily confused, so as he swung, I made my move for survival. Thrusting my foot outward, while twisting backward, I attempted the critical kick—and messed up. Without practice, without Xiong, such combat did not come naturally to me. Instead of striking Gideon, my kick hit the kerosene lantern Miriam was holding. The glass broke, fuel and flame flew into the dry corn, and within seconds the maze was on fire.

I heard a scream, but it wasn't mine. Or Miriam's. Or Gideon's.

The screams came from Hannah. I don't know how long the little girl had crouched amid the stalks, watching our altercation, but definitely too long.

CHAPTER 85

Almost immediately, I smelled smoke. Nearby stalks and tassels were fully engulfed. And the fire was spreading fast throughout the field, much faster than any forest fire I'd ever covered. In the darkness, the danger was vivid. If I waited much longer, I'd be smelling burnt flesh as well as burnt corn.

Gideon and his mother were on one side of the flames, Hannah and I on the other. I grabbed the little girl's hand and ran.

I didn't think about the other two. And maybe that was wrong, but a nine-year-old and I were racing death and losing. And maybe this was the hell that Miriam and Gideon deserved.

Instead of an exit, our path led to a dead end. Fire followed us close behind, and ahead. I tried a new direction, cutting through the corn.

The heat was almost unbearable. Hannah was holding tight to my waist. Burning was such a bad way to go. And while minutes earlier the flames seemed to light the way out, smoke now formed a thick wall obstructing our vision.

We were both coughing. I tore off Hannah's bonnet and held it over her nose so she could breathe better. I once shot a news story about escaping from a burning building by crawling on the floor, where the air was cooler. That technique didn't seem to work in a cornfield because the flames had fuel to burn, from ground to sky.

Then I remembered my tour of the corn maze. And the employee shortcut. I forced myself to concentrate, which was difficult while surrounded by smoke and sparks. Finally I located the homestead's windmill against the night sky and I got my bearings.

By then Hannah was too weak to walk.

CHAPTER 86

Minutes later, I stumbled out of the maze with the Amish girl clutched in my arms, our clothes blackened, faces blistered, and eyebrows singed.

Firefighters eventually arrived and put a plastic mask over Hannah's face and pumped oxygen into her lungs before an ambulance arrived to take her to the hospital. I tried to tell them two more people were trapped inside, but they could do nothing but let the field burn. All twelve acres of corn maze burned like fire and brimstone. Later reports said flames and smoke could be seen in the darkness more than twenty miles away. Like curious moths, gawkers came to watch.

Neighboring fields and other farm buildings would also have been consumed as the corn maze turned into a raging prairie fire, but then the heavens opened up and the promised storm delivered biblical rain.

People sought cover from the downpour. But to me, the water was refreshing, and diminished the smell of smoke. So I stood, allowing myself to become drenched, welcoming the rainfall. Though the inferno had destroyed the corn maze, the squall could not wash the vivid sights and sounds from my imagination of what it must have been like for Miriam and Gideon to burn alive.

CHAPTER 87

I remained standing, almost numb, as ambulances and squad cars pulled out of the corn maze parking lot, sirens blaring. I couldn't understand what could be more urgent than the chaos underfoot. Then I learned a pickup had crashed into a horse and buggy a couple of miles down the road.

Word spread the truck driver had been speeding toward the fire scene to watch the burn. The buggy, without lighting or a reflective triangle, was almost invisible along the dark route.

I headed toward the collision, but traffic was being directed away from the scene. So I parked and walked up to the police line where pieces of broken wood and wheels lay scattered across the road, illuminated by the flashing lights of emergency vehicles.

I showed my media pass to a state patrol officer who had worked on another accident reconstruction case I'd covered years ago. Then I pointed toward the body of a dead horse along the shoulder. "Was that the only casualty?"

He shook his head, telling me the animal had been euthanized. "And we have a fatal." He explained that the buggy driver, a young Amish man, was dead on the scene. However, his passenger was barely injured. "Sad situation." He gestured toward an Amish woman standing in the headlights of one of the squad cars, talking to another investigator. "But we can't release any names yet."

He didn't have to. Even in the dim light, I had no trouble recognizing Miriam.

EPILOGUE

That Gideon and Miriam fought their way free of the corn maze only to meet with more danger might prove that God believes in making the punishment fit the crime. Undoubtedly, Miriam would suffer more living without her son than dying beside him.

He was buried in the plot next to Sarah's grave. I don't think she'd have welcomed her brother as an eternal neighbor, but Miriam made the arrangements. I steered clear of his funeral.

Unfortunately, Sarah's diary did burn. And while I had printed copies of her words and the translation, not having her writing in her own hand damaged the credibility of any sexual abuse charges. And while Amish typically steer away from English law, this was one time the English wanted nothing to do with Amish crime.

The bishop refused to discuss Sarah's shunning. And without victim or perpetrator alive, there wasn't much to accomplish by continuing any investigation of molestation.

Officially, Sarah's homicide remains unsolved. Miriam refused to speak with detectives about my tale of how Sarah came to be injured at Everything Amish and how her body was moved to the sinkhole. If true, the charges were more likely to be manslaughter than murder. So I was surprised authorities took my word seriously.

What I didn't know then was that Sarah's autopsy had showed

a small splinter of wood in her scalp where she suffered the head trauma. Detectives had initially speculated she might have been hit with a club. Now they wanted to compare that tiny piece of oak with the table inventory at Everything Amish for the missing sliver. A match would be as conclusive as DNA or fingerprints. However, most of the furniture had been sold by then in a giant clearance, so that lead was a dead end.

But apparently all this was enough to get Hannah removed from Miriam's custody and placed in the care of Yoder cousins in an Amish settlement in Iowa. Child sexual abuse records are kept confidential, so I never found out whether she was victimized by her brother.

I never saw Hannah again. I just hope she still has the picture of her sister.

Even though I was only heartsick, not dying, Father Mountain anointed me with holy oil on my eyelids, ears, lips, nose, and hands. He prayed with me for the Lord to forgive me any evil I had committed through my powers of sight, hearing, speech, smell, or touch.

"Don't think of this as last rites," he told me. "Think of it as a second first chance."

As promised, I returned to Thao's grandmother, the seamstress, and hired her to sew me a spectacular Hmong wall hanging, because I didn't want to see another Amish quilt ever again.

Deputy Laura Schaefer won the race for sheriff, but a surprising percentage of the voters still cast ballots for the incumbent, even though he faced allegations of assault and theft.

A jury eventually acquitted Ed Eide, but Roger Alton was convicted because of his police interrogation video. I made a copy of it for my parents as a Christmas present. I also gave Husky to them, or perhaps them to Husky, because he seemed happier as a farm dog. And I could always visit.

Brian Kueppers returned a war hero after putting his life on the line for fellow soldiers. He was awarded a Purple Heart and served as grand marshal for the town's annual Fourth of July parade.

Nick Garnett left his government job in Washington and was back as head of security at the Mall of America.

A holiday "smash and grab" flash mob riot recently broke out there involving hundreds of shoppers. Managers of the nation's largest mall had overreacted, going into lockdown mode. Cellphone video of gang members throwing chairs across the food court received network play, so MOA managers lured Garnett back.

Rather than receiving an elated phone call from him, I'd read about his relocation in the business section of the Minneapolis newspaper, so I didn't see any future for us.

As for Channel 3, Nicole still feared that getting her boss fired might hurt her news career. I figured not getting him fired might hurt mine. But she pointed out that our next news director might be even worse, so we worked out a compromise.

Since she had all the evidence, Nicole took it into his office one night after work. I listened with my ear at the door.

"Bryce, there's something we need to get straight." She told him about the sexts she'd saved, and the hidden recording she'd made.

To my surprise, he didn't sound panicked at all. "So let's cut to the chase, Nicole. You're here to blackmail me into making you lead anchor. I'm sure we can work something out." He sounded smooth and confident, making a kissy sound with his lips.

"That's not what this is about," she said. "That's not what I'm after."

She and I had talked. She didn't want a short-lived news career. Sure, accusing her news director of sexual harassment could get her a reputation. But so might landing an anchor job if the rest of the station thought she had something going on the side with Bryce.

"So what are you after?" He sounded suspicious.

That was my cue to enter. Bryce looked pissed. "I might have guessed you were behind this, Riley, when I heard about the hidden camera. How about that lecture you gave me about invasion of privacy?"

He was not just a pig. He was stupid. There's nothing I hate more than working for a stupid boss. "You can't claim privacy to break the law. Besides, that conversation belonged to Nicole just as much as you." I pushed the telephone toward him with a dare. "Call Miles if you don't believe me."

Bryce didn't move. And I didn't want our meeting to drag on, so we gave him our terms for not ratting him out.

No more one-man bands.

Warm water in the ladies' room.

"And one last thing," I said. "Since you've proven you can't be trusted around women, no office walls. The glass has to go back up so we can keep an eye on you."

The disadvantage was that we'd have to look at him.

ACKNOWLEDGMENTS

My editor, Emily Bestler, made *Shunning Sarah* better by encouraging me to find a new ending to the novel. Sometimes authors are so close to a story they can't tell whether their endings are brilliant or over-the-top. As for my readers, if you want to know what the original ending was, ask me sometime. But read the book first. So thanks, Emily—I'm proud to be an Emily Bestler book.

Special thanks also to her editorial assistant Caroline Porter for handling the numerous tasks required to get a book into print. It's all in the details. My list of gratitude for all the things from production to art to publicity to marketing to sales to copyediting also includes Kate Cetrulo, Mellony Torres, Hillary Tisman, Judith Curr, Chris Lloreda, Jeanne Lee, James Pervin, Andy Goldwasser, Susan Rella, Bryan Miltenberg, James Walsh, and John Wahler. And danke to Isolde Sauer, who improved the German in Sarah's diary besides directing the copyediting process.

My agent, Susan Ginsburg from Writers House, also deserves particular recognition for keeping me calm during the current publishing storm. Her assistant, Stacy Testa, is helpful and humorous.

My faithful beta readers—Kevyn Burger, Trish Van Pilsum, and Caroline Lowe—see the manuscript first and are all excellent storytellers themselves with wonderful advice about dialogue and plot. After all, there's a little bit of each of them in my protagonist.

For real-life research, I am grateful to Jerry Youngkin at the Amish Bed and Breakfast near Canton, MN, for allowing me to live like the Amish overnight. I encourage everyone to stay there; to Richard Scrabeck of Amish Tours of Harmony for his insight around the plain countryside. My favorite part of researching this novel involved visiting local farms and buying Amish baskets, quilted potholders, and cashew crunch. Thanks also to Lynn Rogers of the North American Bear Center for sharing his knowledge and passion about black bears. If you've never seen his live bear den cameras, check out his website at www.bear.org. As always, no one knows murder like Vernon Geberth, author of *Practical Homicide Investigation;* and no one has more patience with my forensic problems than Dr. D. P. (Doug) Lyle, author of *More Forensics and Fiction;* Sue Senden shared her secrets to being a forensic artist; Wanda Brunstetter, author of numerous bestselling Amish novels, was generous in guiding me on the difference between German and Pennsylvania Dutch; WCCO-TV photo chief Bill Kruskop kept me up to date about the latest in television news cameras.

Various relatives have become accustomed to seeing their names in the back of my books, and it's probably too late to change that tradition without some pouting on their part, so here's the list: Ruth Kramer; Mike Kramer; Bonnie and Roy Brang; Teresa, Galen, and Rachel Neuzil; Richard and Oti Kramer; Mary Kramer; Steve and Mary Kay Kramer, along with Matthew and Elizabeth; Kathy, Jim, with Adriana and Zach Loecher; Christina Kramer; Jerry and Elaine Kramer; Mae Klug; George and Shirley Kimball; George Kimball, Shen Fei with Shi Shenyu; Nick Kimball and Gannet Tseggai; Jenny, Kile, with Daniel Nadeau; Jessica, Richie with Lucy Miehe; Becca and Seth Engberg; David and Alyssa Nadeau; Mary, Dave with Davin Benson; Steve Kimball with Craig and Shaela; James Kimball; Paul Kimball; and numerous far-flung cousins and other kin.

The life of an author might be lonely without family. I'm thankful for mine: the boys—Alex Kimball and Andrew Kimball—for thriving, at college and soon the world; Joey and David Kimdon for raising Aria and Arbor, a delightful pair; Katie and Jake Kimball as they welcome Barlow, our newest reader home to Minnesota.

I'm especially fortunate for the love of Joe, my soul mate, and glad to be empty nesters together.